Vicky—
In all that
you do...
Take it to the F

Mu

EDGE
OF
CHAOS

MOLLY E. LEE

Edge of Chaos
Copyright © 2016 by Molly E. Lee
All rights reserved.

This book or any portion thereof may not be reproduced or used in any manner whatsoever without the express written permission of the publisher except for the use of brief quotations in a book review. This is a work of fiction. Names, characters, businesses, places, events and incidents are either the products of the author's imagination or used in a fictitious manner. Any resemblance to actual persons, living or dead, or actual events is purely coincidental. This book is licensed for your personal enjoyment only. This book may not be re-sold or given away to other people. If you would like to share this book with another person, please purchase an additional copy for each person you'd like to share it with. Thank you for respecting the author's work.

Visit my website at www.mollyelee.com

Cover Designer:
Regina Wamba at Mae I Design

Editing:
Karen Grove

Second Editor:
Nichole Strauss with Perfectly Publishable

Interior Design and Formatting:
Christine Borgford with Perfectly Publishable

ISBN# eBook:
978–0-9973464–0-4
ISBN# Paperback:
978–0-9973464–1-1

For Daren. The moment I met you I finally started living.

PROLOGUE

A STORM BREWED in Justin's eyes, a ferocity that threatened to shatter everything in my life. He leaned against the wall near the small kitchen with his long arms crossed over his chest, staring at the threadbare carpet like he wanted to set it on fire.

Damn it. I'd been gone *two* minutes. What could've happened in the time it took me to check out the closet in the master bedroom to piss him off?

I paused in the hallway and tested the atmosphere. I knew everything about Justin, had every look memorized. His ultra-short black buzzed hair, brown eyes, and trimmed goatee usually conveyed a mysterious charm, but when he shaped his face the way he was now, I knew we were only minutes from a blowup. He probably would've already erupted—what about, I still didn't understand—if the apartment leasing agent wasn't standing a few feet away in the kitchen pretending to go through paperwork.

I sighed and racked my brain. He'd been quiet on the drive out here, sure, but nothing indicated he was angry. Only two months until my freshman year of college and this apartment was one of the most popular among Tulsa students. We jumped at the opportunity to snag a place so near campus— well, I jumped, Justin kind of strolled.

Two things in my life were certain.

One, I would attend the University of Tulsa. My mother had attended, and all my friends had been accepted and were picking out dorm rooms or apartments, too. I hadn't even applied anywhere else because it just wasn't an option.

And two, Justin.

We'd met when I was ten and he was thirteen during a neighborhood kickball game. He was my first everything. First childhood boyfriend. First real date. First long-term boyfriend. First lover.

"Will you put the deposit down today?" The leasing agent, a blonde woman in a black skirt and blue blouse, asked, and grounded me to the present.

My eyes shot to Justin. He was a statue except for his clenching jaw. My heart plummeted into my stomach, stirring up the two Dunkin Donuts I'd eaten for breakfast.

I swallowed. "Could we have a minute to talk, please?"

"Of course." The agent walked toward the front door. "I'll just leave this folder here for you. It includes the floor plan, estimated water and electric, and the rent is listed at the bottom."

"Thank you," I said as she shut the front door.

The tension in the air mounted. I was so familiar with the sensation. A rough texture, like choking down a Brillo pad. A signature Justin blowup would occur in the next five minutes—he merely waited for me to initiate it, as was his pattern. After years of these, I'd almost rather eat the Brillo pad.

Oh well, fuck it.

"What's up, Justin?" I decided to mirror him and took up my own firm lean against the opposite wall, but opted to put my hands on my hips as opposed to crossing them over my chest.

He finally looked at me, the fuse lit. His brown eyes were sharp enough to cut me as he shrugged, the motion rippling the muscles in his arms.

My heart rate kicked up. A silent start was way worse than an instant outburst.

"Seriously, what is it?" I kept my voice even, not wanting to fan the flames.

He clenched his jaw again, and I almost lost it. I'd been tiring of these blowups for a while now, but I assumed once we lived together they would stop. He'd be happier.

Justin uncrossed his arms and took two strides to the kitchen, flipping open the folder the leasing agent had left on the counter. He scanned the papers and shook his head before meeting my gaze again.

"This is ridiculous," he said.

"What is? The rent? It's very reasonable considering how close it is to campus, and you know it'll be good for me to be able to walk to class."

"Me, me, me," he said, mocking my voice. "What the hell am I supposed to do, Blake?"

I opened my mouth to respond, but the air caught in my lungs. He had a stack of job applications in my car. We'd picked them up while waiting for the apartment office to open. There were over ten mechanic positions available in town, and two of the managers had even said they were interested in seeing what he could do.

"I thought . . ." He'd been excited about the prospect of getting our own place. Finally living together after all these years. He'd said he was looking forward to the move, a fresh start.

"Yeah, *you* thought. Why'd you have to pick a college that is so far away, huh? Why should I have to leave my friends because you suck at picking schools?"

"Are you serious? It's only two hours away! It's not like I'm asking you to move to Canada." I rolled my eyes.

Huge mistake.

Justin slammed his fist against the countertop, making me

CHAPTER

ONE

Three Years Later

MY CHILDHOOD HOME smelled somewhere between chocolate chip cookies, freshly baked cinnamon rolls, and a hint of something spicy. I walked through the entryway, allowing the familiar scents and sights to soothe the anger pulsing inside me.

Justin had forgotten about me. Again. He'd promised to take me out on my lunch break since it was the first day of a new semester. I'd waited on campus half an hour. He hadn't even called.

I heard Mom in the kitchen and I turned down the hallway. She stood in front of the stove stirring a huge pot of home-made pasta.

Everyone said my mom and I looked nearly identical—with long brown hair and the same dark brown eyes—except for our height. She was a foot shorter than me and often was mistaken for my sister as opposed to my mother. I gave her a side hug. "Smells great."

"Thanks, honey. I figured after classes you'd head over here since you never keep any real food at that apartment you insisted on renting."

"That apartment has the sweet perk of being right across the street from campus." In fact, before heading over here I'd walked home to let my English bulldog, Hail, outside and then grabbed my car. After the blow-off by Justin, I craved Mom's company and comfort food. That and she was right about the "no real food" comment. All I had at my place was turkey and crackers. I seriously needed to go to the store, but I'd worked all week.

Mom scraped the pasta from the skillet into a large palegreen bowl and set it on the table. She returned for the bread as I grabbed our plates. She filled them before she sat down.

"It's not that I'm not grateful you decided to go to college closer to home," she said, handing me a full plate, "but I really wish you would've at least stayed with me. Think of all the money you could save."

I sighed, shoving a huge bite of pasta into my mouth. This was a commonly repeated conversation, but I never budged. "Do you feel like you don't see me enough? Because I'm over here every week."

"Yes, here or with Justin. You never go out and do anything else."

"I work."

Mom stirred her pasta. "Sure, you're really living it up."

"So are you upset that I'm over here too much or too little? Because it sounds like both."

"Neither, honey. I'm trying to express the need to explore things outside of your norm, but I'm not sure Justin would ever let you do that anyway."

Mom usually hit the mark closer than she ever realized. I'd never told her the real reason I'd decided to attend Oklahoma University instead of Tulsa. That the threat Justin made on his life had made my decision not to move. But he didn't control everything I did; I simply didn't have much time between studying, classes, work, and him.

"Anyway," she continued, taking a sip of her iced tea, "how are your classes looking?"

"Great. I'm finally getting into the upper level meteorology courses. I'm really excited about this semester."

"And I'm guessing since you're here, Justin didn't meet you for the date he'd promised?"

I huffed, making a mental note to stop divulging all my plans to her in the future. "No, Mom. He didn't. And *I'm* guessing you bet on that, since you cooked enough food for me as well."

She glanced down at her plate. "I told you not to fall in love with that boy."

Those were the first words out of my mother's mouth after she'd met Justin all those years ago. Her opinion of him hadn't changed.

"Where is all this coming from?" I asked.

"Nowhere. It's the start of a new semester for you, and each time you start something new I have the hopes that you'll *experience* something new. I'm your mother. I want you to be happy. I don't want you going through what I did."

I pressed my lips together. My father had cheated on my mother after years of struggling with their marriage. Justin had been my rock during that time, allowing me to cry into his shoulder, making me laugh when no one else could. The comfort of that stability had vanished over the last three years, but the memory conjured up the evidence that those feelings were real at one point.

"I am happy, Mom," I said, smiling in an attempt to reassure her.

"Are you really?"

I swallowed the piece of garlic bread in my mouth harder

than I'd meant to. Sometimes I swore the woman could zero in on the days I was questioning my relationship better than a heat-seeking missile. I don't know how she managed it, but I knew it wasn't something I wanted to get into. Ever.

"Thanks for lunch. I've got to get back to campus," I said, standing quickly and kissing her on the cheek.

"Anytime, honey," she said.

I closed the door behind me, hoping the next time I returned she'd let the subject drop. I was grateful I had a mother who cared and was perceptive to my moods, but that didn't mean I wanted to defend my relationship at every meeting. And lately, defending my choices when it came to Justin was becoming harder and harder.

I LEANED MY head back against a bench on campus. Students shuffled to and from classes, filling the area with chatter. I tuned the voices out and gazed at the slate-gray sky with storm clouds rolling in from the west. The scent of rain misted the air. The grass on campus looked ten times greener with the gray backdrop, and I found myself smiling. From the look of it, a thunderstorm would hit in a little under an hour.

I dug my cell out of my pocket and pulled up Dash Lexington's website. He was a professional storm chaser and the foremost opinion on local weather. I hit his site up more often than checking the news stations. He usually nailed it, and he had awesome chase videos as a bonus.

A late afternoon thunderstorm watch west of campus will be in effect until nine p.m. tonight. #weatherupdate #buybeerearly

I laughed at his most recent tweet displayed at the top of his site. Underneath it was a shot of the current Doppler Radar tracking the storm I had already spotted in the sky.

A picture of Dash sat just off to the side of the storm tracker, his credentials listed beneath it. The image always conjured up a giddy sensation within me, like some high school girl with a celebrity crush. But it wasn't just because he had green eyes and strong features. I liked that his smile wasn't forced. It looked so natural, as if any inkling of a storm could fill him with an uncanny happiness—a feeling I understood well.

Pocketing my phone, I rose and headed to my first day of Physical Meteorology—this one focused on cloud physics and atmospheric dynamics—and found my sour mood from Mom's prying giving way to excitement.

I loved starting a new class because, like Mom had so adequately felt the need to point out to me *again*, my life was one big routine. Wake up, go to class, come home, study, go to work, come home, possibly see Justin, sleep, wake up, and do it all over again. Sometimes, if I was lucky enough, Justin would surprise me and take me to a movie or dinner, giving me a much-needed break from the full schedule of classes I had.

Anticipation soared through me as I neared the science building, something that only happened when heading to a class that pertained to my major—Meteorology.

I'd learned early my freshman year that I got the same thrill when combining weather data to make a prediction that normal people got from doing extreme sports, like skydiving or swimming with sharks. And it wasn't just the excitement factor, either. Interpreting data came easy to me and allowed me to be the first one to know about approaching storms. It put me in a prime position to warn people about what to look for and when to take cover—and I enjoyed that sense of power. I wanted to track supercells and relay coverage on their progress. Submerge myself in storms where I'd always felt happiest.

Only two more years to go and I'd achieve that dream. Well, hopefully. I'd have to find an opening for a meteorologist on a network, but I'd have the degree that would get me there. The only silver lining from Justin's refusal to move to Tulsa and his threat if I left him was the fact that Oklahoma University had a highly respected meteorology curriculum. The prospect filled me with a sense of accomplishment. Like all the studying and working for minimum wage at the electronics store to pay for books and rent was worth it.

The classroom consisted of three rows of long black-topped tables, a large projector screen at the front, and a computer system to the left. I took a seat in the front, pulled a notebook out of my oversized shoulder bag, and opened it to a fresh page. Three guys were the only other students in the room, and they all huddled around one table near the back. They chatted with excited voices and sounded like they were discussing a past road trip, but I tried not to eavesdrop. Their easy camaraderie and banter made my chest tighten—the aching fingers of loneliness wrapped around my heart and squeezed.

Between classes, work, and Justin, I hadn't had much time to make new friends, unless you counted my bulldog, Hail, which I did. She'd been my best friend for the past two years. I had some acquaintances that I talked to in class or at work, but outside of everyday chit-chat, the only person I spoke with was Justin.

I supposed the boyfriend being the number-one priority was natural, though. It's definitely how he wanted it. There had been fewer blowups from him—which resulted in less tears and less broken furniture—since all my friends went off to college. And the few times I'd thought seriously about integrating myself into a new group of friends, Justin would remind me of the sacrifice I'd be making—the little time we had together.

Checking the time on my cell, I noticed the professor was a few minutes late. I tapped the Facebook app and scrolled through my feed. I'd lost touch with all my high school friends, long ago I could barely remember the feeling. It hadn't been mind-blowing. Not in the way I'd read about or even seen in the movies. Something I would never admit to Justin.

We'd lost our virginities to each other, and after the first couple of times, it wasn't so bad. He'd been more tender with me back then.

Over the years, things changed. I'd told myself it was due to all the stress he'd undergone—losing jobs, overdue bills, car wrecks, never reconnecting with his family—and I'd stayed quiet, wanting to give him the time to return to the more gentle man I'd fallen in love with.

After things evened out for him and the sex didn't change, I expressed my willingness to explore and find a better rhythm, but Justin wouldn't hear of it. It was either his way or no way, and he'd been set on turbo-doggie-style mode for years, probably from some god-awful porn he'd watched one too many times.

I racked my brain. When and why had Justin pulled out that surprise? It clicked after a second. He'd gotten drunk the weekend before and called me a C U Next Tuesday for not going out at 3:00 a.m. to buy him a pack of cigarettes. That was over a year ago.

I wrote the name of the class on the paper a little harder than I needed to.

"I know, I know, I'm running late!" A man with a bushy gray beard and balding head bustled into the room, toting a leather satchel and a cup of coffee. "I got caught up examining the atmospheric pressure in Starbucks. A terribly unstable situation there. The air has a scent to it that leads me to believe a supercell could erupt at any given moment. You can't be too careful when studying these things, you know?"

I laughed out loud this time, as did the band of boys behind me. Dash had taken a seat with them, not that I'd checked. I was left alone in the very front.

The professor set down his things. "Now let's get serious and take a look at who the victims are this semester." He trailed his brown eyes over each of us. "I'm Professor Ackren, and I see we have an upright bramble of students dying to take my course." He widened his eyes in exaggeration while scanning the many empty seats in the room. "No matter, only the strong of heart will come out of here victorious and set forth unto the unknown and chaotic profession of attempting to explain, define, and understand weather."

I liked him instantly.

He clapped his hands together. "Now. Who among you is an aspiring meteorologist?"

Only my hand shot in the air. I let it drop slowly, and sank a little deeper into my chair.

Professor Ackren approached my table. "Why, my dear, do you want to be a meteorologist?"

"I want to be the first one to know about the storms and relay the info to the public." The answer rolled off my tongue. It was one reason on a long list.

"You want to predict and track storms?"

I nodded.

"Well, then, your first lesson is that weather is never predictable and anyone—"he eyed the gang behind me—"who thinks it is, plays a very dangerous game. Storms are like poker, just when you think you have the game beat, someone deals you a bad hand and bam! Game over. Money isn't at risk in this profession; it's people's lives. Could be your own, could be those of an entire town. And that is why we must appreciate the nature of weather and its unforgivable unpredictability. You storm chasers should know a thing or two about that by now, right?" He eyed the group of guys behind me. I spared a look, and their faces were more serious now than minutes before.

Professor Ackren segued beautifully into his lecture then,

them every time they came to town or anywhere within driving distance. Justin had always dropped me off and picked me up. He never came in. He'd always said concerts were overcrowded and lame, but he wanted to make sure I made it home safe—like he thought I'd get kidnapped by the band or their crazy fans. I'd laughed at the notion but never argued because if I got to go to the shows without a lecture or a guilt trip over it taking time away from us, then it was worth it.

Justin shrugged. "I'll just drink through it, and besides, it'll make you happy, right?"

"Yes." Maybe he was finally putting forth that effort he'd been promising me for years now. "Thank you!" I stood on my tiptoes and kissed him. "I can't wait."

He smirked and my muscles coiled out of reflex. I knew that look too well. He'd given me a gift and now it was time for his reward.

I barely had time to enjoy the spontaneity before I was hurtled onto the couch, my back hitting the cushions with an audible thud.

I gasped and looked up at Justin as he hovered over me.

His dark eyes held me for only a moment before his lips crushed mine. My mouth opened automatically underneath his, the pattern of his tongue familiar as it jutted against my own. He'd kissed me a thousand times, and it was always the same. His mouth moved hungrily, and he shoved frantic hands underneath my shirt. His intense desire was enough to stave off my resistance, and I tried to mentally switch gears as quickly as possible.

Justin never wasted time, and my jeans were quickly on the floor, followed by my underwear. I wanted to tell him to slow down while he slipped on a condom, that I needed a little more time, but I bit my tongue. It would only lead to an argument over how real men make love, so I took a deep breath in preparation as he turned me over and thrust himself inside of me from behind.

It stung. Not enough for me to cry out but enough for me to dig my nails into the couch cushions. He interpreted the scratching of fabric as a go signal and clutched my hips and pushed himself deeper inside.

"Justin," I whispered.

He moaned in response.

"I'd really like it if I could be on top this time," I suggested, and not for the first time. Despite my many attempts to take the reins and try another position, he'd never once made love to me face to face, and I thought perhaps I might enjoy it more from another angle.

"This is how *I* like it. Relax. I've got this under control," he said, his voice shaking by his quick breathing.

I opted for another tactic. I reached behind me and grabbed his thigh, slowing him down. I closed my eyes and tried to control his movements by rocking forward and backward, but his death grip on my hips made it pointless. He quickened his pace within seconds, and I released a breath of frustration. He never let me be in control, not that I knew much more than him, but I believed my body and understood what it wanted. And this wasn't it.

I breathed deep and let go of my frustration, knowing this would be over in minutes and I could escape to a warm bath⊠a tradition of mine since we started having sex.

In the movies they never showed the girl jumping into the tub for a good soak after she made love to her hero. Guess they didn't want to show the reality of how painful sex could be if paired with a selfish lover in bed, and how the only cure is a good length of time under warm water. I wished at least one movie would, to warn girls like me.

He pumped his hips harder and grunted. I sighed in relief when his body relaxed. He pulled out and retreated to the bathroom for a few seconds before returning. Yanking up his pants, he grabbed my underwear off the floor and tossed them at me. I slipped them on gently, not wanting to increase the soreness already throbbing between my thighs.

"I've got to go. I told the guys they could have a re-match before work."

I kept my face even when he mentioned COD again. I hated the video game because it usually won when the choice came to going out with me or staying in and playing it.

"Will I see you Friday after I get off?" I asked. My shift ended at nine—easily early enough to go out on a real date. One that didn't involve delivery pizza and a marathon Xbox session.

Justin held the door open and paused. "Don't think so, babe. It's double XP points, and I'm having the guys over to pull an all-nighter."

I rolled my eyes. More video game crap.

"You need to study after work anyway, right?"

"Sure."

"Call you later. Enjoy your bath," he said and walked out, shutting the door behind him.

I cringed. He was well aware of my after-sex habit and why I needed it, but he never asked if there was anything he could do to help prevent it.

And every time I'd tried talking to him about it, his response was the same—there was something wrong with me. I wasn't able to handle how endowed he was.

I locked my door and filled Hail's bowl with food. She waddled into the kitchen a few seconds later and inhaled the contents as I scooped the concert tickets off the coffee table to pin them on the fridge.

This was the coolest gift he'd given me in years. In fact, it just topped the geode he'd given me for my twelfth birthday. I'd been a huge rock hound that year—back when I'd found the ground more interesting than the sky—and he'd waited until the very end of the party my mom had thrown me to pull me aside.

I'd followed him to the middle of my driveway.

"What's up?" I asked.

"I want to give you your present. Close your eyes."

I clenched them shut.

"Okay, open them."

He held one hand behind his back and the other gripped a small hammer.

My eyebrows rose. "Um, thank you?"

He laughed and brought his other hand around, revealing a speckled gray rock the size of a softball.

I gasped, excitement soaring through me. "Is that what I think it is?"

Justin nodded. He sat the rock on the ground and handed me the hammer.

I gave him a spare glance before I brought it down on top of the rock with as much force as I could muster. It didn't even crack. My shoulders drooped.

Justin took the hammer from me and let the rock have it.

It cracked like an egg under his strength.

I'd scooped up the pieces and treasured the white crystals sparkling inside.

He'd nailed the present, and over the years I'd often compared him to that rock. Rough on the outside, but so much more underneath. Though, lately, he'd been closer to the sharp points the crystal held as opposed to the beauty.

I took a deep breath and focused on the tickets in my hand. I could only hope the boy who'd given me the geode was slowly returning.

CHAPTER

TWO

I EYED THE tiny clock on the upper right-hand corner of my register screen. Only an hour left to go. Don't know why I was so excited to get off, wasn't like I had a fun date to get ready for, just a mountain of reading from the first week of classes.

Justin had called and said I could come over to his place if I wanted to, but the idea of watching him and four of his closest friends play Xbox and drink beer all night was less than tempting. He wouldn't even know I was there anyway, not with COD on the screen.

Scanning my next customer's three DVDs I tried not to be bitter, but it was hard. Routine smothered me, and I desperately craved to do something, *anything*. I handed the customer his bag of movies. Maybe I'd skip class reading and color my hair tonight, something wild like red or blonde.

"Hey there," a familiar deep voice said, snapping me to attention.

Heat rocketed to my core, and my heart stuttered.

Damn. Dash Lexington. He was gorgeous, but he had an

approachable air, like it'd be easy to carry on a conversation with him.

"Hi," I said, grabbing his CD and scanning it. I held the CD up before putting it in a bag. "You like Blue October?"

His eyebrows raised. "Hell, yeah. They're incredible. You know them?"

"Been to six of their shows. They're even better live."

Dash smiled, and it lit up his chiseled features. "Agreed. I've only been to a few shows, but I'm going next month. You?"

"I'll be there."

He swiped his card and signed the pad with the cheap plastic pen. "So, Blake, who likes to answer every question in class, when do you get off?"

My mouth dropped for a moment. "I don't answer every—"

"Yeah you do, but it's all right," he cut me off, "gets me and the boys off the hook."

I handed him his bag as he stood there eyeing me. I glanced behind him, but there weren't any customers waiting in line since the store would close soon.

"What?" I finally asked, and hoped if I had ink or something on my face he'd have the decency to at least tell me.

"What time are you done here?"

I blinked a couple times. "Oh, less than an hour."

"Perfect, it'll still be happy hour over at Bailey's. You know where that is?"

I shook my head.

"It's a bar the guys and I hang out at near campus. Total dive, but they've got rated burgers and cheap drinks."

"Sounds nice," I said.

"You want the address so you can meet me there, or do you want me to wait so you can follow me?"

My eyes widened for a second, realization setting in. "That's really sweet, but I have a boyfriend."

He tilted his head. "And I have a girlfriend. Overconfident

much?"

"I'm sorry! I just thought . . ." Blood rushed to my cheeks.

Dash chuckled. "Relax, I'm just teasing. I get it. You probably have guys asking you out all the time. In my case, though, it's strictly a friendly invite because I wasn't joking about the girlfriend part."

He smiled at me again. The gesture was so genuine it calmed my embarrassment and tugged on my intense desire to shatter the routine I was stuck in.

"In that case, I'd love to." My answer came quick and I swallowed hard. Usually I weighed the pros and cons on whether an event was worth fighting with Justin over. He didn't like it when I went off script, but something in me didn't want to say no to Dash.

"Awesome, I'll hang around till you get off. Be easier if you follow me."

"All right," I said, the butterflies resuming their flapping in my stomach. I told myself this was because I was thrilled at the prospect of actually making some friends before I graduated college and not at all to do with how his lip quirked when he smiled.

"You should text your boyfriend and tell him to meet us there," he said while walking toward the exit. He had his cell phone out and typed as well. "I'll be out here when you're done closing up."

I watched him walk through the automatic doors. I saw the outlines of defined, but not bulging, muscles through his snugly fitted red T-shirt. I blinked and forced myself to snap out of it. He literally just told me to text my boyfriend!

I pulled out my cell phone from underneath my register and stared at it for a few moments, contemplating the right way to invite Justin. I knew he wouldn't come out, not with his boys' night in full force, but I also knew he'd want me to go home and study. Not go to a bar. The idea of getting to know

Dash—a person I'd admired and respected, who also shared my field of study—filled me with a confidence I hadn't experienced before. I finally shot Justin a quick text, and then proceeded to do my closing duties.

Forty-five minutes later I clocked out and headed to my car. I glanced at my phone for the first time since I'd texted Justin. Six missed calls. My heart pounded a little harder in my chest. Six calls on a COD night was unheard of.

"Hey, you ready?" Dash leaned against his black F150, his hands in his jeans pockets.

"Sure," I said, stopping at my car parked a few spaces away.

He gave me a nod and hopped in his truck. I dialed Justin's number while following Dash out of the parking lot.

He answered after the first ring.

"What do you mean you're going to a bar?" he snapped.

"Hello to you, too." A loud mixture of male banter and video game gunfire boomed in the background.

"Don't get cute with me, Blake. Why in the hell are you going to a bar?"

"To hang out with some people from class. What's the big deal? You're with your friends tonight," I said, sighing.

"That's different."

"Why?" I asked.

"I'm not getting drunk with a bunch of college assholes."

No, you're getting drunk with a bunch of drop-out assholes. "I'm not going to get drunk, and they're not assholes. What's the problem?"

"I know you. Ten to one you're not meeting a bunch of sorority girls."

"They're guys from my class and their girlfriends. You could meet us there, you know." I continued to follow Dash's truck, which took me on the familiar route toward campus.

"I shouldn't have to do that," he said, the anger in his voice mounting.

"You're right. You shouldn't *have* to come out with your girlfriend on a Friday night. You should want to," I snapped and instantly regretted it. Where had my fight-filter vanished to?

"I can't believe you're choosing to do this over your responsibilities. You should be studying, and if not that then you should be here."

I gripped the steering-wheel harder, waiting for the guilt that normally hit me when he pulled those lines. It didn't come. "My classes are under control, and you don't even notice me when COD is up."

"Whatever. This is bullshit. Hope you have a great time tonight. Try not to get roofied." He hung up.

My mouth dropped, and I scoffed at my cell phone, resisting the urge to throw it out the window. I opted instead to shove it in my purse and crank up my stereo.

Going out with a storm chaser from class who had arms that tornadoes would change course for wasn't wrong. I was an aspiring meteorologist. It was networking. Despite repeating this to myself, I was still fuming when I parked next to Dash's truck in front of the bar.

The small brick building had a lone neon sign hanging out front. Posters with specials plastered the windows, and Dash held the door open for me as we walked in. The smell of cigarettes and fried food instantly hit me as we entered. Music blared from speakers in the corners of the small room, and a wooden bar took up most of the space. To the left were a few round-top tables with red leather bar stools and a shuffleboard pressed against the wall behind them.

The place was packed with people, most in OU shirts. Chatter joined the music bouncing off the walls, drowning out the angry thoughts in my head. Dash gently touched my lower back, sending another spark soaring through mc. I tried not to freak out that the creator of the website I practically stalked guided me to a tall, round-top-table in the back next to the shuffleboard.

The other two guys from class sat there with giant frosty mugs in front of them.

"Whoa, who invited the meteorologist?" the dark-haired one asked. He wore an OU T-shirt and jeans, his brown eyes looking me up and down.

"I did," Dash said and turned to me. "Blake, this is Paul Whitmore." He pointed to the dark-haired boy.

"Hey." Paul leaned toward me. "What do meteorologists get after a night of tequila and bad tacos?"

I shrugged. "I don't know, what?"

"Rear-flank downdrafts," Paul said and burst out laughing. He stopped only long enough to take another swig of beer.

I chuckled. "That's so corny it's almost funny."

"Don't mind him, he's an idiot." Dash pulled out a barstool for me to sit on. He pointed to the boy sitting next to Paul. "And this is John Langston."

"Wondered what took you so long," John said, eyeing Dash. "Where'd you have to pick this one up?" He had a perfectly mussed natural red faux-hawk and kind blue eyes.

"I followed him here," I answered and took a seat.

"Worried about me, John?" Dash asked and sat next to me.

I glanced at Dash. "I'm guessing your close friends call you Ringo?"

The two boys laughed while Dash pressed his lips together to stop his smile.

"Nice! We should start calling you that," John said before taking a swig of his beer.

"No way, man. I'd be Ringo if anyone in this group was Ringo." Paul shook his head.

I turned to Dash. "Confession time. I've known who you were since the first day of class. I love your site."

"Whoa, stalker alert." Paul arched an eyebrow.

"Yeah, it'd be nice having someone else to listen to other than these two!" John said. "They think they know absolutely everything, and they never stop at the good gas stations. Pretty girl like you, I bet they'd stop where the clean bathrooms are just to be polite."

I couldn't help but laugh because I never would've guessed a guy with a faux-hawk would care about bathroom cleanliness. "So, what are all of you majoring in then? I thought all storm chasers were meteorologists."

"Common misconception," Dash answered. "Atmospheric sciences is our field. Though I'm minoring in videography and photography as well." He motioned his head toward John. "So is he."

John shrugged. "They really like me for my skills driving the Tracker Jacker."

"Fan of The Hunger Games?" I asked.

"Don't get me started!" John set his beer down. "These two give me so much crap for reading the books."

"I love the series, too," I said.

"Nice." John stuck his fist toward me.

I gave it a bump and asked, "What is your Tracker Jacker like?"

Dash patted John on the back. "A beat-up pickup with instruments hooked to the top that follows my beast of a truck."

John cut his eyes at him. "Yeah, act like you'd get anywhere without me." He turned his attention back to me. "I navigate the paths and am constantly connected to Doppler to help us get ahead of the storms. Can't always rely on Dash's 'instincts.'" John framed the last word with his fingers in the universal quotation mark sign.

Dash motioned to Paul. "He's a double-major, alongside engineering."

"Wow, that's a ton of work."

Paul shrugged. "These two have to have someone who can

build useful and working equipment if they want to be the top chasers in Oklahoma."

"It's nice that you all have an important role."

"Still missing a tried-and-true meteorologist though." John eyed Dash.

He smiled at me. "Don't worry. I'm not planning on forcing you to join the team . . . yet."

I grinned, enjoying the thought of being part of anything outside my boring routine. "Does the University pay you guys to chase?"

Paul grunted. "Nope, all the funds come from Dash's website. We did just get a grant to build some probes—mobile devices with instruments measuring wind velocity, atmospheric pressures, and temperature—"

"She knows what probes are," Dash interrupted him.

"Oh, yeah, of course she does." Paul tapped the side of his near empty beer glass. "Well, ours won't be fully operational until next season."

John set his mug down. "We just have the tools hooked up to the Tracker Jacker for now. That and Dash's abilities to get the best footage out there," he said. "It's going to be a killer season."

"It better be!" Paul interjected. "We've spent the whole winter planning for it. I swear if I look at another map for more than five minutes at a time I'm going to set it on fire."

"Dash!" a high-pitched voice squealed above the bustle of the crowded bar and cut through our conversation.

Dash jumped up and grabbed an empty barstool from the table next to us, dragging it to the other side of him. A few seconds later a blonde who barely came up to my shoulder wrapped her arms around his waist. She wore a blue-jean miniskirt with a white tank top and her lacy red bra peeked through the fabric. Dash kissed her quickly and offered her the barstool.

wonder it was packed.

We talked supercells and Blue October between bites while Lindsay pecked at her bowl of lettuce and pouted. She wasn't obsessed with storms like the rest of us, but she was clearly obsessed with Dash. She hung on every word he said and desperately sought his attention—grabbing at his hand even if he was using it to eat or rubbing his back while he told a chase story. I only noticed because I knew the gestures all too well. I used to paw at Justin that way, desperate for any kind of confirmation that he loved me as much as I loved him. That desire faded after time, natural after being together as long as Justin and I had been.

The thought of him returned the simmer in my gut. My earlier anger had been blissfully forgotten, lost among my new friends and their endless stories about storms I'd kill to see. I reached in my purse and checked my phone. No missed calls. He was really being an ass. I huffed and finished the last of my second beer.

"You all right?" Dash asked, leaning closer to me.

He smelled like Irish Spring soap and pure man. Heat from his body so close to mine landed on my skin. I backed away slightly before noticing Lindsay's absence. She must have snuck off to the bathroom while I revived my anger.

"I'm fine," I said, glancing around for Diana. Once she locked eyes with me, I held up my bottle. She gave me a nod from across the room.

Dash raised his eyebrows.

"It's nothing."

Diana set my third beer down in front of me, and I quickly took a long swig. My head was already fuzzy and my tongue was thick. I really needed to build up a tolerance to this stuff, but it wasn't like I got a ton of opportunities to drink. The disconnected sensation was extremely welcome.

"Want to talk about it?" Dash asked, his green eyes never

straying from mine. He put his hand on my back and tension I didn't know I held uncoiled under his touch. He seemed like someone I could trust.

Maybe it was the beer.

I took another gulp. "It's my boyfriend, Justin."

He nodded, allowing me to continue at my own pace.

"He's just so . . ." Where to begin? "Well, he's super pissed I came out tonight."

"He wanted you to be with him instead?"

"He said he did, but I know better. I'd be nothing but an extra body in the place." I took another drink. It was probably a bad idea to talk to Dash about Justin, but I needed to talk to someone, anyone. And he was here, willing to listen. "He's having an all-boys COD party."

"Call of Duty, nice." Dash smiled, but the grin dropped when I gave him a stern look. "Anyway," he continued, "I'm confused; why is he pissed?"

"Because he'd rather me be at home alone than out with friends." I went ahead and used the word, hoping that after tonight I really would be able to consider them all friends.

"That seems unfair."

I shrugged. "He'll find some way to apologize for everything tomorrow."

"And you'll let him off the hook?"

"It's what I do. After eight years, there isn't anything else to do." Every time I even mentioned taking a break he threatened to kill himself—the last time he'd grabbed a bottle of pain pills he'd recently been prescribed after a small hand injury on the job, and said he'd swallow them all. My chest tightened at the thought, the rope he held me with constricting around my heart.

"Holy shit, eight years. You're practically married."

"Oh no I'm not," I said, my words dragging slightly. Justin had brought up the idea of marriage more times than I could count, but I'd constantly squashed the idea. I always blamed my parents' divorce, but really I couldn't see myself walking down the aisle with him. I already felt bound enough. "It has been a long time," I said and looked around the room for Diana. She handed Paul and John two more frosty mugs where they played shuffleboard. She saw me and nodded. "All my life really," I continued, twirling my third empty in front of me. "It's hard to remember anything before him."

"That must get difficult. Not experiencing anything outside of him," Dash said, his words terribly close to the ones my mother had lectured me with last week.

"Yep." I nearly launched into the University of Tulsa fiasco. Maybe I'd had too much to drink, or maybe it was just Dash, but talking to him made me want to confess all my life's wrong turns and have him tell me they were just detours. I tried to sharpen my fuzzy focus and grinned at Diana's perfect timing as I took my fourth beer from her. "Thanks, this is helping loads."

She eyed Dash. "She isn't driving is she?"

"No. I'll get her home."

My eyelids were heavy, and it took me forever to lock on to him. "Where'd your tiny friend go?" I asked, happy to change the subject from my relationship to his.

He chuckled, the throaty rumble quickly becoming a sound that soothed my insides. "She already left. Never stays here long. Isn't really her scene."

"I get that," I said. "You're so nice. To her . . . you're so nice to her."

"How do you figure?"

"Just a thing a girl can tell."

"A thing a girl can tell when she isn't used to it," he said, his voice growing softer.

"You could say that."

Two more beers later and the crowded bar was on a

permanent tilt. The floor swayed underneath my feet as I walked toward the exit, but luckily I had the strength of Dash to lean on. In the back of my mind I knew I'd regret this all tomorrow and be terribly embarrassed, but those things were hard to focus on—especially with the edges of my vision blurring.

I heard Dash say, "Whoa," before I blacked out completely.

CHAPTER

THREE

GRAVEL FILLED MY head—tiny pebbles that rolled around and caused sharp pains to burst throughout my brain. The smell of hot coffee hit me, and in the back of my mind I figured Justin had come over with it as a peace offering for acting like such a jerk last night. He had a spare key and could easily have let himself in.

The thought triggered my curiosity. I let go of the heavy blanket of sleep, and peeled apart my eyelids.

I saw blond hair instead of black.

The guy leaned over my nightstand only inches away. Adrenaline coursed through my veins. Sleep totally forgotten, I leaped up and hurled a right hook at his face.

He caught my fist a second before it hit him square in the nose.

"Whoa! Easy, woman!" he yelled and let go of my fist, backing up a few feet.

His voice and a clear picture of his face had me instantly sighing in relief.

"Dash?"

He held his hands up in the air as if I pointed a loaded gun at him. I glanced down. I still had my work clothes on from last night. I couldn't remember how I'd gotten home.

Looking at Dash I made an easy guess.

My relief was followed quickly by sheer embarrassment. My very unsexy beige bra hung off my bedroom doorknob, and I had other equally unappealing clothes strung across my floor, plus an array of stuffed animals with their insides spewing out of their eye sockets and earholes, courtesy of Hail.

Between classes, work, and Justin, cleaning was always the last thing on my mind. Of course, if I'd known Dash Lexington would be standing in my bedroom right now, I might've made an attempt.

I relaxed my attack stance—which had to look absolutely ridiculous standing barefoot on my queen bed—and hopped to the floor. Had he taken off my shoes and socks?

Blood rushed to my cheeks, and I swallowed the lump in my throat.

"Sorry," I said.

Dash smiled and dropped his hands. He eyed a tall white paper cup on my nightstand. "Coffee. Figured you'd need it. Hope you like it black."

"Only way I drink it," I said, scooping up the cup and taking a careful sip. The richness soothed the pulsing ache between my eyes.

"Me, too." He put his hands in his pockets and shifted his weight.

I took another drink, swallowing hard. "Can you give me a minute to change?" I decided it'd be easier to ask him about last night in a fresh pair of sweats.

He nodded and turned out of my door. I shut it behind him and quickly ripped off the smokey clothes. I tossed them in the corner next to my small black desk and kicked the other clothes littering my floor toward it.

After slipping on my softest gray sweats and a maroon T-shirt, I yanked my hair into a ponytail and walked down the hallway.

Dash sat on my couch, Hail practically in his lap. She leaned her massive white head into his chest as he rubbed under her neck. Her long pink tongue dangled out of her mouth, and I swear the bulldog smiled.

"What?" he asked, noting my open-mouthed stare.

Hail spared me a glance, her butt wiggling.

I took a seat next to them. "She's never reacted like that to a guy before." Technically Dash was only the second male to enter my apartment, but she'd never once acted like that toward Justin. She barely tolerated his presence. "Are you a dog whisperer or something?"

Dash leaned down and planted a kiss on top of Hail's head. "Nope, but obviously I'm good with the ladies."

I licked my lips, unable to stop my eyes from trailing his body. He looked unbelievably good, despite his slightly wrinkled clothes. I noticed he only had socks on and glanced around, spotting his shoes near the door.

"Did you sleep here last night?" I blurted out. My heart pounded in my chest. How much had I forgotten?

He tilted his head. "Wow, you really are a lightweight. You don't remember me bringing you home?"

I shook my head.

"You were a challenge."

Heat swept across my skin. Like, hard to get me into bed challenge? Had I been that drunk? I mentally searched my body for any sensations that would let me know if we'd had sex.

"You had a hard time giving me directions. Luckily you live so close to the bar. That is a sweet perk. You could walk if you wanted to."

I sighed. Of course. I was terrible with directions—even

sober. That *would* be a challenge.

Hail sighed and dropped across Dash's lap. Apparently she decided he was staying for a while.

He rested his hand on top of her back. "I crashed out here since it was so late. I went out and grabbed us some coffee and came back. Didn't want you to wake up alone and confused. Sorry, was that crossing a line?"

"No. Of course not . . ." I bit my lip. I'd gotten wasted and let a stranger take me home—well, a somewhat stranger. His website *was* bookmarked on my laptop, surely that had to count for something in my way of judgment. Thank God Dash was a perfect gentleman, too. A shudder ripped through me with the thought of what could've happened if he hadn't been.

"It's all right, Blake. I wasn't going to let anything happen to you." He reached across the couch and touched my knee.

My muscles uncoiled. Damn he was good at reading my moods. "How are you so . . . perceptive?"

"I've got two sisters, a great mom, and an amazing grandmother who lives right next door to my parents' place. I never stood a chance." He cracked a half grin. "I had to develop a sharp eye to spot all the mood swings you girls have." He winked at me.

"Well, thanks, for everything. I'm sorry I got out of control."

Dash laughed. "If that's you out of control, then I almost feel bad for you."

I sighed, finally at ease for the first time since I woke up. The possibility of relaxation surprised me, with Dash sitting on my couch, petting my dog, and offering the kind of friendship I'd craved for years.

I leaned back and took another sip of my coffee. Hail snored on Dash's lap, not quite loud enough to cover up the sound of keys jingling outside my door.

Ice shot through my veins.

I jumped up and yanked furiously on Dash's arm. Hail toppled off him with a thunk.

"What the—"

"Shh!" I shoved Dash down the hallway, Hail on our heels, toward my bedroom. I pushed him into my opened closet and gave him a panic-stricken look. I mouthed the words *please* and *sorry* before shutting the door in his face.

By the time I came out of my room, Justin was headed toward it. I closed my bedroom door behind me, cocked my hip to the side, and fastened an angry look on my face. It was harder than I thought, because while I was still pissed at him, I panicked on the inside. If he found Dash here there would be blood, and I couldn't put Dash in that position.

"What are you doing here, Justin?"

He dropped his eyes. "I wanted to stop by before work and apologize about last night. You know how I am when I drink . . ."

"Yeah." I sighed. "I know."

The sound of nails scratching against wood scraped behind me. He craned his head in that direction. "What the hell is that?"

"It's just Hail." Trying to get to Dash. I swallowed a lump in my throat.

"Dumbass dog."

"No one asked you to be here," I snapped.

His eyes turned to slits. "Stop being so defensive of your fucking dog! It's an animal, not a baby. God, sometimes you are so fucking sensitive. Look, it took a lot for me to come here. I *should* be at work already, but I wanted to say I was sorry. Now are you going to hear me out or what?"

My heart pounded against my chest, but I took a deep breath to slow it. Justin's arms were still loose at his sides so I knew his anger was at a safely low level. No need to heighten it. "I'm listening."

"Like I said, I was drunk and pissed off because my truck got towed and Mark had to take me to pick it up. We'd just gotten back to my place when you texted."

My mouth popped open, the question of where he'd parked in order to get towed on my tongue, but I stopped it. He often parked in the covered area of his apartment complex despite not paying extra for the space. I reached for his hand, noticing he wasn't wearing his watch. "Why didn't you tell me?"

He pulled his hand back. "Because I stopped needing a mother years ago, Blake."

The way he said my name hit my chest with guilt, as if the jab was directed at me and not his estranged family. I swallowed hard, now understanding his outburst last night. I'd been the direct catalyst for his family kicking him out, and even though I'd tried for years, I'd also failed to reunite them, and he had no one to help him in tough situations like that.

"I'm sorry I took it out on you, but you going out with a bunch of science-geeks only made it worse. They don't have your well-being as their first priority like I do. You shouldn't have sprung that on me."

"I hadn't planned on going out . . ." I rubbed my palms over my face. Explaining all the reasons he didn't need to worry about me as much as he did was too long a conversation to have while Dash was locked in my closet.

"Where's your watch?" I lightly grazed his wrist, shocked that he didn't have it on. He'd worn the gold piece every day since we were sixteen. It'd been his aunt's father's and she had slipped it into one of the boxes that Justin's uncle had left on the porch the night he'd kicked him out. I'd always believed the watch was her way of saying goodbye and that he wore it as his way of saying he still needed her. In my darker moments, I looked at it and only saw a golden reminder that I was the reason for his abandonment.

He held his wrist out, gazing at the empty spot for a few seconds too long, before shrugging. "I sold it to get my truck back."

I sucked in a breath. "Justin, you could've—"

"Don't. It wasn't a big deal. Thing was a pain in the ass to wear anyway."

I opened my mouth to tell him I knew that wasn't true, but the look in his eyes quickly shut my commentary down. He wasn't in the mood.

"About last night," he forged on, returning to the original reason he came over. "Can we both agree that we're sorry?"

I glanced up at him, his tall frame made his head nearly touch the ceiling in my small hallway. For some reason I *did* feel an urge to apologize, but not because of going out with Dash and the guys. More to make up for the fact that he had no real family outside of me, but somewhere in the far back of my mind I knew it wasn't entirely my responsibility.

Before I could respond he pulled me into his arms and pressed my head against his chest.

"You're all I've got, Blake. I can't stand the idea of what could happen to you when you get reckless."

"I wasn't reckless," I said, despite knowing I could hardly remember last night. I was about to make a case for being able to handle myself just fine, but the angle he held me in gave me a clear view of Dash's shoes by the door, and I jolted within Justin's embrace.

"What's wrong?" he asked, looking down at me.

I took a step back and pinched the bridge of my nose, trying to hide my panic. If he saw those shoes . . ."Nothing. I just don't feel well."

"You see what I mean? You shouldn't hang out with that type of crowd." He shook his head.

"Weren't you already running late?" Anger came to keep

my panic company.

He glanced at his cell. "Shit. You're right. Call you later."

Justin headed for the door quickly, and I thanked God he rushed out without looking down. I locked the door behind him, and waited until the sound of his footsteps disappeared before turning around.

I was surprised Dash hadn't bolted out of my room and left, never to speak to me again. I was clearly more drama than any ultra-new friendship could handle. He probably thought I was a lunatic, shoving him in there like that.

My cheeks flamed as I walked into my room, imagining all the horrible things he could say about me—like how I was so insecure in my relationship I had to hide a boy in my closet even though nothing had happened between us. Or the fact that I was such a lightweight, I blacked out half the night. And then he could always bring up the point that I'd let him, a near stranger, bring me home.

Hail sat in front of the closet, her hips swinging back and forth rapidly. I nudged her aside with my foot and cringed while sliding the closet door open.

Dash held my black sequined camisole over his muscled chest. He glanced down at it before pinning his green eyes on me. "Do you think this top is too much?"

A laugh ripped from my throat. I had to cover my mouth to stop it. "No, it brings out the color of your eyes," I said after gaining my composure.

The tension in my chest burst like a hundred tiny balloons. Dash slipped the cami back on the hanger and stepped out of my closet. Hail got under his feet so fast she nearly tripped him. He righted himself and took a seat on my bed, Hail jumping up beside him.

Dash looked at me then, and the light joking had left his eyes as he glanced toward the hallway.

"I'm so sorry," I said.

"You say that a lot, don't you?"

"What?"

"*Sorry*. I swear, I've only spent one night with you and you've already said it ten times."

My mouth dropped. I didn't think I said it that much. I shrugged. "Well, I am. I know that must've seemed crazy, but if Justin found you in here . . . he wouldn't wait for me to explain. He'd just start throwing punches, and I didn't want you to get mixed up in that."

"Guess it's good I stayed put then. I almost didn't."

"What?"

He stroked Hail's fur. "I was seconds away from shutting Justin's mouth for him. I mean, I know I just met you, but that's no way for a man to speak to a lady."

I felt like I'd been punched in the chest. Justin had always spoken to me like that. I'd never thought of it as anything but normal. "Really?" I asked, imagining the brawl that would've ensued if Dash had followed through with his plan. "You seem like the type of guy who keeps a level head."

He shrugged. "There are exceptions, but most of the time I am. It kind of comes with the job. You have to stay focused when you're out in the field or you can wind up hurt, or worse."

"True." I sighed.

I wished Justin kept calm under pressure, but it wasn't in his nature. Anytime the situation got a little intense, he'd resort to act first think later, and usually that led to me getting hurt—at least emotionally. My belongings were the only things he'd actually physically harmed, and himself. I pushed the thought away.

Dash pulled his cell phone out of his pocket and glanced at it. "Ten thirty. You want to go get some breakfast-lunch?"

"You mean brunch?"

He patted Hail's head before standing. "No. I meant

breakfast-lunch. Men don't eat brunch." He smirked.

A thrill ran through my center, but it quickly fizzled. Justin was clear on where he stood when it came to me going out with anyone other than him. I gazed at Dash, a hollow feeling in my stomach—I'd regret it forever if I didn't get to know him better. I thought about how angry Justin would be if he found out, but I reminded myself he hung out with his friends all the time. This was no different than that.

"Sure," I finally said. "You want to call Lindsay? We could pick her up on the way." I rummaged through my closet for some jeans.

Dash took a step closer as I turned around with my favorite pair in my hand.

"You know it's all right to be yourself around me. I think it's safe to say we're friends. And my girlfriend doesn't have to be there in order for it to be "acceptable" to hang out with you. I'm not sure if he makes you feel that way, but that isn't how I operate, okay?"

The sincerity in his green eyes nailed me to the floor.

"All right," I whispered and swallowed the lump in my throat. "Sorr—"

"*Don't* say sorry," Dash cut me off. He shook his head. "You'd think you never had a real friend before." He chuckled on his way out of my bedroom.

I shut the door behind him to change but didn't laugh. He was right.

"THESE ARE INCREDIBLE," I said after I swallowed another bite of the best Belgian waffles I'd ever eaten. "How do you know all the best places?"

Dash cocked an eyebrow from where he sat across the table. "I'm on the road a ton during storm season, and most of our food comes out of a paper bag. So when I'm home, I only eat where it is exceptionally above par." He took a drink of his iced tea before tackling a massive panini on his plate.

The quaint restaurant had a classic southern appeal with sleek wooden furniture and plenty of painted longhorn skulls hanging from the walls. The place's spread for brunch was stacked with classics from buttermilk biscuits and gravy to chicken fried steak. There were small stations next to the buffet—one cranked out fresh waffles or pancakes, and the other had the made-to-order panini press.

"Are you ready for this season?" I asked, drowning a piece of waffle in the restaurant's special pecan syrup.

"Absolutely. Nothing like the start of it . . . so many possibilities." His green eyes lit up like he could see an endless line of tornadoes begging for capture.

"How does Lindsay take you being away?" I asked, considering the freedom in having a valid excuse for a two-month break.

Dash shrugged. "We only had just gotten together a couple months before last year's season, so she's only been through one with me. And she handled it all right, I guess."

"You guess?"

"Well, she called . . . a lot. And she couldn't really grasp that if we came back for a weekend we might leave again at a moment's notice. One time we decided to track a supercell in Plano, Texas, and she lost her shit over it. Wanted me to take her to a foreign film festival instead. When I got back, she gave me the silent treatment for three days."

"I'd relish a silent treatment." I took a drink of orange juice.

"You're telling me the way he talked to you earlier today is . . . normal?"

"Actually, this morning was his good side. He has an ultra-short fuse. Anything can set him off, and the blowups are horrendous."

"And you stick around because . . ." He let the question hang there.

There were several reasons, but the main one I wasn't ready to tell him. I sighed. "We've grown up together. He's had a hard go of it. His family cut him out of his life at sixteen, and ever since he's kind of lived his life like the world is out to get him. He doesn't really have anyone else besides me."

Dash crunched down on a french fry. "Everyone has hard times. Doesn't give them the excuse to treat other people poorly."

My stomach clenched with the thought that there might be another way relationships worked. One without blowups or threats. Or one where I didn't have to keep an innocent outing like this a secret. "It's not an excuse . . . it's . . . just the way Justin is."

"Has he always been that way?"

"No. When we were kids, he was funny and sweet. Charming even."

"Well, surely he has some of those moments now. Right?" he asked.

I tried to conjure up the last time I'd found Justin charming. The day he'd given me the Blue October tickets came to mind, but the horribly selfish sex afterward squashed the charm right out of the memory. I hoped the kid I'd fallen for was still in there. Justin had lost himself somewhere along the way, and I'd tried to help him find it again for years.

"What keeps you and Lindsay going strong?" I asked instead of answering him. "Magic? I mean, she's obviously not into storms like you are." I challenged him to take the spotlight off my relationship. Speaking about it out loud made me analyze it in ways I never had before, and the result knotted up my stomach.

"Honestly, I don't know. We met at that party and then we just kind of happened. I'm not normally a serious relationship type guy." A flush swept across his cheeks, and he glanced down.

"You played the field," I said. He was smart and gorgeous. He could play all his life and never run out of partners.

"Yeah, you could say that. I'd never been in a relationship longer than a couple months. Thought I'd give it a try."

"Something must've worked since it's been a year," I said.

"She cares for me. It's a little intense at times, but I just got tired of the dating scene after a while, you know?"

I looked down at my nearly cleaned plate.

I had no idea what it was like to be single and have the freedom to browse. I glanced up at Dash, his bright green eyes holding mine. He was fully engaged in our conversation. He didn't check his phone or have that glazed-over, tuned-out look.

If I *could* browse, I'd look for something in his section. My heart stuttered with the thought and heat rushed to my cheeks. Not that he'd ever notice me in that way; Lindsay and I were starkly different. I could never be the girl he wanted, an utlra-pretty, social butterfly, like her.

"You want anything else?" he asked.

I laid my napkin over my plate. "I'm throwing in the towel."

He snatched the paper check the waitress had left at our table. "You did good. I would've had to leave you here if you'd only grabbed a fruit plate." He winked at me and headed toward the counter.

"Don't you want my share?" I asked, placing my hand on his forearm. His skin was warm stretched over the hard muscle. A hot tremble ran through my fingertips.

"No. You can get the next one," he said and slipped out of my grasp.

My heart soared. The next one—and I hadn't even had to beg.

CHAPTER

FOUR

"I 'VE GOT TO meet Paul and John at the lab before we head out on our chase later. You want to come with?" Dash asked as we exited class.

"Absolutely," I said, stopping myself from asking to go on the chase with them. It had only been two days since Dash took me to brunch, and I was still a new girl to their tight-knit group so I didn't want to push.

Dash motioned for me to follow him. We walked a short way to the neighboring brick building where a string of labs were used by students for interpreting data. He turned into the third door on the right of a long hallway. John and Paul were already inside and hovered over a table against the back wall. It had four computers spaced evenly on top of it and there were more scattered throughout the room.

Various maps and pictures of supercells lined the walls, not unlike our Physical Meteorology classroom. The boys had three of the computer screens up and running, each one showing a different image from a weather satellite and a station model weather map beneath it.

I hung back a ways, allowing Dash to join them, but couldn't help smirking a little. I'd learned my freshman year of college that I was sharp when it came to interpreting weather maps, especially station models. The combined data displayed—air pressure, temperatures, wind velocities, cloud cover, and precipitation measurements—gave some people trouble when adding them all together and predicting the outcome. But to me, all the numbers and patterns aligned in my head quicker than if I was doing basic math, and the outcome clearly presented itself in my mind. That is one reason I knew I'd be a great meteorologist, because I could interpret this data on the fly and hopefully provide the most up-to-date and accurate report possible for the people in the path of a storm.

"Hey, Blake," John said over his shoulder.

Paul gave me a nod while talking to Dash in hushed conversation.

"Hi," I said, trying to focus on one of the images of a supercell hanging over some small-town water tower, but my eyes kept shifting back to the screens the boys stared at, begging me to calculate, predict.

"Come here a second," Dash said after a few moments.

I set my bag on the table in front of me and quickly headed over. "Yeah?"

"We need you to settle something for us," he said, eyeing Paul. "We're about to head out on a chase, but there are two locations primed for tornado activity. I think this one with the squall line"—he pointed to the screen in the middle—"has more of a shot."

"And I disagree," Paul said, pointing to the screen on the right. "This one has a better chance."

Dash sucked his teeth. "You see our problem."

I leaned over Paul, who hadn't moved from his seat in front of the screens. I glanced at each image of the sky the weather satellites provided for the two locations and then studied both station models beneath them. I had my answer within two minutes.

"I agree with Paul," I said.

"What makes you do that?" Dash asked.

"Because"—I placed my hand on Paul's shoulder with one hand and reached over to point at the middle of the screen with the other—"while you are correct about this awesome line of organized storms, they'll most likely only produce damaging winds. Intense, sure, but not as likely for tornado activity as this one." I pointed to the screen on the right with the collection of large gray bubble-like clouds covering the sky. "This combination of mammatus clouds and the warm temperature are primed for producing a tornado. Check out the wind velocity already," I said, pointing it out on the surface map. "In fact"—I glanced at the clock in the upper right-hand corner of the screen—"hit refresh on the image. I bet you in the time we've been discussing this there is already an updraft developing."

Paul clicked refresh.

Dash smacked him on the back once the image reloaded. "She's right. Time to go." He turned to me, placing his hand on my shoulder. "Nicely done. That was fast."

"Wicked fast," John said, scooting away from the table and gathering his gear.

Paul flashed Dash a knowing grin before glancing back at me. "Yeah, you did all right." He smiled and walked toward the door.

"I'll give you a call tomorrow," Dash said. "And thanks."

"Anytime," I said, stopping myself from adding a *be careful* to the end of that statement. They chased for a living and knew what they were doing, but the concern for their safety was hard to ignore. I hung back to check out the other images pulled up on the screens, but turned my attention back to the boys as they exited the room.

Dash nudged Paul with his elbow as they walked through the door and whispered, "Told you she could do it."

I sank into the seat Paul had once occupied, my heart swelling. They'd given me a test and Dash had been the one to believe in me. The sensation was new and totally blissful as I turned back to the screens, staring at the location where my prediction sent them.

"YOU READY?" JUSTIN asked once I'd opened the door for him.

I smiled and nodded.

"Great, let's go," he said and swung around.

I climbed into his truck, my stomach twisting in anticipation. Justin had called last night and told me to be ready to go out at noon; he had a surprise for me. My jaw had nearly dropped to the floor, and it had taken me a good thirty seconds to respond. I couldn't even remember the last time he'd been spontaneous.

I'd seen Dash every day since we'd had brunch last week, whether it be in class, hanging out in the weather lab, or going out to eat, and he more than fulfilled the intense longing I had for a true friendship.

But Justin didn't know that.

I'd battled with myself ever since the first night I hung out with Dash, but in the end, I'd decided it was better if Justin believed I was studying on campus or working when I wasn't with him. I didn't like hiding it from him, but I also couldn't stand another ultimatum, and I was sure he'd give me one if I confessed how close Dash and I had grown as friends. Even if it was innocent, Justin would find a way to make me feel guilty about it. So, if I was going to feel guilty anyway, at least this way I got to keep Dash's friendship. And I hoped one day, possibly after I figured out how to get the two of them to meet so

Justin could see how awesome Dash was, that I wouldn't have to be so secretive about it.

"Here we are," Justin said after a short drive. A genuine smile lit up his sharp-angled face. He navigated the truck into a parking spot in front of a bookstore connected to the mall.

"What's the occasion?" I asked, stepping out of the truck.

He reached for my hand. "I feel like I never see you anymore."

"I told you my last two years in school would be heavy," I said. It was the truth, if not absolute. Sure, I'd spent some extra time with Dash and the guys but never when I was supposed to be with Justin. When Justin would call, I was there. It wasn't my fault he assumed I'd just sit at home and wait by the phone until he did. It was better this way. The blowup wouldn't be worth the full-truth, and it wouldn't be merited anyway.

"I guess I didn't realize how engrossed you'd be with it all. You missed my call yesterday. I'd wanted to take you to lunch." He tugged me toward the entrance to the bookstore.

I let the confusion show on my face. I'd had my cell on me the whole day, which I'd spent in the weather lab with the boys. He hadn't tried to call.

"So where were you, Blake?" he asked, as he held the door open for me.

"On campus. Studying. Where else would I be?" I swallowed hard, the sharpness in his eyes making my chest tight. That look was exactly why I couldn't let him know every detail of my free time.

He was silent for a few moments before he nodded. "Next time text me if you're going to stay on campus on your breaks, okay? I go crazy when I don't know where you are."

I forced a smile, wondering why his words irked me more today than normal. He'd said the same things to me since I started school and I'd never questioned it. He'd always wanted me to check in once I got home or went to work, that wasn't a big deal. But now that I had to hide my newly-formed friendships from him, I wondered how much his need to know where I was constantly was out of love or out of the need to control every facet of my life.

The smell of fresh paper and hot coffee wafted over me as we walked deeper into the store, the scents grounding me in the present. I shook my head, tossing the thoughts off as the over-analyzer I was.

"Pick out a couple. Any you want, I'm buying," Justin said and released my hand. His tone was even and he smiled, helping to shove my earlier concerns and irritation down.

"Thank you." I turned down an aisle, gazing at the variety of beautifully covered books.

His gesture made a flood of memories rush through me, like the tide of the ocean that had drawn so far away from my toes in the sand I thought it'd never come back.

Memories of when we were younger—our walks around the neighborhood that seemed endless and yet always ended too soon. Where we would let the moon and lampposts guide us as we walked and talked, discovering each other.

The special expanse of black walnut trees where he'd told me about his mom abandoning him, how he'd never known his real father, and how his aunt and uncle treated him like an inconvenience. I'd held his hand for the first time that day and told him about the screaming matches between my mom and dad, how Dad constantly had to buy new dishes or appliances because he'd break them during a fight, and how the arguments were increasing in frequency. He'd rushed to meet me in that spot, no matter the time, whenever I'd called him, frantic after another fight between my parents.

The phone calls that carried on late in the night—well beyond the warnings from Mom to end the conversation for bedtime—after his aunt and uncle had moved him across town.

The Justin I remembered brought a warmth to my heart and a longing for him to be that compassionate again. He'd lost the sweetness somewhere between high school and now. The blowups started his sophomore year, the same year he'd been kicked out of his home and had to fend for himself.

Now, as he followed me down the adult paranormal section, that sweet side of Justin didn't seem as far away. I'd often hoped one day I'd be able to help draw out a balance in him, one where the boy I fell in love with would merge with the man he could be if he allowed his motivations to go beyond that of Xbox points and most beer cans collected. As he trailed behind me, I thought perhaps this was a small step toward that balance. Maybe he wouldn't care if I told him about Dash and the guys, maybe he'd actually want to meet them.

"I know you'll be a while, so I'm going to look around. Come find me when you're done," he said, cutting through my thoughts.

"All right," I answered, watching him turn and walk away.

I lost myself then, amongst the books and memories of Justin. Like the times he'd show up outside my high school after classes had ended, a new DVD and a sack full of glorious junk food in his truck, and nothing but time to watch it and laugh and simply be together. If I'd known then that those moments would disappear over the years, I may have treasured them a bit more.

I finally settled on a couple of novels, clutching them to my chest as I took a slow stroll through the store, scanning the aisles for Justin. First the Blue October tickets and now this. My chest tightened a fraction, and ice settled in my stomach with the thought of the reward he'd expect when we arrived home.

I pushed the thought away, allowing his sweet spontaneity to take over, and contemplated sashaying through the erotica novels. Perhaps a quick skim of one and I could find the answer to our problem—or my problem as he'd so often put it.

A vibration in my pocket distracted me and I pulled my cell phone out.

Want to grab a late lunch? Dash texted.

A warmth bloomed inside my chest. This was my chance. Justin was in a great mood, and it would be the perfect time to introduce them—put an end to hiding my new friends.

I searched harder for Justin. The thought of the two meeting made me a little anxious. I wanted them to like each other, but they were polar opposites.

When I didn't lock on to his tall frame anywhere in the store, I deflated. I know I'd taken a little over a half an hour in the overwhelming obstacle of choosing just two books, but I thought that was pretty reasonable.

After two unanswered calls to his cell—guess it was perfectly fine for *him* to ignore *my* calls—and twenty minutes of waiting, I gave up and bought the books myself. I grabbed my bag with the novels nestled inside and headed toward the exit leading into the main area of the mall. I had an easy guess where he was.

A short walk and two turns later, I entered the video game store. Huge neon signs reading *One Day Only, 60% Off Store Wide* bombarded the glass windows at the entrance, hung on the walls, and stood on stands throughout the aisles. The store was packed, too, people crowding the rows of games separated into which console they went with, and a line snaked out the exit.

I spotted Justin in the 360 section, four games tucked under one arm as he scanned another with his free hand.

"Justin," I said, weaving through five boys just to get to him.

He glanced up from the game he held. "Some sale, huh?"

"You knew about it." It wasn't a question or an accusation,

just a fact.

He shrugged. "I may have heard about it last week."

I sighed, eyeing the games in his hands. "Don't you already have that one?" I pointed to the one I recognized under his arm.

"Yeah, but this is a special edition. You get four exclusive maps with it." He grabbed it and showed it to me.

My stomach tied into knots. I glared at the games, sizing up my competition. Sadness slithered through my blood when I realized how many times they'd beaten me.

"You found some books?" Justin asked, glancing at the bag in my hand.

"Yeah," I said, holding the bag up and shrugging.

"I'll get the next ones for you, okay?" he said and went back to browsing the games on the shelf.

I pressed my lips together and nodded.

"Actually, I'm going to need to borrow some money." He gave me puppy eyes, but he looked more desperate than charming.

I gripped the bag I held a little tighter. "How much?"

Justin eyed the games in his hands, then looked over the endless array before him. "A couple hundred should do it."

My mouth dropped and I scoffed. "You're joking!"

"This is a once-a-year sale, Blake."

"Why didn't you save up for it then?" I asked. An image of the new stereo he'd bought for his truck last week popped into my mind. Followed by a visual of the subwoofer he had on hold to go with it.

"Oh, come on, it's not like you ever buy anything with your paychecks," he whined.

He knew most of the money I earned went to rent, books, and food. Whatever I had left I saved, other than treating myself to the occasional book or movie.

"I know you've got plenty in your savings. I'll pay you

back," he urged.

He had yet to pay me back for the money he'd borrowed last year for a new set of fishing poles. I sighed. The money wasn't what really bothered me.

"This is why you brought me here today, isn't it?" Anger simmered in my gut, setting the tight knots on fire.

"What is the big fucking deal, Blake? This way we both get what we want."

What I really wanted was time with him that didn't come with conditions or arguments or lectures on where and how I spent my time. I swallowed the lump in my throat. His actions today had nothing to do with me. God, I was stupid sometimes.

"Not this time, Justin."

"Why the fuck not?"

I glanced down. "If you have to ask, then it's not even worth explaining."

"I had to sell my watch for you!" he snapped.

I flinched, as if he'd physically stunned me. "What? You sold it to get your truck back."

"But I wouldn't have had to do that if I hadn't just bought you those Blue October tickets."

My heart sank. I stood there, floundering in my own guilt for a few moments, contemplating pulling out all the extra cash I had and shoving it into his hands. Then I saw the games he held and the guilt turned to a burning anger. "No. I don't buy that, Justin. You could've easily sold your collection of video games and Xbox to get your truck back. Hell, you could've sold that big-ass TV, too, or even asked me then to borrow money. But you didn't. *You* made the choice, so don't you dare put something like that on me."

His eyes popped before narrowing. I saw the shock. It'd been too long since I'd called him on his bullshit. He stomped off without saying a word to contradict me.

Normally I would've followed him and given him the money just to avoid the fight, and being left behind without a ride—which he'd done to me twice in the past.

Not today. I grabbed my cell phone again.

Can you pick me up at the bookstore in the mall? I shot Dash another text, my fingers shaking with adrenaline. Justin blew up all the time, but today it struck a new chord, like a tap to a freshly exposed nerve.

Of course. I know a great Mexican place a block away from there. See you in ten.

AN HOUR AND a half later, I set my napkin on my half-cleaned plate and leaned back in food defeat.

Dash sat across from me and shoveled another chip with a heaping pile of salsa on it into his mouth. The restaurant smelled of peppers and fried chips, and the food, of course, had been delicious.

"Did he say anything when you left?" Dash asked after taking a gulp of iced tea.

"I didn't wait around to hear it this time," I said, still shocked I'd walked away from Justin in the video game store. I'd told him I found another ride home and just . . . left. Never, in our entire relationship, had I had the nerve to do that. I glanced across the table at Dash, knowing our friendship contributed to my new boldness.

"Good job. That was a jerk move, even by guy standards."

"Thank you." I sighed, the relief of being understood was so intense it was almost unnerving. I hadn't been able to unload my fights with Justin on anyone before—Mom, the only other person I really talked to, didn't care for him and would never hear me out.

"Does he do that a lot?"

"What? Act like he's doing something for me and then I

realize it's really about him? Or ask me for money?" I fiddled with the sugar packets on the table.

"Both."

I brought my gaze back to him.

He leaned back in his seat and shook his head. "Can't help you there. Lindsay has got more money than she knows what to do with."

"It's all right. You help just by listening. Sorry I talk your ear off all the time," I said. How much personal history *had* we covered in the past week? Nearly all of it, I realized. Talking to Dash was just so easy. He listened and actually tuned in, like no one else existed outside of our conversation. A stab of jealousy hit me, thinking this is how he must treat Lindsay all the time.

"I enjoy it. Honestly, who else could keep up with me about storms and Blue October? And that's not even mentioning our similar taste in movies."

"You've got a point," I said. Yesterday we'd had an hour-long conversation about why The Departed deserved to be in the top ten best movies of all time list. And then a thought that hadn't occurred to me popped into my head. "Do you talk to Lindsay about us?"

His eyes widened.

"That came out wrong." My cheeks flushed. "I meant, does she get upset about the time you spend with me?" I rubbed my hands together underneath the table, wondering if he had to hide our friendship as well.

"No. We're friends and we have nearly the same career plans; of course we're going to spend time together." Dash nodded at the waitress at the table across from us.

"Oh."

"Does he give you a hard time about it?"

I broke our gaze, staring down at the table. "I haven't told him."

He stayed silent so long I finally glanced up. Damn it, he looked at me with pity in his eyes. I never wanted to see that from him. "I've gathered, from the stories you've told, and what little I heard from him that first day I hid in your room, that he is the kind of man who wouldn't approve of us getting close. Regardless of us just being friends?"

"It'd be a battle, and I'm so tired of fighting. Do you think I'm an awful person for hiding this? Is it . . . crazy?" The more I thought about it the more it felt like I was having an affair minus the whole sex part.

"You're an amazing person, Blake. Never think otherwise. You know him better than anyone. And if you need me to pop the brakes I can—"

"No." I cut him off, hoping he didn't hear the desperation in my voice. My happiness had increased tenfold since he'd come into my life. "This is all on me. It would be fine. I'm just not ready to have that argument yet."

Dash bit the corner of his lip. "Sounds like he gives you too much grief over everything. Do you want to talk about it?"

I did. "No. It's just me. Over analyzing is what I do." I paired my answer with a full smile, trying to shrug off the serious turn the conversation took.

"Well, you do have a talent for it." He leaned a little closer over the table. "But if you ever do want to talk, about anything, you know I'm here, right?"

I nodded because I was afraid my voice would crack if I responded. A warmth soothed the confusion and guilt that bit my insides.

The waitress set down the check and cleared our plates, completely breaking the tension that I had brought to lunch. I reached for the paper, but Dash snatched it from me.

"It's my turn." I tried to grab it from him.

He held it out of my reach. "I know, but you've already had one man hitting you up for money today. I will not be the second." He winked at me.

Heat rushed through my core and kick-started my heart. "This is different. It's lunch, not a stack of video games."

Dash dug in his back pocket for his wallet, the corded muscle in his forearm flexing with the motion. I grabbed my iced tea and took a good long drink.

"I'm well aware of that, Blake," he said, planting his green eyes on mine and daring me to argue. "Just consider it my attempt to show you not all men are self-centered video game addicts." He handed his credit card and the check to the waitress who'd returned to our table.

My eyebrows shot up at his not so backhanded rip on Justin.

"Thank you." I hoped Dash knew I encompassed his kindness and mad listening skills within the phrase.

CHAPTER

FIVE

'D WATCHED COUNTLESS thunderstorms from my back porch and seen clips on Dash's site, but I knew neither of those things could prepare me for a real chase.

My eyes darted between Dash behind the wheel of his truck and the gray sky that filled his windshield. I had a hard time choosing whether to focus on the gathering storm or Dash weaving in and out of traffic.

My heart pounded in my chest, adrenaline pumping to each of my nerve endings. Dash had shown up at my place a little over an hour ago, offering my first chance at a chase. A severe thunderstorm with tornado-producing capabilities was accumulating just an hour outside of town, and when he prompted me to get ready in a hurry, I leaped into action.

"Where's my exit, John?" Dash spoke into a black walkie-talkie, his voice tight.

"Three miles. Exit and then head southeast," John's voice blared from the device. I glanced behind me, easily finding the Tracker Jacker—a beat-up nineties model Toyota 4x4 with long antennas sticking out of the top and two large yellow lights attached to the back corners.

Dash set the walkie-talkie down, and I raised my eyebrows at him when he snuck a glance my way.

"What?" he asked, returning his eyes to the road.

"That's the extent of planning?" I asked.

"We've got tons of routes mapped out already from the grueling prep work we did in the winter, but you can only plan so much before you have to make the call yourself."

"So you don't depend solely on the radar?" I asked, shocked that he hadn't checked one station model before picking this location.

"No. I catch a lot of flak for it, but I use it more like a guideline. Once I set eyes on the storm . . ." His eyes sharpened, focusing on the dark clouds gathering in the distance.

I loved when he got lost in the thoughts of a storm. It proved I wasn't the only crazy one who found beauty in chaos.

"What?" I finally urged him to continue.

"It's hard to explain. I just get a sense of where it'll tighten into something bigger and head that direction."

"Why do people give you crap about it?" I asked, remembering how Professor Ackren had it out for him and the guys since day one. He always harped on them about the technical and scientific side of weather. I tried to answer most of the questions as quick as I could to take the heat off them.

Dash shrugged. "I use more instinct than science, and to some people that's reckless. Also, I've got more up-close images than some veteran chasers, and despite us working toward the same goal, it irks them. Some chasers say I'm only in it for the thrill and for selling my shots."

"I see," I said, but it was hard to really grasp his lifestyle. "Does it bother you?"

"Not really. I mean, sometimes it's annoying because we take the same measurements others do. And next season we'll have the probes to deploy, which will increase the data."

He changed lanes to pass another car. "Plus, the most useful area of study is where the tornado touches the ground, and because so many people are afraid to get that close, I'm one of the only people getting that information. If another chaser wanted the data collected from it, it's not like I'd charge him for it. But I can't deny the rush I get from capturing a storm, and I'm not ashamed of the money I make for it, either."

"Good, you shouldn't." I swallowed a lump in my throat. I'd always assumed from Dash's shots he'd just had an expensive camera with an excellent zoom option. From his words, I had been sorely mistaken.

"Thanks, but can I be honest about something?" he asked, glancing at me for a moment.

"Always," I said, focusing on him.

"It would give our group a lot more credit if you became a stable part of it."

"Me? How?" I asked, shocked. "You all have way more experience than I do."

"You always sell yourself short, Blake. The way you interpret data in half the time it takes even me to do it, paired with the natural instinct you have when the sky darkens? It's incredible. And the fact that you are more prone to check the science and use it to back your predictions like any good meteorologist would do could garner us more respect from those in our field that continue to question my tactics. We'd make a great team."

I swallowed hard, a flush dusting my cheeks. I smiled, not exactly sure how to convey the importance of his words to me. "Thank you. I'd love to be more involved," I said and for a split-second thought about how much more involved I could be with *him*.

Heat rushed to my cheeks and I quickly glanced out the window, wondering where in the hell that had come from. I took a deep breath and assured myself it was due to the gratitude swelling in my chest. Though he'd continuously noticed my abilities with storms and my passion for them, I was still getting used to being recognized for my talents, let alone praised for them.

"Check it out." He pointed at a gray wall cloud to the right. He took the next exit faster than I could blink. Once I laid eyes on the full expanse of the supercell—thick tufts of black cloud with the sun blinding behind it—I was hooked. The power of the storm drew me in, the potential written all over the dark, churning mass.

I pressed my fingertip to the window, pointing at the lower right side of the cloud. "There is rapid circulation," I blurted out, thrilled with the catch. If I hadn't been looking for it I may not have seen it, the solid color made it hard to see the movement.

Dash squinted, zeroing in on where I pointed. "You're right." He grabbed the walkie-talkie. "Blake spotted some rotation in the western portion of the cell. I'm heading that way."

A few seconds later John's voice crackled over the radio. "Nice. Follow this road and take the third right. That should give us the best vantage point."

"On it," Dash said. "Good eyes, Blake."

The compliment added to my already-pumping heart. I forced myself to focus solely on the storm. Lightning crackled, followed by the roar of thunder, loud enough to vibrate my chest. I jumped slightly, admiring Dash's calm and unflinching control of the truck. The closer we got, the stronger the winds pushed against the vehicle, threatening to throw us off the road. Rain pelted the windshield, and the splattering bursts made visibility of the developing funnel difficult.

"Dash," I gasped, as if I chased the storm on foot. "It's transitioning into lower rotation. See the funnel?"

Dash slowed the truck on the rural road leading us closer

to the storm. He set eyes on it and nodded. "It has potential. Here, take the wheel," he said, as if he were asking me to hold his phone.

I gaped for a moment, but then blinked twice and reached over him, wrapping my fingers around the steering wheel. He kept his foot steady on the gas as he shifted in the driver's seat, reaching behind him. The motion made his hard chest graze against my bare arm, and another flush raked across my skin. I swallowed and focused on the rain-soaked road ahead of us.

The minute felt like an eternity until he finally righted himself. With a video camera in his right hand, he retook the wheel with his left, and I scooted back to my seat.

Dash turned on the camera and pointed it at the developing funnel in front of us. Judging from the length of road and the growing mass ahead of us, it was only a mile away now. "It's organizing!" Dash hollered as if we weren't sitting right next to each other, and my heart leaped into my throat.

Another crack of lightning struck the ground underneath the cloud, the bright light leaving an impression on the back of my eyelids. Thunder roared even louder than the first time. The hair standing on the back of my neck confirmed we were well under it now.

"The tail is lowering," Dash shouted into the walkie-talkie. "Paul, I will throat punch you if you miss these shots!"

I would've laughed if I hadn't been so focused on the fact that Dash had just confirmed the tail of the funnel was about to touch down, causing a mixture of ice-cold panic and pure excitement to shoot up my spine.

"I already gave him my camera!" John shouted back, grounding me.

The energy was high in both vehicles; I could hear it in their tense voices through the line. My heart raced and the adrenaline expanded within me, begging for release.

A thicker string of cloud snaked out of the rotating portion of the storm, creating a more threatening funnel. Ice filled my veins. I'd never been this close to a tornado before, and despite the slender size, if it touched down, it would be powerful enough to rip trees from their roots. For a split second I had the urge to take the wheel again and spin us in the opposite direction, instinct shouting at me to flee, but it passed in a blink.

An exhilarating thrill sped through me, replacing the momentary fear, like reaching the top of a roller coaster just before making the first drop.

The grayish-white cloud churned and snaked horizontally to the left, like a long bone-white finger reaching to press a button. The wisps of cloud spiraled in and out of focus, switching from semisolid to see-through, revealing the thundering sky behind it.

"Come on!" Dash yelled at the sky, his impatience with the funnel's horizontal trend evident in his tone.

Static crackled from the walkie-talkie before Paul's voice sounded in the cab of Dash's truck.

"It's roping out," Paul said, his voice dejected. I glanced behind me, seeing the Tracker Jacker and Paul's eyes on his laptop opened before him.

I whipped back around, focusing on the storm again. He was right. The spinning cloud slowly dissipated little by little, shedding pieces of atmosphere like sloughs of snakeskin. The broken sections of cloud wouldn't reconfigure, not with the predominant cloud breaking apart, too.

My stomach sank, the disappointment heavy. We'd been so close to seeing a tornado on the ground I could taste it, but the potential was gone now. My building anticipation shattered, like I'd shown up late to a concert and missed my favorite band. We'd gotten to the top of the roller coaster but weren't allowed to fly down it.

"Damn it!" Dash yelled, finally setting his video camera in the space between us.

We both sighed and then then truck filled with silence.

"We had the perfect vantage point," John said after a few minutes, the disappointment clear in his tone as well.

Dash took a deep breath before pushing the button on the walkie-talkie. "You're right. We couldn't have asked for a more prime spot. Just wish we could've gotten ahead of it in time to pull off-road and film better. Paul, anything on Doppler?"

"Nothing, man," Paul shouted across the line. "A strong gust of cold air must have just blasted through here, killing all potential."

Dash set the radio down. We didn't need Doppler to tell us that, not for this location anyway. I could easily tell just by looking at the broken clouds in the sky and the lessening rain that this storm cell was done.

My hands trembled from the adrenaline slowly leaving my body. "I know that was probably nothing for you, but I've never seen something so incredible."

Dash sighed. "Yeah, but I really wanted you to see one touch down today. It'll change you."

I already counted the minutes until another chase opportunity presented itself. It wouldn't change me, though . . . it already had.

CHAPTER

SIX

"YOU'RE NOT SERIOUSLY bailing on me again, are you?" I held my cell to my ear and tried to stop my hands from shaking.

"I actually worked all week! I didn't just sit in a comfortable classroom and read books all day, or check out customers looking for the newest DVD."

"But you promised—" After the video game store fiasco a couple of weeks ago, Justin had promised he'd make it up to me for being a jerk. I'd seized the opportunity to test the waters, explaining to him about the new "study-friends" I'd made and wanted him to meet. In the moment, he'd agreed to anything to get back in my good graces, but in the time since he'd failed to deliver.

"This is bullshit! I have *two* days off. I'm exhausted and want to relax."

Tears stung the backs of my eyes, but I pushed them away. I paced the concrete walkway outside of Bailey's. This was the second weekend in a row Justin had flaked on that promise. Last week's excuse was he didn't feel well, which I would've totally understood if he hadn't spent both nights drinking with his boys while watching a Die Hard marathon. He'd invited me over, but I wasn't in the mood. He'd texted me throughout, giving me crap over studying with the guys over watching movies with him. The way he harped on me about it only reaffirmed my decision on not fully disclosing just how much time *not-studying* I did with Dash and the guys.

"It's not like I'm asking you to run a 5k, Justin," I said, returning to myself. "Just come out for a couple hours to meet my friends." I stopped mid-pace and leaned against the outside of the bar. People went in and out, ignoring the girl close to losing her cool.

"Your friends? God, Blake, you've known them for a week." He scoffed.

Over a month now, actually. And I'd spent nearly every day with Dash. After class we'd go to lunch and rehash the lectures or he'd tell me one of his countless storm-chasing tales. Sometimes he and the guys would drop by my work before I got off and then hang at my place after.

John and Paul loved Hail, and she surprised me with her acceptance of more males, but she doted on Dash. I hadn't been out this much or had more fun in my entire college career. Possibly high school, either. And I wished Justin could be a part of that, but he wasn't. I couldn't even be honest with him about it, because if he knew how happy Dash made me he'd squash it. Twist it and make me the bad guy. Maybe I was. Or maybe Justin really didn't want me to have any source of happiness outside of his control. I didn't know what made sense anymore.

"You know they only want you around to help them get ahead in class or chases or whatever the hell it is they do. They don't like *you*, Blake. They only like where you'll get them."

It wasn't true, but his words stung. He made the idea of someone else actually liking me for who I was sound ridiculous.

"Fine. You have fun playing video games," I snapped.

Stupid of me.

"You're being an immature bitch, and I won't stand for it. I'm a grown man, and if I want to drink beer and play COD on the weekends, then I will."

"Funny how that is more appealing than spending time with your girlfriend." Grown man my ass.

"You're always welcome over here. You know that."

I sighed and rubbed the back of my neck. I hated Justin's apartment. The normal state consisted of wall-to-wall Keystone Light cans, half filled with chew-tainted spit, and the other half crushed and thrown across the room sporadically. Fast food bags, empty dip cans, cigarette packs, and dirty laundry rounded out the decor. The only pristine thing in his apartment was his fifty-inch flat screen and the fully loaded entertainment center beneath it. When he first got the place I'd made a habit of going over there on Mondays after school when he was at work and cleaned. I did it for months and the place always smelled fresh and looked like a real home afterward. Though, after months of never getting so much as a "thank you", I'd given up and had him over at my place instead.

"Come on, Blake. I'm sorry I snapped before. It's because I need to see you so bad. Just ditch those guys and come over. We'll watch a movie. Just you and me." His voice had softened.

I glanced at the bar, picturing Dash and the guys inside.

"Just you and me?" I asked, wondering if the time alone would give us the opportunity to find a common ground again. It *had* been two weeks since he'd seen me. Maybe that was why he was in such a mood. He needed me. I could make him happy and set things right.

"Yes, just us."

"All right. I'll be over in half an hour."

"See you then."

I gave him a little time, hoping he'd clean the place up a bit before I got there.

I walked back into the bar and slid my fresh frosted mug of beer toward Dash. Lindsay eyed it but quickly looked away when I glanced at her. "You can have this. I'm heading to Justin's."

"I thought he was coming here?" He scanned the bar as if Justin would magically appear. I wished.

"He's beat from work. We're going to do a movie night." I made it sound like a normal thing we did.

"Your loss, Meteorologist. We're about to engage in an epic shuffleboard battle," Paul said.

"I'll catch the next one."

"Hey, wait," Paul stopped me before I could turn to leave. "What do meteorologists call a row of martinis?"

I rolled my eyes but indulged Paul's need to crack a corny weather joke every time we saw each other. "What?"

"The Dry Line!" He laughed at his cleverness, and I released a small chuckle.

"Good one," I said.

Dash shook his head. "Paul, man, where do you get this crap?" Paul just smirked as Dash hopped up from the table. "Hold up, Blake. I'll walk you out."

We cleared the crowded bar and stepped into the cool night air. I stopped before my car and glanced at Dash who was awfully quiet. "What's up?"

He shoved his hands in his pockets and shrugged. After spending so much time with him, I knew that meant he was holding something back. I'd seen him do it with the guys plenty of times, especially when they argued the wrong side of a debate regarding why tornadoes occurred predominantly in the afternoon. Honestly, I think Paul only said it was due to atmospheric pressure as opposed to the more likely reason of temperature and moisture levels to get a rise out of Dash.

"Come on, just tell me."

"I don't want to upset you," he finally said, meeting my eyes.

The notion almost made me laugh. We agreed on almost everything. "I highly doubt there is anything you could say that would upset me, Dash. Out with it."

He shrugged again. "You let him off too easy."

A rock lodged itself in my throat. Dash normally avoided speaking his mind in regards to Justin and settled on eye rolls when I relayed stories to him. It was nice, to just talk about things with him without being judged. I knew it could only last so long.

"What do you mean?"

"This is the hundredth time he's flaked on you."

"He's only done this twice."

"To meet us, yeah, but to you . . ."

I took a deep breath. Maybe I'd been too liberal when sharing past stories with him.

He took his hands out of his pockets and raked them through his hair. "You don't have to cater to his schedule, you know. If he wanted to see you . . . he'd see you."

A sharp pain twisted in my chest. Dash was right. Damn him. Of course I knew that, but I couldn't change Justin. He'd been this way since the beginning. All I could do was take what he gave, no matter how little he offered.

"Well, he's about to see me," I said angrily and dug my keys out of my purse.

"So you're just going to run to him? Let him dictate how you spend all your time?"

"He doesn't decide how I spend all my time."

"Oh really? Why are you going to school here? Not that I'm not happy you are, but really? Why is it that you haven't been to one party since you started school? Or why do you feel the need to lie to him about all the time we spend together?"

Shame clawed at my stomach having the fact that I had to lie about my friendships thrown in my face. "It's easier if he thinks we only study together—"

"You've got to be joking." Dash jerked his hands in the air. "Tell me you can at least see that he isolates you for a reason?"

My heart pounded anxiously. Dash didn't know the truth. He couldn't understand I was the only person in Justin's life who hadn't abandoned him. My presence kept Justin from slipping into that dark place where everyone else in his life who was supposed to love him had pushed him. A place where his life hung in the balance. "You don't know him—"

"I know *you*, Blake," he interrupted me. "I know that you can't stand tomatoes but are too nice to ever ask the waitress to leave them off. I know that the only other artist you blare as loud as Blue October is Elvis. I know the look in your eyes when you see the sky darken and you hear that first clap of thunder. And I know that every time he hurts you, I want to introduce his face to the curb."

My mouth dropped open. Dash continuously shocked me with how well he understood me in such a short amount of time. The sensation of completeness was new and almost jarring. I took a deep breath and let it out slowly. "Dash . . . if you only knew—"

"I'd still probably think he was an asshole," he cut me off.

Why were the men in my life picking fights with me today? My stomach boiled. "Fine." I shrugged. "Think what you want." I opened my car door and sank inside. Dash stomped toward the bar, and I drove off before he'd made it in.

I gripped the steering wheel so hard my knuckles turned white. My insides trembled and I screamed.

I took a few deep breaths to calm down, eased back in my seat, and focused on the road. Even Justin hadn't pulled a reaction like this out of me from a fight in a long time. Maybe because I avoided fights with him at all cost. Dash had blind-sided me, though.

Why had he chosen tonight to speak his mind? He'd had plenty of opportunities in the past month when I'd basically relayed Justin's and my entire history to him. Instead he'd just made his faces and given his own war story involving him and Lindsay. We'd laughed about it.

I let myself in to Justin's apartment, excitement replacing the anger within me. Justin and I were about to have a much-needed quiet night together, just the two of us. Dash couldn't possibly understand the need because Lindsay was at his beck and call. He had no idea what it was like to have to fight for time with your partner or to get to a place where you were so lost you didn't even know where you stood anymore. I had to find solid ground again.

My heart sank a fraction as I made my way to the living room. I stepped over opened stereo boxes, their wires and cords strewn everywhere, and then tiptoed across the room to avoid crushing empty beer cans with my boots. The place smelled faintly of smoke and fried food, but not in a good way like at the bar. This was more of a stagnant scent that had hovered who knows how long. It'd been a while since this place had a good cleaning. Probably since the last time I'd done it, months ago. I glanced at the kitchen on my way and cringed. A tower of dishes filled the sink, some moldy, others cracked, and the countertops were littered with McDonald's and Wendy's bags. My fingers itched to give it all a good scrub down, but I squashed the urge.

Justin sat in the middle of his couch, his Xbox controller in hand and his eyes fixed on his massive flat screen. The living room fared no better, and I sighed.

"Just a minute," Justin said without looking up.

I continued to stare at the mess he lived in, a wave of unease sweeping over me. This was worse than I remembered.

Was work riding him so hard he couldn't manage the effort to keep the place even the slightest bit tidy? Or had I never realized it was always this bad? Kind of like I never noticed there were men in the world who actually listened, and got excited about things other than video games? Damn it, Dash's challenge tonight shook up my thoughts so much I couldn't see straight.

I took a seat on the edge of his couch, noticing the sunken-in form underneath Justin had molded even more to his body than before. My stomach simmered—this is where he'd rather be than out with me.

He clicked off the Xbox and laid his controller gently on the entertainment stand. He turned to me. "Glad you came over," he said and stood, taking my hands and pulling me to him.

The simmering stopped. Maybe I wasn't seeing things differently. Perhaps he didn't even realize how bad the place was. Work had to be exhausting him. I'd help him get the place back to livable again. Maybe tomorrow.

I wrapped my arms around his middle.

Before I could speak, he swooped an arm underneath my legs and held me against his chest. He rushed us to his bedroom, crunching beer cans as he went.

"Whoa, where is the fire?" I asked when he tossed me on his twin-size mattress. It laid on the floor, which I was thankful I couldn't see because he'd neglected to turn on the light. I heard the clanking of his belt and then his pants unzipping.

"Right here," he whispered and tugged at my jeans.

"I thought we were going to watch a movie?" I said as he frantically kissed my neck.

"We will after."

After the argument with him and then Dash, all I wanted to do was spend some time having a real conversation with Justin. I didn't want another fight, though. He was right, we'd have good quality time after. And he'd definitely be in a better mood.

My jeans scraped against something cardboard as he tossed them on the floor and my underwear followed two seconds later. He didn't bother with my shirt. He kissed me hard, his tongue meeting mine with a jarring thrust before he turned me and gripped my hips from behind.

I held my breath as he entered me, trying to think about something that would get me in the same mood as him.

"What is it?" he asked when I hadn't moved to meet his thrusts.

"Hurts a little," I whispered.

Justin pushed himself inside again. "You'll warm up in a minute."

After a few minutes I slowed him down by moving forward and said, "Justin, kiss me."

"What?" He grunted, trying to maintain his speed.

"Kiss me," I said again, this time glancing over my shoulder. My eyes had somewhat adjusted to the darkness, and Justin's face was easier to see. I wanted him to look at me, to see the plea in my eyes to make this more enjoyable for both of us. I wanted him to kiss me, thinking perhaps a little more time would change things.

He didn't look at me, though. He just arched his head back.

"Nope. I'm almost there," he said, clutching me harder and picking up the pace.

I turned back around, a combination of sadness and disappointment curling around my chest and squeezing.

He gave one final thrust and groaned, his body slackening behind mine, then he jumped off the bed and dressed in a hurry. "I'm gonna get a drink," he said and bolted out the door before I could ask for something myself.

I winced getting off the bed. Justin had gone faster than normal tonight.

I took my clothes into his tiny bathroom and attempted to clean up. I slipped on my underwear carefully, desperately craving a warm bath. I glanced at his tub and shuddered. A dirt ring wrapped around it and orange stains clung to every corner. I'd rather take the pain than climb into *that*. We needed to have a serious talk about the state of this place if he ever wanted me to come back over.

After gathering myself, I made it back to the living room, totally prepared to take a spot next to him on the couch and try to start a conversation, one that would help us find each other again, and one, I hoped, that would bring balance back to my life. I froze two steps in.

Justin's best friends Mark and Andy sat on either side of him on the couch, a beer in each of their hands. His flat screen had the COD menu up.

"Hey, Blake," Mark said, and Andy gave me a nod.

"Hey?" I said, but it sounded like a question. The earlier simmering heated to a roaring boil now. This was why Justin had hurried. He'd probably told the guys to meet him at a certain time. "Justin, can I talk to you for a minute?"

He glanced up at me and handed his controller to Andy. I turned and stopped in front of his closed bedroom door with him following behind me.

"What is it?" he asked.

I put my hand on my hip. "Are you kidding me?"

"What?" he snapped.

I flung my hand in the direction of the living room. "I thought it was going to be just us tonight."

"It was just us. Now I want to hang with my boys and play COD. What's the big deal? You can watch."

I pinched the bridge of my nose. I would not cry. Not here. Not with his friends only feet away. "I really needed this tonight."

He scrunched his face up. "Needed what?"

"To be with you."

"You just were with me."

"Not like that!" I scoffed. "I needed to just . . ."

"What, Blake? You always need me to do something. To talk or to go somewhere or to meet people who won't matter after school is done. Why can't you ever be happy with just me?"

"I am! But it's not just you tonight, is it? Don't you play games with these guys all the time? Couldn't you give me one night?"

Justin crossed his arms over his chest. "I am. I have! God, you act like playing video games is worshiping the devil."

"I do not."

"Yeah, you do. I don't know why you can't get that this is my downtime. It's like you and your books."

"I don't ever blow you off to read a book, Justin."

"Whatever."

I sighed and took a step toward him, opting to take a different approach. I pried his hands away from his chest and took them in mine.

"Please. Can you tell the guys to go?" I couldn't walk out of this door, discarded once again for a game. Maybe telling him outright would make the outcome different.

Justin arched his head back, staring at the ceiling.

Good. He at least considered it.

He yanked his hands out of mine and slammed his foot into the bedroom door. The force of the kick knocked the door back so hard it hung crooked on one hinge, and I flinched as the air whooshed past my face from the momentum.

"No. I shouldn't have to choose!" he yelled.

I jumped and took a few steps away from him, eyeing the broken door. I crossed my arms to hide the fact that my muscles trembled.

"I shouldn't have to turn my boys away," he said, more of

a hiss than a yell. "If you want to spend time with me, then this is what we're doing." He turned and stomped back to the living room.

I stood there for a moment as my heart plummeted into my stomach. How many times would I let him do this to me?

CHAPTER

SEVEN

HAIL SAT BESIDE my bathtub with her big head leaning over the edge as I soaked and cried my eyes out. No amount of scrubbing my face could stop the tears. I didn't *want* to cry over this. This wasn't new behavior from Justin. I knew how he operated, knew how this relationship worked. What was wrong with me?

I submerged myself completely under the warm water and stayed there as long as I could. Dash's face popped behind my eyelids. I came up slowly, inhaling the steaming air. It was *his* fault. If he hadn't said anything, I wouldn't think I deserved any more than Justin gave me. He didn't understand the loyalty that came with years of being together, of growing up together. But his words rang in my head and made me expect more from Justin.

And damn him if he wasn't right. At least in tonight's situation. I'd let Justin off the hook, and what had it got me? A blowup and blown off, once again.

I dried off and slipped into my softest T-shirt and sweats combo, pulling my wet hair back in a ponytail. I sank onto the couch, welcoming Hail and her fifty-pound butt into my lap. She licked my chin and pouted at me. She could always tell when Justin and I had fought. I scratched behind her ears and leaned my head back, contemplating hunting for the remote and staring at the TV all night until my brain stopped working.

A knock on my door startled me. Hail slid off the couch and waddled to the door, her butt wiggling. I peered through the peephole, my heart pounding.

Dash stood on the other side. I quickly touched my face, wishing I'd tried to hide the redness surrounding my puffy eyes, but I hadn't expected anyone to show up outside my door.

Damn. Oh well.

Dash's green eyes went wide when he got a look at my face. He stepped past me without an invite in. Hail jumped and wiggled at his feet. "What happened?"

I sighed. "What are you doing here, Dash?"

He knelt to pet Hail. "I drove by on the off-chance you'd be home already and saw your car. I felt bad about earlier and wanted to talk."

My heart lifted. We'd only argued a few hours ago and he already wanted to talk it out? Normally I had to wait a whole twenty-four hours, sometimes more, for that.

"It's all right. Really, you didn't have to," I said and shrugged. I was used to arguments and on the fight scale, Dash's and mine wasn't even a blip.

"No, I do have to. I'm sorry. I should've kept my mouth shut. I have a problem with that in case you haven't noticed." He smiled, and I automatically returned it. "I can't judge a guy I've never met. I just hate seeing you get walked all over . . . but again not my place. It's just . . . ."

He focused his gaze on Hail for a moment.

"What?" I finally asked.

Dash shook his head. "I shouldn't . . . ."

"It's fine. I promise."

He sighed and stood up, meeting my eyes. "Don't tell the guys, all right?"

I raised my eyebrows and nodded.

"You've become the closest friend I've ever had. I know that sounds crazy after only a month, but I've never met anyone like you before. We're the same in so many ways. And it's made this annoying urge to protect you crop up inside me and I can't stop it. That's why I ran my mouth off earlier. Can you forgive me?"

My heart swelled and then instantly deflated. The nicest and most sincere thing anyone had ever said to me in my entire life came from someone I'd only known a month. Not from the man I'd been more or less dating for eight years. The reality of that hit me like a punch to the chest, and what happened earlier tonight replayed in my head all over again.

Tears streamed from my eyes before I could stop them. I quickly covered up my face with my hands.

"Whoa, woman," Dash said, and a second later his arms wrapped around me. "What did I say?"

He smelled like the air just after a rainstorm. How had I never noticed that before? Butterflies flapped inside my stomach uncontrollably. I had the undeniable urge to slip my hands underneath his shirt to touch his skin, to find out what his body would feel like against mine. I wondered if he'd take his time with me. I shook my head against his hard chest, but it did nothing to push the involuntary thoughts away.

"I'm so . . . sorry," I stuttered.

"For what?" He stroked the top of my head.

"For crying like this. I'm so stupid."

"Hey." He tipped my chin up toward him. "No you're not. Talk to me."

I sucked in a shaking breath and wiped my eyes with my palms. I took a step back, unable to concentrate with his strong hands rubbing my shoulders and his green eyes offering such honest sincerity.

"You were right. Justin totally bailed on me. He only wanted me to come over for . . ." I shut up real quick. Dash didn't need to know. "Anyway he chose the Xbox over me again. A fucking console wins every time. Am I really a needy psycho chick because I ask for some alone time every now and then?" I sank on the couch and Dash took up the spot next to me. Hail made herself comfortable on his foot.

"No. A psycho chick would've taken a baseball bat to the Xbox long ago and probably his head, too. Trust me, you're far from one of those."

"The thought had crossed my mind."

"I can't imagine you ever doing that. You're too nice."

If I adopted a bitch attitude, would I get more out of my relationship? Lindsay snapped at Dash over little things like ordering the wrong drink or whining about the music he picked out. And Dash still treated her well, pulling out her chair for her or attending parties he had no interest in just because she wanted to go. Why couldn't Justin be like that?

Dash smacked my leg and jumped up. "Come on." He opened my front door.

"What?"

"Get up. We're going out."

"No. I'm in my sweats."

"I don't care. You're on the verge of crying again and I really don't want to see that. You need chocolate. I've got two sisters, remember? I know when to arm myself with the good stuff."

I grinned despite my efforts not to and met him at the door. He whistled at Hail. "You, too, girl."

She waddled over to him excitedly.

Dash opened the passenger door of his truck and lifted Hail into the center seat. He waited until I'd climbed in before closing the door. I scratched Hail's ears as she panted and wagged her little curl of a tail.

Hail tried desperately to squeeze between Dash and the steering wheel to talk to the girl at the drive-through window of my favorite all-night ice cream place. Dash won the battle, but watching it made me laugh so hard my sides hurt.

Dash was right—like he often was—the heavenly, creamy, crunchy, chocolate-Oreo mixture was exactly what I'd needed.

He parked in the near empty lot and munched on his chocolate-Kit-Kat combo. Hail panted between us, her tongue hanging out, happy we didn't leave her behind.

"One time Lindsay called me from this frat party," Dash said, twirling his spoon. "She was so drunk, she'd thought she had called one of her girlfriends to come pick her up. I showed up and she flipped. Had a screaming fit in the middle of the packed house, said I was keeping tabs on her. That I didn't trust her. She smashed an almost-empty Vodka bottle by throwing it against the kitchen wall."

My eyebrows rose. "What did you do?"

He shrugged. "I talked some sense into her and drove her home. Put her to bed. She barely remembered the scene the next day."

I shook my head. "One time, Justin and I were playing Monopoly. He'd had a few beers, but he wasn't drunk. I made a crack about his total lack of property buying skills and he turned the whole table over. The game flew against the wall and the pieces went everywhere. He stormed out of his place. Went and drank all night at one of his friend's houses."

"All over a game?"

I nodded.

"Tell me you didn't clean it up," he demanded.

I gave him a weak smile.

"Of course you did." Dash sighed. "Don't hate me, but I honestly can't figure out why you've stayed with him for so long."

I swallowed the bite of ice cream in my mouth a little too quickly. The freezing burn almost made me choke. I'd never lied to Dash, so why start now? My chest tightened as I tried to formulate the words.

"You remember how I told you about Tulsa?"

He nodded and waited patiently for me to continue, like he always did when listening to me.

"Well, that day I actually suggested we break up. He wasn't willing to move a couple hours away for me, so I honestly didn't think he loved me like he used to." I took a deep breath, forcing myself to continue. "He grabbed his pocketknife, put it to his wrist, and cut himself. Threatened to end his life if I ever left him. Said he'd die without me. And though that was the first time, it wasn't the last. It's happened a few more times, whenever I've broached the subject of even taking a break."

The weight that had taken up a home in my chest for the past three years lifted. The simple act of confiding in Dash released tension I didn't realize I'd had.

"It's really fine though . . . I'm the last person he has . . . I—"

"Stop," Dash cut me off. "You don't have to cover yourself with me, Blake. Never with me." He sat up straighter, setting his ice cream on the dashboard. "Tell me how you really feel about it."

I stopped breathing for a moment, thinking it over. "I feel . . . trapped . . . sometimes. Other times, I don't know, he reverts back to the boy I fell in love with. It's complicated. I can't leave him, he'd have no one left, no reason to continue living."

Dash pressed his palms together, the tips of his fingers touching his lips as if to stop himself from saying more. His shoulders coiled with tension, but after a few long moments, he sighed and glanced at me with a mixture of pity and anger in his eyes. "It makes more sense now, all the shit you let him get away with, and why you can't be completely honest with him. But, Blake, you have to realize you deserve so much better—"

"Why did you stay with Lindsay after her irrational outburst?" I cut him off, wanting desperately to change the subject. Each time Dash and I talked about the serious side of my relationship it was like cracking open a previously locked box and revealing a truth I wasn't ready to handle. It was one thing to hold myself responsible for Justin's happiness, his life, when I thought he loved me just as much, but if he didn't . . . if he was just using me all these years . . .

"She hasn't done it as many times as Justin has." Dash's voice stopped my dark thoughts in their tracks.

I shoved another bite into my mouth.

"Things with Lindsay are . . . I don't know. In the beginning she was different. She found the fact that I was a storm chaser interesting. Supported it. Now, it bothers her. Everything bothers her." He glanced at me before quickly looking down at Hail. "I keep waiting for the day she'll ask me to choose between the storms and her."

I completely understood the sickening trapped sensation an ultimatum like that could conjure up. "What would you choose?"

"I've been in love with storms all my life. I think the perfect woman would be one who'd never ask me to choose. Does that make me an asshole?"

"Of course not," I said. "It makes you a man who knows exactly what he wants."

He scooped up his ice-cream again before holding my gaze. "So, what does Blake Caster *really* want?"

Heat rushed across my skin as I stared at his lips and the way they shaped themselves around the blue plastic spoon. The thoughts from earlier about him shirtless and what all *he* would do to me made my heart race, and suddenly the cab of the truck shrunk ten sizes.

"I . . ." I couldn't think straight. An ache pulsed low in my belly.

Hail took the opportunity to shove her massive face in my lap, begging for a lick of my treat, and the tension broke immediately.

Dash patted Hail's butt and started the truck. "All right, girls. Let's get you home."

Ten minutes later Dash hefted Hail out of his truck without a complaint about the mess of white dog hair she'd left behind. He kissed the top of her head and watched her waddle inside.

"I love that dog." He shook his head.

"The feeling is mutual. You know it'll break her heart if you ever decide to stop coming over."

"Good thing that won't happen anytime soon." His quick declaration shot another burst of warmth through my heart.

"Thanks for tonight, Dash. And sorry about earlier."

"I'm going to start charging you every time you say you're sorry. Seriously, woman, you've got a complex."

I smirked. "So, if I really am the best friend you've ever had . . ."

"Yes?" he asked.

"What's your real name?"

He cocked an eyebrow at me. "Never."

"Seriously?"

He shook his head.

I squinted at him. "I'll get it out of you one day."

He took a step closer to me. "You won't"—he said, and pushed some hair that had fallen out of my ponytail over my shoulder, causing chills to shoot across my skin—"but it'll be fun watching you try."

CHAPTER

EIGHT

"I KNOW SOMETHING that will cheer you up," Dash said as he walked into my apartment.

I'd just opened the door for him, surprised at his visit. It felt like he'd just left. I'd slept half the day, and still had on my sweats. I hadn't even brushed my hair yet. Fabulous.

Dash rubbed Hail's ears and patted her wiggling butt before looking back at me. "Don't you want to know what it is?"

I blinked a couple of times, not quite awake. I'd slept hard last night, a shocker since usually after a fight with Justin I couldn't sleep worth a damn. I'd spend the whole night analyzing what I could've done differently to make the situation better. I suppose Dash's ice cream therapy had worked.

"Of course," I finally answered him.

He stood up, looking entirely too good in a pair of jeans and vintage Blue October tee. "We're heading out for another chase."

My eyebrows raised.

"You want to come?"

"Of course!" I said instantly. "Do I need to pack anything?"

Now that I'd shaken off the shock of my first chase, I was able to think more clearly about important things, like extra clothes and if someone would need to watch Hail. Last time I hadn't given those details a spare thought I'd been so excited.

"No. It's only a couple of hours away. We'll drive back after."

"Awesome!" I stood there smiling like an idiot, anticipation filling my veins.

Dash eyed me up and down. "You might want to change, though."

I snapped out of my thoughts, glancing down at my sweats and oversized T-shirt. "Right. On it," I said and sprinted down the hall. I returned in less than five minutes wearing jeans, a snug black tee, and my boots. I threw my hair back in a ponytail.

After a quick text to Mom, asking her if she could stop by and let Hail out in a few hours, I poured enough food in her bowl to last her until later tonight, and told her I'd be back before heading out the door.

I climbed into Dash's truck with nervous energy coiling around my muscles, the image of the horizontal tornado that roped out before it could touch down fresh in my mind. The visual was intense enough and I couldn't imagine what it would be like to actually see one hit the ground.

"You can relax, you know," Dash said, glancing at me from the driver's side before returning his eyes to the road. He drove well above the speed limit, passing cars with the ease of someone who didn't worry about getting a ticket.

I let out a breath and sat back against the seat, only then realizing I'd been sitting on the edge of it, the seatbelt stretched to capacity. "Sorry, just nervous."

He shook his head. "Always sorry."

I shrugged and bit my lower lip. At the rate Dash drove, we'd make the two-hour trip in an hour and a half easy.

A burst of static blared from his walkie-talkie. A few seconds later John's voice sounded from it. "Tracker Jacker has caught up and has team leader in its sights."

Dash scooped up the radio and clicked the button down. "About time. What'd you do, stop for Red Bulls?"

"Burritos," John answered.

"Did you get us any?" Dash asked.

"Negative. We're approaching you now."

"Jerks." Dash chuckled.

I spun in my seat to look out the back window. Sure enough, the Tracker Jacker changed lanes and slid in behind us.

"What's the best route?" Dash asked.

"There are two possible locations with potential. One is more toward the east . . ."

I could see John behind the wheel and Paul in the passenger seat looking at his opened laptop.

"I think the one farther west has the best chance," Dash said.

"In that case, you need to stay on this until we reach 136th. We'll follow that until we get sight of the storm. Doppler has it converging near Owasso, but you'll have a better idea once you see it."

"All right. Thanks, John. Keep me updated if anything more develops."

"Roger that."

Dash set the walkie-talkie in the empty cup-holder.

The ride continued in charged silence as I kept my eyes trained on the sky and my thoughts firmly on the chase. I wanted to be a part of this team, to help spot anything that a computer might not be able to. I couldn't do that if I worried about what would happen if Justin knew what I was doing—regardless if I was still furious with him—or if I thought too hard about the uncontrollable desires I continued to have about the man sitting next to me.

John's voice crackled over the radio again, refocusing my attention. "Take the next exit and then head down 136th."

"Got it," Dash replied and pulled off the highway.

My heart beat a little harder as buildings gave way to farmland. Once we caught sight of a fair-sized wall cloud hovering to the west, Dash hit the gas even harder.

The closer we got, the more massive the thing looked, like a bottle of ink had been upturned, blotting out huge chunks of blue-gray sky. Dash reached behind him and withdrew his video camera case from the back without asking me to take the wheel again. With one hand he managed to get the thing out, turned on, and handed it to me.

"Point and shoot. You've got the better vantage point," he said.

I took the camera from him and rolled down my window. I'd never captured a storm on film before and was surprised Dash even wanted me to since he was the expert.

"Why don't you ever ride with John so you can film while he drives?" I asked, keeping the lens focused on the dark wall cloud as Dash took a hard right turn down a graveled road.

"I used to."

"What changed?"

"He always wanted to book it when I wanted to stay. I drive myself now so they can bolt if they want."

"Is that safe? Staying behind by yourself?"

"I always manage," he said and winked at me.

Dash picked up the radio again and clicked the button down. "Pulling off about a mile ahead."

"Right behind you," John answered.

Dash pulled the truck off the road next to a freshly plowed piece of land. Rolling green pasture bordered a few acres of upturned red earth, which sectioned in evenly spaced rows. He threw the truck in park, grabbed the camera from me, and hopped out. I followed him, John and Paul meeting us in the middle of a patch of flat packed dirt separating the road from farmland.

The sky was light behind the dark-gray storm cloud, which made the green grass and red dirt below it seem more vibrant. Dash's eyes fixated on the storm before us, their green shining with an intensity I now realized he only held when a storm was in sight.

"It's got potential," he said with a wicked grin on his face. "Maybe you'll see one touch down today, Blake."

I swallowed hard, both excited and scared of the prospect.

"I wish it was more organized," John said, letting his camera hang against his chest.

"Me, too," Dash said, pointing at the northeast portion of the wall cloud. "Look, there's a little rotation."

I focused on where he pointed and saw the slightest bit of movement within the cloud, shocked he'd spotted it so quickly. Nothing as extreme as last time, but I knew it would only take seconds for a tornado to develop out of a rotating wall cloud. My nerves stood on end waiting in eager anticipation.

A crack of lightning bolted from the sky and thunder rumbled a few seconds later. The wind speed around us increased, enough to whip my ponytail back and forth and spray our jeans with red dust. My heart rate spiked with the wind and an excited but terrified sensation shot throughout my body.

"Tighten up!" Dash hollered as if commanding the sky. His eyebrows were drawn as he watched the too-slow churning rotation in the cloud.

The light broken-wisps stemming from the edges of the cloud made me think it was losing steam, but I didn't want to say anything to jinx it.

Chill bumps erupted across my arms, the air turning a few degrees colder. The excited and hopeful energy coursing between the four of us instantly deflated.

Cold air killed the chances for a tornado.

"Damn it," Dash snapped, his shoulders dropping. "It's fading."

Paul booked it back to the Tracker Jacker and leaned over his laptop.

The wall cloud still hung low and was ominous enough with its dark broken sections looking like jagged claws reaching to tear up the earth, but it wouldn't produce anything more than a thunderstorm. The sky rumbled once again as if to prove to us it held all the power. Lightning flashed several moments later, the wicked zigzag bolt striking only a few hundred yards away.

"Shit!" Paul yelled and slammed his fist on the hood of the Tracker Jacker.

"What?" John jogged over to him, took one look at the laptop screen, and dropped his head.

"Don't tell me . . ." Dash's eyes jumped back and forth between them.

"Yep," Paul answered through clenched teeth.

"Damn it." Dash jerked the camera to his side and stomped to his truck, shoving the camera in its case.

I walked slowly toward him, completely baffled.

He read my utterly confused face. "Where at, Paul?"

"Twenty-five miles east of here." Paul shut his laptop with an audible click. "It's weakening like crazy, though. No chance of catching it now, and there will probably only be scattered thunderstorms for the rest of the night."

Dash sighed. All his previous intensity and excitement completely vanished. He looked at me, his eyes completely defeated. "Tornado touched down at the other location east of here. We missed it because I thought this cell's chances of producing were higher." He eyed the clouds behind me like they'd played a cruel trick on him and slid behind the wheel of his truck.

"You know where we're headed," Dash hollered at John before motioning for me to get in.

I gave the underdeveloped storm one last look and sank into the passenger seat. Dash spun the truck around and headed toward the highway. The energy was completely different from minutes ago, our spirits crashing from the high hopes we'd had to capture the storm. The sensation was sickening, knowing a tornado had touched down so close and we'd missed it, knowing the last two chases had technically been busts. The sheer disappointment resembled how I'd felt the day I'd given up my dream of going to the University of Tulsa and went home with Justin instead.

And this was only my second chase. I couldn't imagine how Dash felt, who did this regularly throughout the season.

"Sorry, Dash," I said, even though I knew it wouldn't help.

He shrugged. "It's part of it. Sometimes you get lucky, others not. I should've had you look at the images before we chose a location. I won't make that mistake again. You probably would've told us to go to the other site."

"Maybe not. It really looked like it would tighten up there for a second."

He smiled. "You're starting to sound like me."

"When it comes to storms, you're the expert, so I'll take that as a compliment."

"You should."

"Where are we headed now?"

"The only place that can make a bust better."

DASH LED ME inside a bar three times the size of Bailey's. It was after seven p.m. by the time we made it back to town—thanks to the late start on the chase day and the dinner we stopped for on the trip back. Loud top-40 music blared from massive speakers stationed against the walls, and a huge dance floor took up the entire right half of the place, a bunch of college kids moving to the beat of the music underneath a flash of colored lights. The rest of the place was darkened, only lit by low-hanging lights covered in red-colored glass. A huge bar made up the center, and over a dozen pool tables occupied the left half of the room.

John and Paul headed straight to the tables while Dash pulled a stool out for me at the bar. I took the seat with a thank-you and grabbed the drink trifold that rested against a small container of cardboard coasters.

A beautiful red-headed bartender walked over to us. She wore a tightly cinched black vest with only a bra underneath, a small strip of her flat stomach exposed above her tight red jeans. She smiled brightly, and I tried not to hate her for making me feel plain in my dust-covered pants and wind-warped ponytail. Sure, my snug tee showed off my nicely sized breasts, but the bartender's vest made hers look like they were on their way to a red-carpet event.

I hadn't even contemplated asking Dash to take me home so I could change once we rolled into town. I sighed and reminded myself it didn't matter. Dash had seen me in the same clothes all day, and Justin wouldn't be caught dead in this place. Luckily I had no guilt about not telling him where I'd been all day. He'd picked the awful fight last night so I didn't owe him any explanation today, and could rest easy until he decided he was ready to talk.

"What can I get you two?" Her voice had a husky quality, and the same sexual prowess radiated from her skin. She reminded me of Lindsay, not in looks—except they were both equally gorgeous—but they had a sexual spark that buzzed around them. Every time I met a girl like them I wondered how they did it. Did they learn something I didn't in school, or were they born with it?

My shoulders sank a fraction remembering the many times

Justin had told me I lacked that sexual bombshell edge, but he always backed it up by saying he loved me regardless.

"I'll take a Briar Patch Ale," I answered after scanning the micro-brew section of the menu.

Dash grinned at me, and I wondered why he wasn't using that charm on the bartender to get us free drinks. "I'll take a 405 Oklahoma Lager," he said without looking at the girl. I glanced down at the list in my hand.

"Copycat," I said. He'd chosen a beer made by the same brewery as mine.

"Please, woman. You wouldn't even know what a micro-brew was if it wasn't for me."

"Touché." Before he came along, the extent of my alcoholic adventures had been cheap champagne and Keystone Light.

The Megan Fox-worthy bartender hurried back, placing our brightly labeled bottles in front of us before rushing off to tend to other patrons. I took a fast drink, the taste of pear and apple bursting on my tongue and zinging me in a sweet way. A few more swallows and I didn't worry about my attire anymore. Red dirt covered Dash's clothes, too, though it made him look more rugged than worn out.

Halfway through our beers, bombshell bartender smacked two shot glasses full of an amber liquid in front of us.

"We didn't order these," I said.

She motioned toward the pool tables. "Those two did."

Dash and I followed her gaze to where Paul and John stood in front of a pool table, cues in one hand and raised shot glasses in the other. They nudged their shots in the air before swigging them down and returning to their game.

Dash scooped up his shot and held it toward me. "To the next chase."

I tentatively picked up mine. I'd never taken a shot before, but I'd done a lot of things I'd never done before because of Dash.

"We'll catch it next time!" I said.

Dash clinked his tiny glass against mine before throwing it back.

I did the same, filling my mouth with the entire contents of the glass and swallowing a few seconds later. The burn was instant, but not unpleasant. A sweet and near smoky taste hung on the back of my tongue and made my jaw tingle. The liquid warmed my belly, and I hissed once I could breathe again.

Dash chuckled, adding to my already unwinding state. The tension that my muscles had held like a live grenade since we started the chase melted away with each deep breath.

"Got to love bottom-shelf whiskey." He set his glass back on the bar.

My head instantly buzzed. "I think I do. Let's get another one."

His eyebrows rose for a spilt second before returning to his normal relaxed expression. "Whatever you want." He motioned at the bombshell, and she sauntered over to refill our glasses.

I lifted mine and turned toward him, my knee brushing against his leg. "What should we toast to now?"

"How much fun lightweights are?" He raised his glass.

"Ha, ha," I snarked back. "How about to a night with no drama besides a missed storm?"

He nodded and we threw the drinks back. I didn't hiss as loud this time.

"He hasn't apologized yet, I take it?"

"Nope," I said, setting the glass down with a smack. "But it's only been a day. He'll most likely call tomorrow and all will go back to normal."

"Just like that, huh?"

I shrugged. "It's the pattern."

"That's"—Dash sucked in a breath and let it out slowly—"understandable after so many years, I guess." He said the words through clenched teeth. I could tell it had taken a huge effort to bite his tongue.

My tummy simmered with a whiskey warmth and my head buzzed with bursting bubbles. I blissfully slipped into a sweet place where worry didn't exist, and I *so* didn't want another fight with Dash over how I let Justin off too easy—especially since every time he pointed out the flaws in my relationship, I questioned it more and more.

I quickly finished the rest of my beer.

Paul put his hand on my shoulder, materializing directly behind us and startling me so much I nearly fell off my seat. "Whoa," he said, steadying me. "Someone cut the meteorologist off."

"Oh, please." I rolled my eyes but thought about ordering a water before my next beer.

"What happens when a male meteorologist forgets his anniversary?"

"Nothing," I said, thinking of all the times Justin had missed our anniversary. Not that he was a meteorologist, though.

"Wrong," Paul said. "An approaching cold front with explosive storm development."

I smacked him on the shoulder. "Clever, as always."

"Can't help it. Anyway, I lost so John could play a sophomore chick. Want to dance?" He offered his hand to me.

I reached out to take it happily, but Dash stood up and stepped between us. "I'm not leaving her in your incapable hands. You have near nonexistent rhythm."

Paul pretended to look offended while Dash grabbed my hand. "Why don't you save our spots and talk to the redhead," Dash suggested, waggling his eyebrows from Paul to the bombshell serving bright green drinks to a group of girls a few seats down.

"Nice. Thanks, bro," Paul said and took a seat.

I stifled a giggle at the thought of him stealing her heart away with bad weather jokes as Dash tugged me toward the dance floor.

The music rose to an exceptionally loud level as we zigzagged our way through the throngs of grinding couples and into the middle of the floor. The song transitioned to Awolnation's "Sail" as he found a clear spot and stopped.

Dash nodded to the beat and moved his hips back and forth, pulling me closer with a wicked smile on his lips. I moved effortlessly toward him and didn't even flinch when he wrapped a strong arm around my waist. He swayed us to the rhythm of the music, the sweet drawn-out beat thumping from the speakers and into the floor, vibrating my bones.

He spun me out with a simple flick of his wrist, and I arched my head in a slow circle before he drew me back in quickly, the momentum causing me to crash against his firm chest. He didn't miss a beat, steadying me with his hands on the small of my back. Heat flushed under his touch, a spark of tingles shooting across my skin.

The music and my buzz created an awesome sense of floating detachment. I hadn't felt this great in months. Years maybe.

He twirled me again, and this time I had more grace when he tugged me back. I moved in sync with him, and his strong lead made me feel like a puppet helpless to his direction. A combination of sheer blissfulness and a twinge of guilt hit me.

Justin hated to dance. I'd nearly gotten him into a club once, but he'd had a classic blowup and bailed before we'd even made it to the parking lot. I sighed, swaying where Dash directed me, and forced myself back to the present.

And then I realized how close we were. Heat from his skin radiated beneath my thin tee, my breasts grazing his hard chest, and I was once again overcome with wonder of what Dash would do to me in bed. My core hummed with an aching need and I sucked in a sharp breath. Had I crossed a line dancing with him like this?

As Dash grinned down at me, moving me so easily to the steady thump of the music, I shook my head. No, this was fine. More than fine—it was completely natural for me to be curious after only being with one person my entire life—and everyone had fantasies. I was allowed to enjoy a night out with my best friend, especially since my boyfriend hated doing pretty much anything that involved separating from his Xbox and hated it even more when I did anything beyond study.

"What are you shaking your head at?" Dash pressed his cheek against mine and spoke into my ear so I could hear him over the loud music. His breath on my skin made my heart stutter involuntarily and I wanted to shower in the sensations he awoke in my body for a little longer, despite knowing actively enjoying it took it one step closer to not being a harmless fantasy.

"Do you have to be so great at everything?"

He pulled back for a second, arching an eyebrow at me before returning his lips near my ear. "Of course. It's what I do."

I laughed again and thought about how half the time I was with Dash we spent it laughing. I would have killer abs if we kept it up. "You know what would make this even better?"

"Justin being here instead of me?" he quickly replied.

My stomach sank with my instant internal denial. Not that he'd ever be up for anything like this, but if he were here, he'd be sulking at the bar and lecturing me on the immaturity of dancing. "Sorry Lindsay didn't come," I said, my train of thought broken. He'd texted her on the way in, but she'd never responded.

"Not what I meant." He gently rocked me backward before bringing me up against his chest again. "What would make it better?"

The notion seemed silly now. "Never mind."

"Tell me, woman!"

"If I knew your name!" I relented.

"Of course, anything for a friend," he said in a mocking tone. He tugged me closer, inching his leg between my thighs until our bodies were flush. My pulse quickened, and I swallowed hard. His lips grazed my ear. "It's"—he held me in agonizing anticipation—"Lexington, Dash Lexington." He burst out laughing.

"Ha, ha." I smacked his chest.

One song faded into another, and we danced until my legs were on fire. Dash never faltered, and damn it if he didn't show me a good time. When he finally carted me off the dance floor, sweat popped from both our foreheads.

We found Paul chatting up the bombshell where we left him. She actually had a genuine smile that lit up her eyes as he said something funny. I found myself hoping he'd score her number as I took a seat next to him, Dash standing close behind me due to the lack of available space.

Once they took a breath from their in-depth conversation about why the best tequila chaser was the lime, I ordered Dash and me two more beers. They were cold and so refreshing after the vigorous dance session.

"Not a bad way to mend the wounds of a bust." I held the tip of my bottle toward him.

"Can't remember ever having more fun after such a letdown," Dash said and clinked his bottle against mine.

CHAPTER

NINE

JUSTIN SAT ACROSS from me at our regular high-top table at Bailey's. I couldn't freaking believe it. He'd showed up as a way of an apology for being a complete asshole last weekend.

I wrung my hands out underneath the table, my knee bouncing uncontrollably. I wanted Justin to like Dash and enjoy being out of the house, but I was equally hoping Dash or Lindsay wouldn't slip up and say something about all the non-educational outings we had. I'd grilled Dash on the reasons why that would be a bad idea even though he already understood and I could only hope Lindsay would respect it as well. Of course, I wanted everything out in the open, but on my terms. After tonight, I prayed I could tell Justin how close I'd grown to Dash and the guys without any problems. Once he saw how awesome Dash was he couldn't scold me for the friendship.

John and Paul played shuffleboard as Dash told me about his latest idea for the design of the probes they were working on. Lindsay sipped her cranberry and vodka, sitting next to him with a dazed look.

"You're really into all this weather shit, too, huh?" Justin interrupted Dash.

Dash cut his eyes to Justin. "Yeah, you could say that."

Justin finished off his third IPA. "Don't you think it is a little cliché?"

"What?" Dash asked.

I swallowed hard. Arrogance colored Justin's tone.

"Oh, come on! We live in Oklahoma and you're a storm chaser? Technically isn't every other person in this place one? At least being a meteorologist is a *real* job. Chasing isn't very original," he said and took another drink.

I opened my mouth to defend our shared passion, but Dash was quicker.

"There's a little more to it than standing on your back porch and snapping a photo with your iPhone."

Justin shrugged. "Whatever. You ride around in a car and point a camera out the window. Hardly rocket science."

I placed my hand on top of Justin's wrist. "There is actually a ton of science involved." He'd understand that if he ever paid attention to any of the weather maps I brought home or the station models I studied.

Lindsay giggled and nearly spit her drink all over the table. How many had she had?

"Dashy, he's right; you do point a camera out the window. It's not like you're in a lab conducting experiments or anything. Though the way you and Blake talk about it, you'd think you were." She patted Dash's shoulder like he was a silly puppy.

I ground my teeth together and stopped myself from smacking my forehead. Dash and the guys worked in the weather lab on campus almost every day, and I'd been joining them more frequently, helping them interpret the tons of data they gathered. They also designed probes, tested instruments, plotted courses, and ran through preparation scenarios. Hell, all three of them were up to date in first responder training, too, just in case they were the first ones on a damaged site after a storm. They spent the entire winter preparing for the storm season, and Lindsay had the nerve to brush it off like it was as easy as buying a video camera and driving to the nearest pasture.

"You know, actually—" I started with a snark in my tone before she cut me off.

"What do you do, Justin?" she asked, her voice sickly sweet.

Justin lifted his chin a fraction. "I work over at SprayGoods."

"That huge warehouse off 77?"

"That's the one. I'm on the line every day. Using my hands to build things. You know, actually making a real contribution to the world."

I stifled a snort by taking another swig of my Native Amber. Lord, he made it sound like he built solar panels for industrial companies or high-grade water filtration systems for the ocean. He pressed a button and watched the line to make sure the machinery didn't back up while it assembled the nozzles that went on squirt bottles. He hated it, but tonight he acted like it was an honor to work there.

Dash chuckled. "Nothing like assembly work to really make a man feel more . . . manly." He finished off his beer and signaled to Diana for another one.

I raised my bottle, too, though I hadn't even finished it yet—the tension between the two men was palpable. I'd wanted tonight to be a fun, easy way to introduce them, not a competition for who has a bigger piece in their pants. The thought made me ponder Dash's equipment for one second too long, and heat rushed to my cheeks. I couldn't lock those thoughts down even if I had a safe.

I took the last few gulps of my beer quickly. Why had I even bothered begging Justin to come out? He was obviously pissed about it and being rude as a punishment.

"This coming from someone who sings in the rain?" Justin laughed, and to my shock so did Lindsay.

"Dashy doesn't sing! But that would be funny." She stroked Dash's arm. "You could narrate your little clips by singing!"

"Have you even seen his site?" I snapped, my filter growing smaller with each beer I drank. The videos on Dash's website were all up-close footage of tornadoes in their strongest capacity. Little clips my ass.

"I've been on there . . . once." Lindsay shrugged. "Dashy knows I don't believe in that stuff anyway," she said, smiling at him.

Dash pressed his lips together, and I could tell he held back a laugh with difficulty. I eyed him with an *are you serious* look.

"Believe in it? Are you saying extreme weather is something you can choose not to believe exists if you don't see it in person? Like ghosts or unicorns?" Whoops, I'd blurted that out a little too bluntly.

Dash sprayed his last sip of beer back into the bottle as he laughed.

Lindsay rolled her eyes. "Of course not," she snapped. "Unicorns definitely don't exist."

I sighed, and Dash wiped his mouth off with a napkin. Diana brought the next round to our awkwardly silent table. *Damn it, could this night get any worse?*

"This place is lame." Justin broke the silence.

I cringed. He'd declare his undying love for his Xbox in three . . . two . . .

"We should all go somewhere else," he suggested, shocking the hell out of me.

"You're so right," Lindsay agreed. "Where did you have in mind?"

"Blake, you mentioned ghosts. How about the Ponderosa bridge?"

"You're not serious."

"Why not?" Justin asked.

"Because that was fun when we were kids . . ."

We'd made the trek there on our bicycles numerous times when we were younger. It was an old wooden bridge still intact over Black Bear Creek and legend had it Ms. Ponderosa was supposed to meet her fiancé there to elope in secret when her parents denied him her hand in marriage. He'd either never shown and she'd jumped off the bridge, or he *did* show and threw her off in a fury at being denied her inheritance. Either way, we'd never encountered anything, just royally freaked ourselves out.

"Making the trip out there now sounds like a pain in the ass," I continued. Now that we had cars instead of bicycles, we'd have to park blocks away and make the rest of the trip on foot. A less than desirable idea in the dark and buzzed.

"Yeah, man, people stop doing that around age twelve." Dash backed me up.

Justin scowled at him before shrugging. "If you're a scared little bitch, then just say so."

My mouth dropped open. "Justin!"

"What? I say we take a six-pack out there and have a little fun. The two of you are acting like I suggested we run a half marathon. Sounds more like an excuse because both of you are scared."

Lord, he *acted* like a twelve-year-old.

"It sounds fun to me!" Lindsay chimed in, and Dash and I shook our heads at the same time.

"Fine." Dash sighed. "Let's go." He swished back the rest of his beer and slammed it on the table.

After my invite was received with a laughing decline from John and Paul, I left a ten dollar bill on our table for Diana. Dash stopped Justin outside the door by placing a hand on his chest. I held my breath as Justin's eyes turned to slits.

"Just for the record," Dash said, "you may not want to call a man who chases tornadoes for a living a scared little bitch. It could come back to haunt you." He walked to his truck, and opened the door for Lindsay.

I grinned despite myself, but it instantly faded when Justin caught my eyes.

"What a fucking tool," Justin said. "I can't wait until this semester is over and you don't have to study or run in the same circle with this guy anymore." He brushed past me without a second glance and climbed into his truck. My heart sank at his words. He'd never approve of my friendship with Dash, and if I admitted the truth now, he'd force me to choose between them.

I opened the door of Justin's truck, the conditions revolving around my relationship smothering me, and I wondered what it would be like to be Lindsay for just one night.

THE MOON SHONE bright silver against the night sky and a cool breeze made chill bumps burst on my arms. I rubbed my hands back and forth on them, wishing for my jacket. The grass nearly came up to my knees as we made the long walk to the bridge. Dash had a flashlight he'd brought from his truck, but other than that the stars and moon lit the path before us.

Justin carried a six-pack he'd picked up at the gas station on the way over. He'd already cracked open a beer, and every time he took a drink my stomach churned. A fine line rested between a fun Justin and a blowup-worthy Justin on a normal day. When he drank too much that line disappeared. I prayed by us actively doing what he'd suggested that Dash wouldn't have to see it.

"You know," Lindsay said, "I heard that the lady was pregnant and that's why he pushed her off the bridge." She clutched Dash's hand and giggled.

"That's awful." I had no clue how she could find that notion funny.

She whipped her head around. "You're so sensitive. Lighten up."

Justin tossed an empty bottle on the ground. "She really is! God, Blake, you need to learn how to let things go."

I hung back a beat and picked up the bottle to throw in the trash on our way out. Whenever that would be. Lindsay and Justin may be enjoying themselves, but both their attitudes were borderline juvenile and I found myself exhausted at the high-school feel of it all. I seriously considered turning around and driving myself back to Bailey's to enjoy another Native Amber and a big-ass burger. I smacked my forehead when I remembered I hadn't driven and I'd most likely have to drive Justin's truck home with the way he tossed the beers back.

"Not that any of the stories are true," Dash said, suddenly beside me. "But that one is particularly gruesome."

I spun the bottle slowly in my hand. "Right? Thank you." I shook my head. "You'd think I cried over a puppy commercial."

He motioned his head to the side. "Come on, I've never chased a ghost before. You'll have to show me how."

"Ha! I haven't, either. Well, not since I was little. And back then we basically stood around and made each other jump at random times."

Lindsay giggled from several yards ahead of us, drawing our attention. Apparently Justin was a riot. Funny, he hadn't made me laugh in a long time. Maybe I'd just heard all of his jokes.

Oak trees bordered the land across the old bridge and there were a few scattered amongst the tall grass on the side we approached from. The railing was made of rusty old metal spaced out in large Xs with a flat piece on top, and wooden planks connected the walkway. Black Bear Creek trickled underneath it more than forty feet below, a slow and steady stream that added to the crickets chirping in the night.

Despite the dark rumors surrounding it, I'd always enjoyed the bridge as a kid. Probably because I'd watched a thunderstorm roll in from the west one time. The afternoon sky had lit up with white-hot lightning strikes and illuminated the thick cumulonimbus clouds—which back then I'd called "the big scary ones." Everyone else had grabbed their bikes and hauled ass home, but I'd stayed behind and watched the storm unfold until it rained so hard I had to walk my bike home.

Of course I had. How had I not known from the beginning I was born to study storms?

The shattering of broken glass cut through my thoughts, and Dash and I picked up our pace, catching up to Justin and Lindsay who stood in the middle of the bridge.

Justin peered over the railing. I followed his gaze and sighed. He'd tossed an empty over, and it'd smashed on a huge rock sticking up out of the creek. Another beer down quick. I swallowed hard instead of chastising for the broken glass.

"Nice," Dash said sarcastically, and I sucked in a breath. He was unaware of the lengths I took not to trigger an eruption from Justin.

"Something wrong, chase-boy?" Justin turned toward Dash, his eyebrows drawn.

Dash smirked. "Not a thing. So where is this ghost of yours?"

Justin motioned toward the railing. "A girl has to stand where she did in order to draw her out." His words bordered on the thick side, and I tried to do a mental recap of how many he'd had tonight.

"'Course. Makes sense," Dash said and tossed me another *are you serious* look. I grabbed two beers out of the pack Justin had set on the bridge. I handed one to Dash and shrugged. Living in the moment, plus if we drank them then that made two more Justin couldn't.

"Ew, I'm not doing it! I'll ruin my heels, plus my skirt isn't really climbing material. Blake, you have to! You can't mess up those old boots any more than they already are."

The hack about my boots only stung a little. I glanced down at the scuffed black leather, my jeans shoved into them. They were well broken in, just the way I liked them, and they were damn sure more comfortable than the four-inch red pumps she wore. How did she even make it through the grass without falling or at least getting mud on them?

"No thanks." I took a generous pull on my beer, then scrunched up my face and glared at the bottle. Justin had picked the cheapest, skunkiest beer he could find.

A light mist fell around us, and Dash and I both instinctively looked at the sky. No storm clouds indicating anything major would drop down on us other than the light sprinkle.

"Oh, you're no fun!" Lindsay whined and stomped her foot, drawing our attention back to earth. Did she really just do that?

"Come on, Blake. You used do it all the time," Justin said.

"When I was ten!"

Justin threw his head back. "Ugh, you were more fun back then. Now, you're just . . ."

A hot anger simmered in the pit of my stomach. Him and Lindsay were a perfect pair tonight, and I wanted to tell them both to go to hell.

"Boring," he finally finished.

Dash flinched beside me, and Lindsay's mouth dropped.

The anger soared to a roaring boil. "Boring? Your idea of excitement is not getting killed in a COD match," I snapped, my thoughts traveling to the bedroom and how he'd only make love to me one way—flipped over and fast.

Justin's face turned a dark shade of red, and the muscle in his jaw flexed. "Don't be a bitch." His eyes dared me to take his bait for a fight.

I shook my head.

Fuck it.

I smacked my beer down on the wooden plank and walked to the railing. The metal was slick against my palms with the light mist of rain but I ignored that. I was *not* boring, and maybe it was the fact that I had three beers in me, but I was damned if I'd let him call me that.

"Blake, don't," Dash said as I hitched my foot within the X shape, climbing up until I straddled the wet beam. I completely ignored him and the cold wet metal soaking through my jeans.

I pushed onto my feet and tried not to think about plummeting off the railing. Instead I assured myself that the wonderful air barrier between me and a forty-foot drop to the creek below would be sufficient protection. Rolling my eyes, I slowly turned my back toward them and looked outward, not down.

The air flowed past me in a steady not-at-all-threatening breeze, and the fine spray of rain kissed my cheeks. My heart pounded against my chest as I held my arms out horizontally, and it wasn't from fear of a damned ghost, either. It was exhilarating being up this high, the night sky laid out before me with crystal stars shining through the broken string of rain clouds.

"Blake!" Justin screamed so obnoxiously his voice cracked the silence worse than a clap of thunder, and I startled—clearly his intention.

The railing, slick beneath my boots, seemed to tilt, and I quickly lost my footing. My heart in my throat, I windmilled my arms until I somehow managed to fall backward instead of head first into the creek far below.

Where I expected the hard, wooden bridge to break my fall, a warm body sank beneath me. My head knocked back against Dash's chest, his arms gripping me as the momentum from my fall jerked us to our backs. I heard the thunk of his body take the full impact, but all I felt was . . . safe.

Then embarrassed. And then pissed off.

Justin and Lindsay roared with laughter, but Dash's lips were at my ear, his breath warm on my neck.

"Are you all right?" he asked, his arms still held me against him.

I did a quick internal check and, besides my pride hurting something fierce, I was practically melting in his embrace. God, could I be more of a damsel in distress?

"Fine," I said over Justin and Lindsay's laughter and rolled off Dash to kneel beside him. "You're the one who took the hit, are you okay?" I eyed him, but he'd already jumped up, his T-shirt didn't even have a wrinkle in it.

He kept his mouth shut, the fire in his green eyes so hot they were molten.

"I'm sorry I nearly crushed you," I said before I could stop myself.

He shook his head and brushed some dirt off the side of my thigh before he cut his eyes to Justin.

"You're too easy, Blake." Justin smacked his thigh as if my falling was the funniest thing he'd ever seen.

Dash walked toward Justin, stopping an inch from his face. "She could've been killed, you fucking idiot!"

I gasped and reached out for him as if I could pull his words back. It *so* wasn't worth it.

Justin's happy face quickly turned to a scowl I knew all too well. "She's fine. You didn't have to be the hero-boy and catch her either. Don't be such a tool."

"That's hilarious coming out of your mouth," Dash snapped.

Justin crossed his arms over his chest and lowered his voice to where I just barely made it out. "You should stop worrying about Blake so much and focus on yourself."

"You have no idea who you're threatening."

Lindsay clicked up between both of them, swishing her hips as if she were going to ask one of them to dance. I didn't understand how she could be oblivious to the severity of the situation, but perhaps it was because I knew Justin better. "We're out of beer," she practically purred. "Can we stop this testosterone match and get a girl a drink? Blake's fine, right?" She eyed me and I nodded, stepping closer to them.

The tension in Justin's shoulders melted and my heart slowed a fraction. He turned and looked down at Lindsay. "I've got another six-pack in my truck." He motioned his head and walked back the way we'd come.

"All right! Come on, Dashy!" Lindsay didn't wait for Dash but hurried after Justin in the short-stepping way one can only do in pumps like hers.

I stood frozen, shocked that Justin hadn't taken a swing at Dash. Maybe he wasn't as drunk as I'd thought, or maybe he knew how upset I'd be if he did.

"Blake are you coming?" Justin called, looking over his shoulder.

I pointed at the empty beer bottles on the bridge. "Just want to gather these first."

He kept walking. I didn't move until he and Lindsay were barely shadows through the darkness.

I let out a long breath and knelt to pick up the bottles. Dash helped, grabbing two from the other side of the bridge. "Thanks," I said as we stood and walked slowly back to the trucks. I stopped in the middle of the tall grass. "I'm so sorry."

Dash craned his head back to the sky. "You know I hate it when you do that."

"Do what?" I asked.

"Take the blame. Say sorry for things out of your control."

"I just wanted tonight to be fun. I wanted you two to like each other."

"He's a complete dirtbag, Blake. The way he treats you . . ." He clenched his eyes shut. When he opened them again, he registered my completely defeated expression.

He took a deep breath. "I don't think I'll ever like this guy. But I'm willing to try."

I swallowed hard to stop the tears from reaching my eyes. Justin wouldn't be as courteous of my wishes. Dash was too good a friend, and I put him in a situation—again—where he could've been the subject of Justin's rage. The morning I'd hidden him in my closet flashed in my eyes. I seriously didn't deserve him.

"Thank you, for breaking my fall."

He took a step closer to me. "Someone has to save you sometimes, since you're constantly doing it for someone else."

He looked past me then, to where I knew Justin had to be, and my chest tightened. I didn't regret telling him the truth about Justin's threats every time I tried to leave, but when Dash said things like that it made me question . . . everything. And my mind was overrun with the guilt and the worry and the curiosity of how different things could be if Justin wasn't the way he was, if he was more like Dash. If he *was* Dash. The thoughts raced together in a jumbled mess of a traffic-jam and I had no idea which way was straight anymore. So instead of trying to talk it all out with Dash, I simply gazed at him, and admired the ease of his presence next to me.

"How'd you adapt this stoic calm you possess?" I asked as we continued our walk. The trucks came into sight, Justin's headlights and music blaring.

"Please, woman. Think about what I do for a living."

"Right, duh," I said, but my laughter died as Dash and I stopped a few feet away from Justin's truck.

Lindsay leaned against the driver's side door, her hip cocked against one of Justin's thighs as she peered over him, sipping on a beer as he talked.

"Just installed these myself," Justin said and pointed to something near his dashboard. Most likely the new stereo he'd bought recently.

I shook off the shock of someone as gorgeous as Lindsay so close to Justin rather quickly and wondered idly if it should bother me more. I glanced at Dash. He stared at the two with a distant gaze, more inside his head than standing in the tall grass next to me.

"What's up?" I nudged him with my elbow.

He blinked a couple times and gave me a half smile. "Nothing . . ." He chuckled quietly to himself. "Absolutely nothing."

CHAPTER

TEN

SLIPPED MY black calf-high boots over my best skinny jeans and tugged at my sleeveless black lacy top. I wanted to look hot tonight. Blue October only came to town once or twice a year and I looked forward to it more than my birthday. I'd even dyed my hair an espresso brown a couple nights ago for a fresh look. Not much darker than my natural color, but the change lifted my spirits, and with the concert only hours away I was practically flying. And despite Justin's outburst over the tickets a few weeks ago, I was determined to have a good time.

I finished my look with some red lipstick—choosing to go bolder than I ever had before—just as I heard the jingle of keys outside my front door. My heart galloped. Justin was here. I half expected him to call and bail on me after the disaster of his meeting Dash last week. I told myself tonight would be different. Who couldn't have fun at a concert?

I heard Hail growl from the couch and him hiss back at her.

"Stop it, both of you," I yelled from my bedroom.

"She started it," he said.

I shut my door and caught Justin staring at the large tub of

Nutella brownies my mom had dropped off the day before. She had the habit of coming over to my place when I had a long day of classes to "drop things off" and ended up cleaning, too. I'd continuously tried to get her to stop, but the baked goods were beyond hard to turn down.

The look in Justin's eyes as he skimmed over the sweet note she left on top of the tub made my chest clench.

Longing, wonder. Anger, regret.

Each emotion flashed in his eyes in the span of a few heartbeats before he decided to stick to one. He shoved the tub away on the kitchen counter, like it had personally offended him.

I gulped down the guilt, letting it settle in its usual spot in the center of my chest. These moments weren't completely unheard of. Moments when I'd catch him longing for that special bond only a family could provide.

Holidays. Tough times. Each could've been an opportunity to try to reconcile after all these years, but he never tried. And from my many phone calls in the past, I knew his aunt and uncle wouldn't try if *he* didn't, so I'd given up on the idea long ago. Justin knew all this, of course, but it didn't change things. He was set in the way his life worked and wouldn't budge. That left me set with my guilt, and the constant overwhelming urge to fill that gap for him, despite it never being enough.

He finally registered my presence, catching me watching him.

"You look nice, Blake," he said, his eyes distant, gentler. He blinked and the rare tender moment was gone. He stepped away from the counter quickly, scrunching his eyebrows. "Are you ready? I want to get there and get a spot near the exit so we're not stuck in a logjam when this thing is over." He swung his keys back and forth between his fingers.

I sank a fraction, wishing his default mood wasn't anger. "Yeah, I'm ready."

"Good. Let's go."

I climbed into his truck, shocked it'd been cleared of food bags and other trash.

"We'll do breakfast tomorrow, too. And then maybe a movie?" he said as he navigated the roads.

I had to shut my mouth it had dropped so fast. "I'd love that."

"Good. I've been wanting to see the new Bruce Willis movie for a while."

I wondered if the moment I'd caught him having earlier was the reason for his long-lost sweetness. I kept my hopes in check, though, knowing that those kind of promises usually came with a price. I sighed with the thought, wishing I could just enjoy his spontaneity and focus on the fact that maybe he was finally, if not slowly, changing into the man I knew he could be when I'd fallen in love with him as a boy.

The line outside The Starlite wrapped around the brick building's corner despite Justin's insistence to rush. I'd told him we would've had to arrive two hours early to be the first in line, but he didn't believe me. He'd been so sure he hadn't even let me grab something from the drive-through and I was starving. It'd be hours before I could eat now.

Excited butterflies flapped in my stomach, helping distract me from my hunger. Each time I saw Blue perform was like the first time—the eager anticipation, the rush of adrenaline, and then the release after an incredible high—something I savored.

"Holy shit. This is ridiculous." Justin looked over the line as we took our places in the back.

"Told you." I shrugged. The minimum hour-long wait didn't bother me because I knew that after it my favorite band would be two opening acts away from taking the stage and performing the music I loved.

Justin cut his eyes to me. "You didn't tell me we'd be

standing here for hours just to get inside and stand for another four hours listening to a band you can hear on your iPod."

"Geez, loosen up. Concerts are a blast." I tried to hug his arm, but he pulled away.

"It'll be fun when I can get a beer." He grabbed our tickets out of his back pocket. "I bought these weeks ago. I should be able to get in before all these jokers paying at the window."

"You can"t—"

"Stay here." He took off toward the front of the building.

I didn't try to stop him. Maybe it would take up half the wait time for him to figure out we'd have to stand in line like everybody else. Glancing across the street, I noticed several people wearing Blue October shirts crowding around a small display. The guy behind it also wore the band's gear. Since we were still the last ones in line, I decided to give in to my curiosity and headed over.

An array of baked goods, from cookies to brownies, sat on the display. One girl shoved half a dozen cookies in her purse as she walked away. A small neon sign read: Support Local Artists.

My stomach growled. "What artist is this for?"

The guy behind the display had blond dreads covered partially by a Blue October beanie. "My band and a few others. We're raising money for new instruments. We have a similar sound to Blue."

I grabbed an individually packaged brownie the size of my hand and over an inch thick. "Awesome," I said and handed him a ten dollar bill. "Keep the change. Good luck with your music."

I hurried back to the line only to find someone had taken my spot. "Hey, jerk, this was my spot!" I yelled in my best high-pitched whine.

Dash whipped around, his eyebrows scrunched together. "You want to fight over *this*?" He eyed the very end of the line we occupied. "And that was a terrible voice by the way. Knew it was you."

"Sure you did," I said and unwrapped my brownie. "Where is Lindsay?" I glanced around, shocked she wasn't attached to his hip.

Dash cleared his throat. "Well, she and I—"

"They won't let us in." Justin's voice cut off Dash, and I turned to see him behind me. "Even though I bought *you* these tickets way ahead of time." The mention of buying the tickets for me turned my stomach. I knew he'd just been delivering a low blow when he'd blamed this present as the reason he had to sell his watch, but it was hard to take, and I resisted the urge to apologize for something I knew I wasn't responsible for. He had plenty of things he could've sold and more so, his truck wouldn't have been towed if he'd simply parked in a space that wasn't restricted.

Instead of saying anything along those lines I shoved a huge bite of brownie in my mouth. Not the best I'd ever tasted, kind of dry actually, but I was starving so I didn't care. I slowed down, nibbling it as Dash filled the tense silence with one of his awesome chase stories. Nearly an hour later the line moved forward inch by inch and we finally reached the front. Justin had been glued to his phone the entire wait, and I glanced up at him, wondering how I could make him enjoy this night more.

"I just noticed you changed your hair, Blake. It looks amazing," Dash said, regaining my attention.

Heat rushed to my cheeks. "I colored it. Thanks," I said before taking another bite of the brownie, which was now more than half gone.

"You colored your hair?" Justin finally pried his eyes away from his phone, looking at the hair framing my face. He glanced at Dash before returning to me. He didn't smile. "You know I liked it the way it was."

My chest tightened and I shook my head. Why did anything involving the slightest hint of change have to irk him so much? I wracked my brain, wondering if he'd always been this way or had I just started to notice it because Dash was so starkly different? *His* notice of me was so welcome I had the urge to wrap my arms around him.

The idea made my entire body tingle, and then I laughed so hard I shook.

"What the hell, Blake?" Justin asked after I couldn't stop the giggles for two minutes straight.

I sucked in gulps of air and wiped under my eyes, finally reeling myself in as we moved into the lobby of the building. "Sorry," I said. "Don't know where that came from." "Where did you get that?" Justin eyed the half-eaten brownie in my hand.

"From the guys across the street raising money for their instruments," I said, motioning toward the building's doors.

Justin raked his hands across his buzzed head. "You idiot!"

I burst out laughing at the sight of his scowl. He really had that look down. He needed a beer quick. I thought about getting a drink, too, but I suddenly realized I felt like I'd already drank four.

"What?"

Justin lowered his head. "That brownie is laced. Probably with a whole bunch of different drugs. Now look at you."

My laughter died instantly and I froze, staring at the brownie in my hand like it would bite me. "Drugs? Like cocaine? Meth? Oh my God, did I just eat meth?"

"Probably," Justin said. "You shouldn't buy shit off strangers like that."

Dash gently grabbed my shoulders and looked me in the eye. "It's just a pot-brownie. You'll be fine, Blake."

"No, no no no. It's meth. I'm going to freak out like that guy on Breaking Bad . . ."

"You are not. Relax." He chuckled, and the sound cut through my terror.

"How can you be sure?"

"Always a first for everything." Dash grabbed the remaining half of the brownie from me and shoved it in his mouth.

"Better?" he asked after swallowing. He flashed me a huge smile, tons of brownie still stuck between his teeth.

Justin's eyes jumped between the two of us again and he shook his head. "You're both fucking idiots."

It wasn't at all funny but I laughed again, and this time I didn't stop until we'd found our spots on the floor.

BLUE STAGE LIGHTS sparkled off thick layers of smoke in the air. My head buzzed with a wonderful mixture of loud music and floaty-sensation. My muscles had never been so relaxed as I swayed rhythmically to the sound of the electric violin and closed my eyes as the lead singer crooned the first note of my favorite song. The music touched me, soaked through my skin, and hummed in my bones. The pleasure built inside me until I couldn't hold it in anymore. I let out a scream and threw the rock sign up. Dash followed suit, and so did a bunch of others in the crowd.

Dash stood next to me, nodding his head to the music. I glanced around at Justin, who was behind us with his hands crossed over his chest. He stared at the stage but remained still. I couldn't fathom how he could be surrounded by such awesome music and not move.

I turned my attention back to the stage and nudged Dash when the band segued into his favorite song. He let out a holler of his own. We both mouthed lyrics at each other over the next few songs and banged our heads to the beat. I'd never been to a show with someone who loved the band as much as I did, and I instantly decided it was the absolute best way to experience it. Blue slowed down to a soft tune and my heart jumped when Justin left the bar and pulled me closer to him. My shock of him asking me to dance quickly vanished when he continued to tug me toward a clear space closer to the bar where I could hear him easier.

"We have to go," he said.

"What? No. They're not even close to finished yet."

"Look, I'm sorry, but the guys have this major tournament up. They can't finish it without me. Our team will forfeit."

I freed my wrist from his fingers as an angry response churned itself up in my stomach. "I can't—"

"I can take Blake home." Dash cut me off, and I only then realized he stood next to us.

Justin's eyes went to slits, looking Dash up and down. Of course he didn't know that Dash knew exactly where I lived and had hung out with me—John and Paul as well—plenty of times. The battle in his eyes was clear, but I couldn't tell where he'd land.

"Fine." Justin took my hand again. "We will do breakfast tomorrow though. And the movie. I promise. Be at my house at eight. Okay?"

I nodded. "Thanks for bringing me," I said as he walked out of earshot.

Dash grabbed my hand and guided me back to the dance floor before I could contemplate how, or *if,* I was even upset.

I quickly focused on the band who launched into a fast-paced number that I knew by heart. The sweet, bubbly sensation still popped underneath my skin, and chased away any thought I'd have given to Justin's departure. Instead, I let loose the moves I normally saved for my kitchen. Bouncing from side to side, I grabbed Dash's hand and spun myself around, the night from our failed chase fresh in my mind. It wasn't anywhere near club music, so Dash didn't take control and draw me close like he had before, but he twirled me a couple times before letting go and matching my steady bounce.

Soon we each played an air instrument in perfect synchronization. Caught up in my mad air-guitar skills, I didn't see a man the size of a linebacker making his way toward the bar and stepped right in his path. The sheer mass of his movement knocked me off balance, and I toppled hard into Dash.

I gripped his shoulders, and he steadied me with one strong arm wrapped around my lower back.

"Sorry!" the man shouted and continued to the bar.

I glanced up at Dash, my lids slightly hooded.

"You all right, woman?"

"Couldn't be better." The truth rang clear in my voice and I don't know why I was surprised at the notion. Justin had left, had bailed once again, and I just . . . didn't care.

Dash raised his eyebrows but didn't break our gaze. I stared back at him, enjoying the hard press of his body against mine. My eyes trailed to his lips. I wondered what he tasted like? I imagined something sweet and intense, like dark chocolate and cayenne. I blinked a couple times and realized I hadn't let go of his shoulders. I slowly pulled away. He unwound his arm from my waist, and my heart raced.

He winked at me, and my limbs melted. I quickly bounced up and down to the next song, desperately grounding myself in the present and forcing my mind to stop fantasizing about Dash. I blamed the brownie.

The band did an encore, but it still ended too soon. I'm pretty sure I could watch Blue perform for well over their normal two-hour limit.

We funneled into the line of a hundred or so other people exiting the building at a slow crawl. There were only inches between me and the person in front of me, but Dash's chest pressed against my back as he stood behind me. I couldn't deny how safe I felt with him there. And I couldn't stop my body from reacting the way it did, or my mind from trying to make the friendship I had with Dash into something more. I focused my thoughts on Justin and our breakfast date tomorrow, instantly deciding I'd use the time to talk and find common ground again. I assured myself that is all it would take to end the madness filling my head.

Then Dash shifted his weight behind me, his hand accidentally grazing my hip causing an electric current to run through the center of my body and crackle.

HAIL SAT ON the floor, resting her head on Dash's knee, the perfect pout plastered on her face. We were devouring the two pizzas we'd brought home after the concert, and she was in a mood since I wouldn't let Dash give her any. She already weighed fifty pounds and didn't need any more jiggle. I told her she was perfect the way she was, but she continuously begged for food like I starved her.

"Did you get a good look at Ryan's new violin? It was badass!" Dash said, stuffing another slice of pepperoni in his mouth.

"Yeah, it was wicked! I loved the bright blue flames." I finished off my fourth slice and carried the empty box to the kitchen. I set it on the counter and grabbed two more beers from the fridge, twisting off the caps and tossing them in the box. I stopped when I turned back around, finding Dash petting Hail as she leaned against his legs. I swear both of them were smiling, and the sight warmed my insides.

"You going to drink both those beers, woman, or are you sharing?"

I handed Dash one of the bottles and sat back down.

"So, Dash Lexington, what's your real name?" I asked, hoping the abrupt shift in conversation would shock him enough to tell me.

"Nope."

"Seriously? Beer and a pot brownie and you still won't let it slip?"

"Never going to happen, Blake." He took another swig from the bottle.

I sank further into the couch and fake-sulked while nursing my own longneck. The beer tasted unusually good tonight, as did the pizza. The credit could go to the brownie, but I suspected it was because the night had been utterly awesome.

"So, are you upset that Justin bailed to play video games . . . again?"

"No."

"Really?"

I shrugged, unable to convey the battle of thoughts raging in my head. "He promised breakfast tomorrow. What more can I ask for?" The question sounded much more depressing than I'd meant it to.

Dash sighed, shaking his head. "I don't know. Just seems like he should be here and not me."

My stomach sank. "Do you not want to be here?"

He glanced at me, his green eyes intense as ever. "Not what I meant. I love being around you, Blake. You know that if the choice came down to it, I'd rather be with you than do almost anything else in the world. But I also want you to be happy."

"I'm happy—"

"Tonight," Dash cut me off. "And it's not due to him because whenever he does something for you, it's *still* about him."

He was right; I couldn't deny it. A slow, familiar dull ache surfaced in my chest. "I know that, but what would you have me do?" He knew the reasons I stayed.

Dash set his beer down and gently clutched my shoulder, pinning me with those damn green eyes. "I'd have you realize that the woman you are deserves better than the man he is."

"But . . ." It wasn't that simple. "Who's to say I deserve

better than what Justin gives me? It's been like this forever. I don't know anything outside of it." I chided myself, because I *did* know better. Because of Dash.

The warmth from his hand slid across my skin as he moved it to my neck. "Don't think that. You deserve more, Blake. And you need to understand that you are so much more than how you see yourself and a hell of a lot more than how he treats you."

My breath caught in my throat, and I tried to ignore the sparks erupting low in my belly from Dash's words and touch. I licked my lips, my mouth suddenly dry. He studied me, gauging me for a response, but I didn't have the words.

"Do you . . ." I inhaled sharply. "Do you want another beer?" I asked instead of opening the door he knocked on.

He let out a long breath, like he'd been holding it. I glanced at him and his eyes were on me. Really on me, with a deep, almost magnetic stare I'd never seen before. It made my heart race. He reached his hand up and touched the ends of my hair where it lay on my shoulder. The light caress sent a wave of heat throughout my entire body.

"You deserve to be free." His voice was soft and low and different, like I was hearing it for the first time.

I parted my lips, but only air escaped.

Dash sighed. "I better go before I have too many and have to crash here again," he said, standing from the couch. The playful grin he sported set my nerves at ease but didn't erase the seriousness of his earlier words.

"Yeah, my couch isn't much to sleep on," I said and couldn't stop the blush that flooded my cheeks. The first night Dash and I hung out he'd ended up sleeping over. And look how far we'd come. My best friend—I couldn't imagine life without him.

Dash took a step closer after kissing Hail goodbye. He looked down at me, his eyes hopping from mine to my lips and back again. My hands trembled.

"I didn't mind it." He winked before he turned and walked to my door. "See you later."

I stared at the door long after he'd left, desperately trying to ignore the shockwave of heat pulsing throughout my entire body.

CHAPTER

ELEVEN

I STOOD OUTSIDE Justin's door, thirty minutes after eight a.m. I'd wanted to give him some extra time—knowing mornings weren't his strong suit—to start our day on the right foot. I heard laughter from the other side of the door, followed by insults and playful shouting. The boys were over and still playing COD. Had they even slept?

Done with the idea of knocking, I pushed open the door and walked inside.

Justin's focus was intently on the flat screen in his living room, but Mark and Andy saw me. All their eyes were rimmed in red. So they'd been up all night, and from the look of the amount of beer cans strewn across the floor, they were probably still drunk.

Wonderful.

"Hey, Blake," Andy said, rubbing his eyes before grabbing the controller sitting next to him. I gave him a closed mouth-smile, trying to keep the adrenaline in my veins from fully unleashing. Justin hadn't officially bailed on me . . . yet. I took a deep breath.

"Justin?"

He finally noticed I stood in his living room. His eyes grew wide, recognition flickering behind them. "Oh, yeah, sorry. I meant to text you."

My heart sank, the sensation so familiar it made me angry. I think I'd already known he would do this.

"Why?" I managed to ask.

He glanced around the room and then at the screen. "Isn't it obvious? We're still playing."

"But you promised. We were going to . . ." The fight went out of me. The main hope I'd had for today was a good talk with him to clear the air but it quickly vanished.

Justin glared, visibly upset by my plea. He stood up, coming closer and lowering his voice. "Damn it, Blake, was the concert not good enough for you?"

"What?"

"Seriously, I took you, played nice all night. That should've bought me time. I shouldn't have to do anything for a while now."

My mouth dropped. "You only took me because you were . . . buying me off so I wouldn't ask you to do anything with me?"

"Well, it sure as hell wasn't because I liked the band." He had the audacity to laugh then, turning to fist-bump Andy.

The laugh, paired with his nonchalance about blowing me off, for the umpteenth time, broke something within me. The last piece of my heart that cared about him, ached for his attention, his love, died. With it came a rushing sensation of clarity, and it was like my eyes were open for the first time in years.

Justin would *never* change.

And I was done being afraid to leave him. I chased tornadoes for God's sake—I could do this, and I wasn't waiting one more second. I would not be treated like garbage. Never again. I don't know if it was Dash's words last night, the fact that I *could* chase down a tornado and barely flinch, or the culmination of one too many emotional blows from Justin, but I was so fucking done.

I took a deep breath. "We need to talk," I said, not letting my anger seep out. I would end this maturely. I glanced at Mark and Andy, suddenly grateful for their presence. Hopefully they could keep him calm and rational, prevent him from hurting himself . . . *if* he resorted to that again. Even if he did, though, I couldn't take it anymore. Dash was right; real love wouldn't place that on someone, and Justin's actions made it clear he didn't love me anymore.

He walked past me toward his bedroom. I followed him, pausing in the entryway, the door having disappeared from the last time he'd kicked it in. I shook my head at the memory, and it was like I saw it from a different angle—how the hell had I let it go on so long like this?

"What is it now?" Justin stood in the middle of his room, arms crossed.

Icy fingers curled around my heart, the image of him grabbing the nearest knife flashing in my mind. My fingers trembled, but I pushed on. "We have to stop this."

Justin's jet-black eyebrows scrunched his forehead. "Stop what?"

I motioned between us. "Us. All we do is fight—"

"Yo!" Mark called from the other room, cutting me off. "Justin, man, you're up!"

Justin made to return to the living room, but I stepped in his way, placing my hand on his chest to stop him.

"This is really important, Justin," I said, pinning him in place with my eyes.

He sighed. "So is this tournament we're in."

"No. Not now. We need to finish this conversation."

Justin jerked away from my touch and nudged me out of

his way. The ice melted, damn near evaporated with the rush of anger that flared within me.

"Justin," I snapped, sharp enough to get him to stop before he made it to the living room. "I'm done," I said as he turned around.

He tilted his head, giving me a look like he doubted my seriousness.

I walked toward him, stopping only a foot away. "I'm done. Now, we can talk about it like adults or you can go play your game. Either way, I'm sorry, but I'm done. I can't do this anymore."

His eyes cleared and he focused them more fully on me, as if he just realized I'd shown up at his place. "What are you saying?"

"I'm saying we're through. And since we've been together so long, I thought you deserved a rational explanation, but if you're more concerned about your video game tournament, then I don't think it'll make any difference."

He glanced over his shoulder at Mark and Andy who were failing at acting like they couldn't hear everything I'd said. He then turned back to me, grabbing my hand. "This is all over me not going to breakfast?"

"This has nothing to do with that. This has to do with the fact that we aren't right for each other. That I've been drowning for the past few years and you haven't even noticed."

"Don't do this now, Blake. Just . . . can't we talk about this after the tournament is over? They need me."

I jerked my hand away, his declaration of need for an on-line tournament sealing in my anger like a pressure cooker. I huffed and reached in my bag for my keys. "There is no later, Justin. There is now." I gripped the cool key fob in my hand. I felt the need to explain myself, to even say I was sorry to leave him like everyone clse had in his life, but he looked over his shoulder again, toward his friends, toward the game, and the words died in my throat.

"If the game is more important than hearing the end of us, then go. I don't care. Honestly, you've done it to me so many times it doesn't even sting anymore. But, Justin? Don't hurt yourself, all right?"

He focused on me again, his eyes turning to slits. I was aware that Mark and Andy heard my plea, and I was fine with that. I wanted them to keep him level if he went off balance after I left.

"This is that asshole Dash's fault." He flexed his hands into fists at his sides.

"What the hell would he have to do with it?" I took a micro-step back, like his accusation had physically pushed me.

"Don't play dumb! I saw the way you acted around him. He's more than a fucking study-buddy and you know it."

I opened and closed my mouth a few times before sighing. "You're right. He's actually become a really close friend, one I couldn't tell you about—not because of anything awful like you assume—but because I knew you'd make me choose. You've *always* made me choose. You put your life in my hands every time I had an inkling of becoming someone other than your girlfriend, and I can't do it anymore. I just . . . won't."

"I only force hard choices on you to keep you safe . . . which is with me. I've loved you since we were kids."

The words stung, and maybe in some twisted way he believed them, but I didn't. Not anymore. Not after realizing the way he treated me was no better than a doll he used to fuck. I sucked in a deep breath and shook my head.

He unclenched his fingers before balling them into fists again. "You're really ending this? You're leaving me after everything?"

"Yes." Guilt threatened to swallow me whole. My worry over his safety had been a constant for years, and I couldn't change that right this second. But the anger was there and the pain and the now crystal-clear knowledge things would never change. "We aren't right—"

"Don't," he cut me off, raising his hand. "Don't bother with the excuses." He gave Mark and Andy a sideways glance before returning his focus on me. "And just so we're clear, I only ever made that threat to keep you."

An ice-cold bucket of water doused the fire burning in my veins. The cold was so instant my stomach rolled. "What?"

He shrugged, smirking at his friends. "Worked for a while."

My mouth dropped, and I couldn't find the right words. There weren't any. Wait, yes there were. *Blake you've been a fucking idiot.* Those fit me to a T. I swallowed hard and steeled my nerves. I'd seen the blood drawn from the knife. Maybe he had done it to keep me, or maybe he only said that now to save face in front of his friends. Either way, I wasn't sticking around to find out.

I gave him a slight nod, holding back tears.

"We're done." I turned on my heels, not bothering to shut the door behind me.

NO SLEEP AND a knock on my door before ten in the morning. I rubbed my palms against my cheeks, trying to restore life into my face. I swallowed hard, assuming I'd find Justin on the other side of the door.

Instead I found Dash holding two white paper cups. "I was hoping you'd left something in my truck after the concert so I'd have a legit reason to come over here this morning, but you're annoyingly non-forgetful. Figured coffee was the next best excuse."

I chuckled, the sensation breaking the sour fear that still churned in my stomach. "You know you never need an excuse to come over."

"Good to know," he said, setting the cups on the coffee

table and petting a sleepy Hail. She'd agonized with me last night, despite not understanding what it was about.

I sighed and pinched the bridge of my nose, a fierce headache throbbing like an ice pick lodged in my brain.

"Hey," Dash whispered, suddenly standing so close I could feel the heat coming off his body. "What's wrong?" He pried my hand away and forced me to look in his eyes.

I pushed past him, sinking onto the couch and grabbing the coffee he'd brought. After a quick hot gulp, I found my voice. "I ended it."

His eyebrows shot up before he smoothed his expression and took a seat next to me.

"Are you all right?" He didn't need to ask why I'd done it.

"I'm more all right than I thought I'd be."

"Why don't I believe you?"

I glanced at him, my eyes squinting. "I hate it, but I'm worried about him. He didn't give me a chance to explain or talk it out."

"And you think that would've made a difference?"

I shrugged. "I thought it would. It meant something to me. To explain myself. To get closure. I was so angry with him because he was more concerned with his video game tournament. And the fact that he said he'd only ever threatened suicide to keep me with him. But I don't know if that's the truth or if he was just playing the tough man-card in front of his friends. I just left him there yesterday morning. Anything could've happened to him."

"I've always thought it was a trap for you."

A cold chill ran through me. "I know, but after all the threats and what I've seen him do . . . You can't blame me for still being worried."

He placed his hand on my back. "I don't blame you. It's natural you'd worry, but I don't think you need to torture yourself over it."

"Don't I? I was all he had left. Everyone else left him, too, because of me."

Dash shook his head. "Not possible. No matter what event led up to them kicking him out, their minds were already made up. It wasn't your fault. And if you were really all he had left to hold on to in the world, he would've treated you differently."

I pressed my lips together, the truth in his statement making me feel better and worse at the same time. "I'm so torn. Happy to be free, but terrified of bad news just around the corner. It's like in a horror movie, you know something is about to jump out and scare the crap out of you, but it just hasn't happened yet."

Dash rubbed his hand up and down my back. After a few moments he stood up. "All right, you need distraction. That's the key. So, you want me to go grab food or you up for a breakfast-lunch outing?"

"I think I'm up for a little distraction. I'll go get dressed," I said and stopped on the way to my room. "Thank you, Dash."

BRUNCH TURNED INTO a two-hour event, followed by a trip to the weather lab on campus. After four hours of checking forecasts and mapping routes for the next week's upcoming storm cells, we'd landed at Bailey's for dinner and much needed beers.

I smiled at Dash over my half-eaten basket of chicken fingers. I had to give him credit. He'd successfully kept me busy all day and my thoughts well accounted for. My enthusiasm vanished as I set my beer bottle down on the table. Now that we weren't moving, or talking, the thoughts I'd managed to keep at bay crept back inside.

Glancing at my cell, I sighed. Still no missed calls. This could be a good thing, but my mind conjured up the worst possible scenario for Justin's silence.

"Blake," Dash said, touching my forearm.

I blinked a couple of times, focusing on his knowing gaze. "Yeah?"

He placed a barbecue-stained napkin in the empty basket before him. "You're really testing my distraction skills. I was doing so good, too. Maybe I need to pull out the big guns?"

"And what would those guns be?"

He cocked an eyebrow, leaning closer over the table. "Well, first off I'd—"

His words were cut off by Awolnation's "Sail" blaring from his cell phone resting on the table next to him. The night we danced to that song flashed in my head. He answered it, and I tilted my head when his gaze turned fierce.

He slowly brought his hand down without saying anything and ended the call. He stared at his phone, contemplating something.

"What is it?" I touched his arm, and he finally snapped out of it.

"It was Lindsay . . ."

"And?"

He worked his jaw back and forth. "We need to go somewhere." He laid two twenties on the table and headed toward the door. I followed him without hesitation and climbed into his truck.

Dash looked at me, his hands pausing on the keys in the ignition. He opened his mouth, nearly saying something, but started the car instead. He hit the gas, taking the usual route toward campus. I held onto the bar above the window, heart pounding.

"What's going on?" I asked, noting his hardened expression hadn't changed since the phone call.

"Not sure, but we're about to find out."

"What did Lindsay say?"

He cut his eyes toward me and they softened.

I reached across the cab and gently clutched his forearm, which was rock hard with tension. "Talk to me."

He slowly let out a held breath through his nose. He made a hard right into the parking lot of the Alpha Chi Omega house.

Dash jumped out of the truck and hurried around to open my door for me. He took my hand and led us up to the giant front porch. The frustration came off him in waves, filtering through our joined hands and finding a home in my stomach. Guys in OU shirts and girls in sparkly tops and tanks littered the porch, all drinking beers or other beverages out of red plastic cups. The large doors were wide open, and people strolled in and out of them as they pleased. Loud, thumping music spilled from the house, and I wondered if all college house parties were the same. We got a nod from a few of the guys parked on the porch.

Dash glanced at me, all the anger in his eyes melting into a sea of hurt. He battled with himself—over what I had no idea. He sighed and something settled inside him. I could see it in his eyes, the anger slipping to a stoic calm.

I opened my mouth to speak, but he already stomped through the place.

The only bright light came from the kitchen, the countertops near invisible due to the wide variety of half-empty liquor bottles covering the area. The rest of the house was coated in muted colored lights and a strobe light flashed in a large room to our right, where throngs of students ground against each other to the music.

Liquor, beer, and smoke hung in the air, so potent I thought I'd get drunk just from inhaling it. My heart raced as I followed Dash helplessly as he pulled me through crowds of people, his eyes sharp as a hawk and tracking.

I didn't know what to do other than follow his lead. I'd

never been to a party like this before, but clearly we weren't there to meet Lindsay for drinks. He was on the hunt, and I sort of hoped we wouldn't find her.

Dash led me upstairs once we'd finished searching the main floor and the basement. We walked down a long hallway lined with four doors on each side. Most of them were open, some filled with people playing video games or shamelessly making out.

He stopped in front of the only closed door and glanced at me apologetically. Dash reached out his hand, hovering over the doorknob. Clutching it, he hesitated and pressed his ear to the door.

I put the pieces together and anger flared in my gut. If he opened that and we found Lindsay cheating on him, I might punch her in the face. Surely there was a mistake, though. How could she ever cheat on someone as great as Dash?

Dash startled, hearing something I couldn't, and yanked the door open.

I stood next to him, frozen.

Lindsay was on all fours in a bed that took up most of the small room. Her skin practically glowed in the dark, and her bare breasts flopped back and forth as she got pounded from behind. I quickly averted my eyes as if witnessing a car crash.

Her high-pitched moaning didn't stop, indicating the two hadn't heard the door.

"I fucking knew it." Dash didn't yell, but his tone was absolutely lethal.

Lindsay gasped.

Dash made to step farther into the room, but I yanked on his arm.

"Oh shit."

I recognized the voice but didn't immediately make the connection.

Dash tugged out of my grasp. The motion forced my line

of sight back into the room, and the floor fell out beneath me.

Justin was naked, a sheet barely covering his lower half.

Lindsay quickly scrambled for her clothes strewn out on the floor.

"Why would you bring her here, Dash?" Lindsay whined, slipping on her skirt.

What an odd thing to ask.

She'd cheated. With my boyfriend . . . my ex-boyfriend. My hands trembled, and hot tears welled beneath my eyes, but the sight of Justin in that fucking bed stopped them. The anger raged hot and irrational in my chest. I was livid with Justin but equally pissed at Lindsay for doing this to Dash.

Before I could mentally arrange the barrage of emotions exploding inside me, I stomped across the room and shoved Lindsay so hard she tumbled backward, her ass hitting the floor next to the bed with a thunk.

"Stupid bitch!" I yelled and pulled my fist back, adrenaline surging through my veins, readying to punch her.

"Blake!" she screeched, putting a hand up defensively. "Dash, stop her!" She focused her wide eyes on Dash.

Dash's arms slipped around my midsection, and a fraction of the anger pounding against my chest cooled.

"What the hell are you doing, Lindsay?" he snapped as he tugged me away from her. Only a portion of me wondered why he didn't sound as mad as I was. The other part thought up ways to slip his grasp and beat the shit out of both of her and Justin.

"You have no right to be mad!" Lindsay yelled and sloppily finished dressing.

"Are you serious? You're cheating on him!" I screamed. Somehow that pissed me off more than anything in this entire situation.

Lindsay's mouth dropped, and she cocked her head to the side. "You didn't tell her?" She laughed a high-pitched laugh.

"Oh, that's priceless, Dash!"

"Tell me what?"

"Shut up, Lindsay," Dash said, raked his fingers through his hair.

She sucked through her teeth. "He dumped me the day after we went to that stupid bridge. I can do whatever and *whoever* I want!"

"You have to know they just broke up yesterday!" Dash snapped.

"I'm so sick of hearing about *Blake*," she whined like I wasn't standing right there.

I turned to Dash with questioning eyes. "You didn't tell me . . ."

Justin moved, garnering my attention. He'd gotten dressed in his signature jeans and a cut-off shirt when my focus had been solely on Lindsay.

"Blake, I'm drunk . . . I'm sorry," Justin said, his arms reaching out to me. Funny, he didn't sound drunk.

My eyes were slits as I stared up at him. "You're sorry? Are you fucking kidding me?"

Justin took another step toward me as if to wrap me in his arms. "I was mad at you for ending it, but I still love you, still want to be with you. Let's talk this out."

"Don't touch me," I said, taking a step back. My heart pounded furiously in my chest. "And you want to talk *now?*" I shook my head. "All these years you threatened to *kill* yourself if I ever left you. You literally drew blood over it! And you pushed me down until I was a shell of the girl I should be . . . I still am that shell—and now what? It's been less than forty-eight hours since we ended things, and this is what you do?" I raked my hands through my hair. "How could I be so stupid? I've done nothing but worry about you since yesterday, thinking you may just follow through on the threats you never let me forget . . ."

"Blake, I'm hurt. I can't live without you . . ." Justin placed his hand on my shoulder and I lost it.

I pulled my right hand back and slapped him across the face as hard as I could. His head snapped to the left and he stumbled back a couple steps. "I said don't touch me!"

Dash laughed, the warm sound so out of place in this fucked-up room. "That's what you get, asshole," he said, placing a hand on the small of my back.

I flinched away from his touch, too. "You knew," I said, realizing that Dash had brought me here for a specific reason. A new wave of hurt crashed over me.

Dash's green eyes softened as they met mine. "You were torturing yourself. You needed to see . . ."

Something jerked in the corner of my eye, but I couldn't react in time.

Justin slammed his fist into Dash's jaw while Dash was focused on me. He pulled back to do it again, but I hurled myself between them and took the full force of the hit on my back.

A white-hot pain burst beneath my left shoulder and the air whooshed out of my lungs. I dropped to my knees at Dash's feet.

"Blake!" Each boy screamed my name. Only Justin's made my skin crawl.

I sucked in the air as my lungs slowly opened back up.

"You're fucking dead!" Dash yelled, and I swore the room shook.

"Why'd you step in front of this tool, Blake? Babe, I'm so sorry," Justin spoke, but the words didn't find a place in my heart.

Dash swung next, and Justin's head snapped back, stopping his pathetic attempt at apologizing.

Justin recovered quickly, and before I could blink the two wrestled on the floor next to me like two wild dogs. Fists hit flesh, the sound sickening.

Lindsay gasped and bolted barefoot from the room, clutching her red pumps to her chest.

Icy cold fear doused my red-hot anger. I'd witnessed too many of Justin's fights. He never played fair and wouldn't hesitate to pick up the heaviest object in the room and use it to bash Dash's head in. It took everything in me to stand up, the pain in my back pulsing.

I reached for Dash, who'd gained the upper hand for the moment, pinning Justin to the floor. The pain from the action was so much I thought I'd crumple to the floor again. I sucked in a deep breath and grabbed Dash's shoulder. It jerked under my grasp as the two tried to rip each other's head off. I squeezed harder and Dash snapped out of it, quickly glancing behind him.

"Not. Worth it," I said, each word hard to get out because I was still trying to remember how to breathe. I let go of him and clutched my side where the pain had made its way down.

Dash glared at Justin for another moment before jumping off him.

Despite my anger, I let Dash slip my free arm over his shoulders and bear most of my weight. He walked me slowly toward the door.

"Blake, wait—"

"Stop," I said, looking at Justin with tears in my eyes. All the anger and guilt twisted inside my chest until I thought it'd burst and spill my heart onto the dirty floor of the sorority house. "I'm almost glad this happened. Now I have no guilt whatsoever walking away from you."

Dash led me out into the hallway and down the stairs. With each step an explosion of pain screamed in my back. I swallowed the pain as we made it to the front porch. I looked at Dash, a sharp sting in my chest, and withdrew my arm. "I wanted you out of that room," I said, taking a few shaky steps away from him, "but I'm walking away from you, too."

Tears coated my eyes, blurring the image of Dash standing on the porch, speechless. My apartment was at least two miles away, but I couldn't handle being next to Dash, who'd put me in that situation on purpose.

CHAPTER

TWELVE

THE WHITE-HOT PAIN in my back and side had made the walk home seem endless, but finally I turned the keys and made it inside. Hail jumped off the couch and wiggled her butt back and forth vigorously as I walked in. I winced as I knelt down and rubbed her head. I wished love was as simple as Hail made it—unconditional and uncomplicated.

I limped to my bathroom and splashed cold water on my face. I pulled my hair back, changed into some pajamas, and took three Tylenol.

Thank God I had plenty of beer at my apartment because I needed more than my fair share. I cracked one open, preparing to down it on the couch, when a knock on my door stopped me dead in my tracks. Ice filled my veins, thinking of Justin being outside the door.

"Blake, please," Dash pleaded from the other side.

I sighed, the ice retreating and anger returning.

"I'm not ready to see you, Dash," I said, even though it wasn't true. I placed my hand on the door, knowing I could never really shut him out.

"You said I never needed an excuse to come over."

Especially when he said all the right things. I huffed and opened the door.

He looked defeated, his shoulders drooped and his eyes were filled with pain.

Damn it. I was still outraged and yet the urge to comfort him overwhelmed me. I resisted the need to wrap my arms around him and instead backed up a few spaces.

He stepped in and pet an extremely wiggly Hail. He took a seat, and I eyed the gash on his face from Justin's sucker punch. I handed him my freshly cracked beer and headed to the bathroom, returning with an alcohol-soaked cotton ball and a bandage. I gently wiped at the cut, shocked when he didn't flinch. I slipped the bandage over the wound and sat back, only wincing a little, the Tylenol taking effect.

We sat there with Hail's panting the only sound between us.

"Why didn't you tell me you two had broken up?" I finally blurted out.

Dash jerked up from the couch so fast it startled Hail and she whined. He quickly patted her, but then paced the length of my living room. Finally, he shrugged. "I don't know. I thought it might sway your thinking, and I wanted you to leave that asshole on your own. Then you did, but I didn't want to shove it in your face that I was single, too. I mean, you *just* broke up with him yesterday."

Justin and Lindsay. How long had it been going on? Since the night at Ponderosa Bridge? "She didn't accidentally pocket-dial you. She meant to hurt you, or both of us. And you *knew* what we'd find when we went there." I knew this for a fact, but a part of me wanted him to deny it. Even if it was a lie, I could get past it easier.

"I didn't think about her doing it on purpose. I heard . . . them, and I lost it. I thought if you saw, you'd stop torturing yourself with worry and guilt and finally realize who he really is," Dash said, his voice soft. He'd stopped pacing and stood clutching his longneck at his side.

"You could've handed me the phone. Let me hear. Or told me. I would've believed you."

I caught his eyes, and pain coated his normal fiery emeralds. "I thought this was my chance to free you from the guilt he's held you in for years."

Dash's reasoning was sound, but it still hurt like a bitch. "Pretty painful way of getting free." I shrugged and crossed the room to get my own drink.

"I see now I shouldn't have taken you there. I didn't think of the pain it'd cause you to see that. All I could think about was you realizing who he was and what he was doing to you." He jerked his bottle to his lips and chugged.

Tears welled in my eyes. "Eight years. All the bullshit. All the blowups and the threats . . ." I sighed. "There must be something wrong with me."

"No there isn't."

"Yes there is!" I yelled through my tears. "I gave him everything, and it was never enough. I wasn't enough . . ." I let my head fall into my hands and cried harder.

Frustration and anger whirled inside me, threatening to bring the beer up. The bitter sting of betrayal was raw, like pouring salt in an open wound, but the realization that the last eight years of my life had been wasted hurt worse. I couldn't be angry over this. It was my fault. I should've ended it sooner. "How could I have been so stupid?"

"You're not stupid, Blake. You're the one with the incredibly huge heart who sees the best in everyone. *He's* the asshole."

I glanced up at him, wiping the tears from my eyes with the back of my hand. I sniffed and took a deep breath. "You're right."

There were more bad memories than good, and despite

what Dash said, I really was stupid. Justin and I hadn't been right for each other for a long time. We were toxic. It had taken Dash entering my life to realize how lost I really was. I just wished it hadn't erupted like that, that we could've ended things on a mature note. There was no chance of that now.

I crossed the room and stopped before Dash, realizing how selfish I'd been. I was letting my anger over the situation get in the way of comforting my best friend, who had seen his girlfriend with another man. He had to be hurting over it, too. Dash and I may not have love for our exes any more—but it still wasn't something we should've had to see.

"Even though they technically didn't do anything wrong—unless Justin had started it up before I broke things off—it *feels* wrong," I said. "I'm so sorry about everything."

"There you go again. Apologizing for something completely out of your control. I'm the one who fucked up and took you there, and still you're trying to comfort me." Dash shook his head. "I don't know if that's something I hate about you or one of the reasons why I love you."

I nearly choked on his use of love and hate in the same sentence. Wait . . . what? I looked up at him, my tears stopped short from shock.

Dash's green eyes filled with the intensity he reserved for chasing storms. He set his beer down on the coffee table behind me, cupped my cheek in his hand, and crushed his lips on mine.

I gasped and held my hands out horizontally as if to back away from a loaded gun. His lips were warm and fierce, and the sensation of them against mine ignited a fire in the pit of my stomach. My eyes closed automatically, and before I could stop myself I clutched the back of his neck and pulled him closer.

He sighed and grabbed my hips, pushing me backward until we hit the wall. My back screamed in pain but quickly drowned in a tingling hunger as his hands slid down the sides of my thighs. His tongue slipped between my lips, making my heart soar like it had wings. He pressed his body against mine, and I could feel his hunger for me through his jeans.

"Blake," he groaned and nibbled at the spot behind my ear.

I raked my hands through his hair and brought his lips back to mine, kissing him harder, losing myself in him, his touch, his scent.

Dash grabbed behind my knee and hiked my leg around his hip. He leaned into me until a pulsing ache throbbed between my legs and I could do nothing but rub against it. He slipped his free hand underneath my shirt and explored my bare skin. When he went for the string on my sweats reality struck me harder than a lightning bolt.

"Wait. Wait, wait, wait." I unhooked my leg from around his waist and gently nudged him away.

"Did I hurt you?" he asked, eyeing around me toward my back.

"We can't do this." I wanted to punch myself in the face. My body screamed at me to grab Dash's hand and yank him to my bed, but my mind conjured all the reasons why we shouldn't do it. "We just caught our super-recent-exes having sex . . ."

"I know that," he said, taking a step closer. "Why do you think she's my ex?"

I put my hand up to stop him, sure that if he kissed me again I wouldn't have the willpower to stop. "I'm not sure. You never explained it to me. You didn't even bother to tell me you'd split."

"You should know the reasons why I left her."

"Because you had nothing in common?"

"That and the fact that I couldn't rightfully stay with her when I'm completely hung up on you."

The floor seemed to drop beneath me I was so stunned.

The kiss wasn't about revenge on our exes? "Why . . . why haven't you said anything?"

"I didn't want you to leave him for me. I wanted you to leave that asshole on your own. And to choose me when you were free to think clearly."

There was no way. Dash was out of my league, and we were best friends. "You're not thinking straight."

"Yes I am—"

"No, you're not." I cut him off. "Dash, you're my best friend. If we do this, it'll change everything."

"And that's a bad thing?"

"I don't know!" I couldn't wrap my head around anything. My eight-year relationship had only just come to a crashing end yesterday, and the way Dash touched me had my head spinning. What if we went through with it and tomorrow he decided it truly *was* a mistake?

"Blake," he whispered my name again and caressed my neck. I shut my eyes, and his lips were against mine in seconds. I kissed him back, my resolve weakening. His lips worked over the skin of my neck before returning to my mouth, their power the only thing strong enough to erase tonight's memory.

Almost.

The image of Justin pounding Lindsay from behind flashed in my head and I flinched away from Dash, pinching the bridge of my nose.

"Damn it!"

"What?" he asked.

"I can't get tonight's visual out of my head! I never will! Why did you have to take me?" I yelled, the memory running on repeat in my mind.

He reached for me. "I said I was sorry."

"No. You can't do this to me." Another apology for something that hurt like hell, despite the deliverer, was too much. I couldn't take it.

"Do what? I'm finally doing what feels right. Tell me this doesn't feel right to you." He trailed his lips to my collarbone, making my eyes roll back in my head.

"It's incredible, but I can't get over the fact that you put me in that situation tonight! What did you expect to happen? That I'd get over it in two seconds and then hop into bed with you? I won't be a revenge fuck." The words came out harsher than I'd intended, and Dash jerked away from me.

A new wave of hurt coated his eyes before they turned sharp. "So that's what you think of me."

"Dash, I—"

He raised his hand, stopping me. Then he grabbed his keys off the counter and paused as he opened the door. "I know taking you tonight was a mistake. I acted on impulse and I'm sorry for that, but, Blake, I've never once given you a reason to think I'd use you to get even with them. I thought you knew me better than that." He slammed the door on his way out.

The words stung like a knife slipping into my chest. I stood there staring at the door, desperately wishing he'd come back and let me apologize. Let me work through my anger and think rationally. Figure out where my heart was. But I didn't even know where to start.

CHAPTER

THIRTEEN

M Y CELL BUZZED on my nightstand. I glared at it through squinted eyes. I'd worked till closing last night and was dead set on not budging from bed until well after nine a.m. The home screen blared brightly with Dash's number. I picked up instantly.

We hadn't really spoken in days. Not since the disastrous night at the sorority house. I'd tried to flag him down after classes, but he'd rushed off claiming he had tons of research to do and neglected to invite me. I tried to be understanding, but it stung. I wanted to talk about what happened, but he clearly wanted to avoid it. I was sure I'd lost him as a friend forever— the one thing I had tried to avoid. If I'd known this was going to happen I might as well have gotten in bed with him. Heat flushed my cheeks, and I blinked hard to snap myself out of the fantasy. I sucked in a deep breath and decided to act completely normal.

"It's six thirty in the morning, Dash," I groaned despite the building elation that he'd called.

"Beautiful morning you happen to be missing, Blake." He

was way too happy for this hour and way too normal for our first time speaking since the night we nearly slept together.

I wondered if he felt the same as I did every time I thought about it, a mixture of insane sensations that hummed beneath the skin.

"Ugh." I rubbed my eyes in an effort to get them to open more. "What do you want?" I asked, ready to play the whole let's-act-normal game.

"If you keep giving me attitude, woman, I'm not going to tell you."

"Dash," I whined, but internally relaxed for the first time in days. Maybe I hadn't ruined things. Maybe everything would be all right.

"Fine. Doppler is predicting a string of supercells just north of Bartlesville. Tornadoes are highly likely. You in?"

My eyes popped wide open and I shot up straight. "Are you serious?"

"Now look who's happy at six thirty in the morning."

Adrenaline coursed through my veins. I'd wanted to go on another chase the second the last one had ended.

"Are you in or not?"

"I'm so in! Just tell me when and where." I hopped out of bed. Hail grunted but didn't budge.

"I didn't know if you'd want to after . . ."

"I've been wanting to talk to you about that night, to apologize—"

"Don't," he cut me off. "We both said and did things we didn't mean. Let's leave it at that, okay? I don't want to lose my best friend over one bad decision."

Did he mean kissing me or taking me to the party or both? My chest tightened, but I focused on the bridge he'd rebuilt just for me. "You'd never lose me, Dash."

"All right then. I'll pick you up at ten. You should pack a bag this time."

I hung up and scrambled to get ready, even though I had plenty of time. Excitement built inside me, making my nerves feel like firework fuses, and successfully pushing all other thoughts away.

I managed to wait an hour before dialing my mom and asking her out to breakfast. She agreed and met me at a local cafe near campus.

Mom arrived before I did and picked a table near the back. I hugged her once I reached the table.

"You look great," she said as she sat back down.

"Thanks, Mom." I took the seat across from her. I hadn't even put makeup on, but she was always ready to tell me I was beautiful. I kind of loved that about her.

We ordered our breakfast, and I caught her up on everything that had happened in the last few weeks. Minus one breakup and a night involving my new best friend and his body pressed against mine. Damn it, every time I stopped thinking about it, the scene popped into my head and replayed in high-def.

Focusing extremely hard on normal chatter with Mom helped cool the fiery thoughts, and I quickly arrived at the reason I'd called her after filling her in about the storm chase.

"Could you watch Hail for me?"

She sat her half eaten egg-and-turkey-sausage sandwich down. "You know I will, but do you have to do this?"

"Yes. Going on chases is an amazing experience. I can probably use it to write a paper for my Physical Meteorology class."

She reached across the table and squeezed my hand. "I just worry about you." She shuddered and pulled her hand back. "Chasing tornadoes. Honestly, I should've known you'd do something like this."

"Why do you say that?" I asked and finished off the last bite of my chocolate croissant

"When you were a baby, the only way I could get you to

sleep was by playing a cassette recording of a thunderstorm."

"I didn't know that."

She shrugged. "You about wore that tape out. Listened to it almost every day when you were seven, too. After you got caught in that thunderstorm on your way home from riding bikes."

The image of a small cassette case with a lavender sky, dark clouds, and white lightning striking the ground popped behind my eyes. "I remember I found it in one of your old boxes of photos."

"If I would've known I'd be sparking inspiration for a dangerous career I might have chosen to play ocean waves instead."

"Then I'd be studying oceanography and flying to the coast for deep-sea diving excursions." I took her hand and squeezed. "I'll be fine, Mom. Dash will be there. He won't let anything happen to me."

Mom dabbed at her lips with a napkin. "How are you and Justin doing?"

Damn. I knew I couldn't get away with her not asking.

"Well," I said and took a deep breath before relaying the short version of the breakup. "We just weren't right for each other," I finished.

I expected her to do a victory lap around the table, but she only smiled. Of course she'd tried to tell me this numerous times over the years but it had never sunk in for me. I wished it would've. If I had listened to her I could've saved myself a hell of a lot of hurt and even more embarrassment over staying with him so long.

The tightness in my chest loosened as I took a sip of my orange juice.

Mom raised her hands and set them back down on the table. "I just want you to be happy, honey. You know I've always wanted that." She reached for her drink. "This Dash must be really something."

My eyes widened and I almost choked on my juice. Could she see the lust in my eyes every time I said his name? "Why do you say that?"

"All throughout breakfast it's been Dash this and Dash that. I'd really like to meet this fellow."

I breathed a sigh of relief. At least she hadn't shoved an *I told you so* in my face.

"He's my best friend. And we spend a lot of time together." Time I now realized I didn't have to hide from anyone anymore. A hot hunger flared within me. Dash's lips on mine, me grinding against him, the delicious weight of him against me all flashed red in my mind. My hand trembled as I scraped a smear of chocolate off my plate.

"Plus we're going on a chase in"—I glanced at my cell—"an hour!" I squeaked and stood up. "I've got to go." Mom reached out to me, and I hugged her. "You remember how much to feed Hail every day?"

"Yes, honey. Goodness, you'd think I was incompetent."

"You know it's not that!" I had to measure Hail's food out on a daily basis or she'd gain weight. Extra pounds on a bulldog equaled added breathing problems and heart stress. Something I didn't need my only other best friend going through. "Thanks. Love you, Mom," I said before power-walking to my car.

I GAVE HAIL a brand-new bone and kissed the top of her head before grabbing my duffle and waiting outside for Dash. My excitement bordered on insanity, but I really couldn't handle him coming inside—the couch wasn't far from the door and part of me wasn't sure if I could see him on it again without wanting to rip his clothes off.

I focused on the sky to stop the train of thought. A normal

clear blue stretched above me, but I knew when we made it to Bartlesville we'd see a whole lot of action. I'd checked out the predictions online and Dash was spot on. A supercell headed that direction—much larger than the last two chases. My knee bounced up and down, the uncontrollable energy working its way out of my body.

Dash's truck pulled into the parking lot. He honked the horn four times, hung his head out of the window, and whooped like a maniac as he parked. I practically sprinted to the passenger side, tossing my duffle in the small space behind the seat.

"You ready for this?" he asked, flashing his damn smile that melted my insides. I swallowed hard and tried not to think about his hands on me.

"Yes?" I was ecstatic, though I couldn't deny the cold hands of fear clutching my spine. I thought since this was my third chase I wouldn't be as nervous, but the idea of actually seeing a tornado up-close produced an undeniable combination of anxiety and excitement within me.

"Awesome, let's get to it!" He pulled out of my complex and broke the speed limit once we hit the highway.

The entire hour and a half drive Dash talked about everything but *that* night. I was sure by the time we stopped at a local motel that he'd decided kissing me really was a mistake and didn't merit further exploration. Which was good, right? Our friendship was more important than seeing just how far we could push each other over the edge . . . physically. My heart sank. Yeah, I'd just keep telling myself that.

Paul and John stood outside of a room with the door open. Dash and I walked inside and set our stuff down. Four laptops were up and running. Two on one of the double beds and two on the small round table near the window. Each one had a different image or map up, showing the locations for the string of storms forming across the area.

The energy inside the room was palpable, like someone had pumped vaporized Red Bull into the AC vents. John's faux-hawk wasn't as perfectly put together, like he'd run his hands through it too many times. He and Paul were busy watching radar and tracking the storm. Dash worried over all the camera equipment.

"Paul, tell me you didn't forget the shutter trigger for the Olympus! If you forgot it again and we miss getting the lightning still-shots I'm going to ice you."

"Relax, bro, it's in the other bag." Paul glanced at me sideways once Dash turned his back. "You see the way he treats me?"

I laughed and rocked back and forth on my heels near the doorway, too excited to sit down. Since I wasn't a cool storm chaser with a special decked-out laptop I elected to watch the sky.

It was slate-gray and moving. No funnel formations yet, but the dark clouds hung low and wide, and wisps of their structures swirled slowly as they migrated east. The rain hit a few minutes after we arrived and it plinked off the asphalt in tiny bursts. A few people got out of cars, dragging luggage to their rooms. A wave of icy fear crashed inside my chest and I whipped my head around.

"It isn't predicted to hit the town is it?"

Each of them glanced up at me.

"It shouldn't," John said. "Doppler is placing it farther east where there's mostly farmland. But you know we can't pinpoint it, Blake. It could happen."

My shoulders dropped. Of course it could. I glanced at Dash, who stared into the distance lost in thought. He knew all too well what a tornado could do to a town. I swallowed hard. Did he see the destruction and devastation from his past every time he went on a chase?

I crossed the room and leaned over John's shoulder, eyeing

the satellite images he had pulled up on both his laptops.

"Don't worry, Blake," John said, turning his head to look up at me. "I'm sure the news is on right now, warning people about this."

I sighed and nodded. He was right. Meteorologists would be showering the locals with information. The same data we were accessing now. Of course, they'd be warning people away from the storm as opposed to searching for ways to get in front of it.

I pointed to the screen on John's left, noting the surface map's data. "The air pressure on this location is increasing along with the temperature. Keep an eye on this one. It looks prime to fire." I returned to my spot in the doorway, eyes trained on the sky. I wrung my hands out, the anticipation coiling inside me like a spring.

"This will help you relax," Paul said, glancing at me over his opened laptop. "What does a meteorologist cry before she tees off?"

I rolled my eyes. This was not the time for one of his jokes.

"Fore-cast!" He dragged the punch line out without me baiting him.

I laughed despite my efforts not to.

Paul gave me a sincere smile and went back to staring at the laptop screen.

"You were right!" John hollered. "The cell is about to fire. We need to head north on 75 if we want to get ahead of this thing." He slammed his laptops shut.

Suddenly the room was in a frenzy. Dash shoved the cameras and recorders inside their bags, and John slipped all the laptops into their cases. Each slung bags over their shoulders and scrambled toward the door. I quickly jumped out of the way.

Dash stopped outside the door and turned to me. "Blake, we have to move!" He bounced on the balls of his feet.

My heart surged with adrenaline and excitement fluttered inside my stomach. And if I was being totally honest, I couldn't decide if the thrill was from the storm we were chasing or the look in Dash's eyes.

CHAPTER

FOURTEEN

I F I'D THOUGHT Dash drove fast on the way here, I was totally wrong. He was now close to breaking the sound barrier
and John was right on his tail in the Tracker Jacker. I gripped
the handle above the window so hard my fingers ached.

Dash had both hands on the steering wheel but continued
to push himself over it to look up at the sky. Each time, his
green eyes flashed with an unmistakable passion that made
me feel like I was spying on an intimate moment between him
and the clouds.

Rain came down in sheets, slapping the windshield as if
someone tossed giant buckets of water at us. Thunder roared
above, so close it shook the truck. We sped past other cars and
trucks that had parked on the side of the road. Several were
from local news stations identified by the logos on their vehicles and others were chasers like us, cameras in hand and
laptops sitting on the seats of their cars.

"We're pulling off soon," Dash said into the walkie-talkie
before glancing at me. "Stick close to me and follow my lead.
I know you predicted this location, but this is bigger than the

last two times. And if I tell you to get in the truck and drive, you do it. Understand?" He slowed the truck and took a turn down a rural road that ran next to a flatland of green pasture whose grass rolled in waves from the wind.

"Yes." I swallowed the rock in my throat, noticing that no other chasers had chosen this path.

He pulled the truck to a stop on an even piece of grassy land off the road. Thick wooden posts lined the pasture, barbed wire snaking between them. The prickly wire trembled in the strong blasts of wind.

Dash reached behind him and grabbed one of his video cameras. He fiddled with some complex buttons and the lens. His chest rose and fell rapidly. "You ready?"

"Yes," I said, letting my breath out slowly.

He tossed me a still-shot camera and hopped out of the truck. After getting the lens off and the strap around my neck, I jumped out, instantly soaked by the rain. John and Paul were already behind us, each holding their own cameras and pointing it toward a large wall cloud about six hundred yards to our right. I followed suit and snapped a series of shots.

Outside of Dash's video clips he'd posted on his site from past chases and other weather channel shots, it was the scariest wall cloud I'd ever seen. It stretched at least three hundred yards wide and hung so low to the ground I was sure it would touch down with a spinning tail any second. The dark gray color clashed with the smooth bright sky behind it, and the upward rotation quickly gained momentum.

I stood close to Dash, thankful I'd worn my flat leather boots because the ground was squishy with grass and mud. Somehow Paul had thought it a brilliant idea to wear flip-flops, but he didn't seem to notice his feet were caked with slimy dirt and water.

"Look at that updraft! Can you believe it?" Dash hollered over the rain.

I hadn't been able to take my eyes off it since we arrived. "It's going to come down any second!"

Dash let out a whoop, and John and Paul screamed with him. They were like a pack of wolves howling at the moon. My heart raced and instinct told me to run in the opposite direction and take cover, but I fought the urge and let out a holler of my own. Dash locked eyes with me, and in that moment the world dropped away. Nothing else existed but me and him and the purely primal violence of the storm.

The rain instantly died, grounding me firmly in the present. The abrupt silence nearly deafened me. I glanced at John and Paul, their clothes stuck to their bodies in a soaked mess. Their eyes locked with the formation before us, not even blinking.

Dash held the same intense stare. His wet blue T-shirt clung to his carved stomach, outlining the defined ridges in his skin. Heat rippled through my body, and I shot down the image of me running my hands over his abs. I trembled but assured myself it was from the rain coating my skin.

Sirens blared in the distance, a faint sound of warning. I hoped it was early enough for everyone to get to safety, and then I prayed the storm would stay out of populated areas. I realized, for the first time, how extremely close we were to it, and every nerve in my body sparked with ice.

"Here it comes," Dash said, his voice excited as he held the camera up.

He was right.

He was always right.

A funnel cloud snaked downward and spiraled until it touched the ground, instantly transforming into easily an F-2 tornado. The ground beneath the tip of its tail swirled in a brown dusty mess, turning the once grayish-white beast black. It roared and screeched louder than a freight train, the sound a kind of terrible awesome. Every inch of my body trembled, but I couldn't pry my eyes away. The tornado mesmerized me, twisting and turning sporadically like a caged animal that had finally been freed.

A magnetic force throbbed within me, and I stepped closer to the wired posts we stood outside of. Life had never been so clear or real as in that moment. I'd never been more in the present, been more aware of each sensation soaring throughout my body—fear, excitement, awe, and wonder. I watched one of God's miraculous creations—a terrible and fascinating thing—and knew I was where I was meant to be. Storms had always been a part of my life, always filled me when I was hollow, but now they were in my blood.

"Dash, Blake!" I heard John scream over the roar of the tornado. I turned to him. He stood halfway in the Tracker Jacker, Paul already buckled into the passenger seat. He waved at us with a hurried hand and then pointed to the tornado.

It moved closer to us. How had I missed the change of direction?

I tugged on Dash's arm, who still hadn't taken his eyes off it. "Dash, we have to go!"

He held his position as if he couldn't hear me.

I whipped my head around. John swung his arm, beckoning me to hurry to his truck. I shook my head. I wouldn't leave Dash. Paul yelled something at John. He gunned the Tracker Jacker a few seconds later, reversing onto the road before spinning it around in retreat.

"Dash!" I screamed and yanked on him so hard the camera moved in his hand.

He finally looked at me, his green eyes wild. "This is amazing!"

"We need to move!"

He glanced back at the tornado heading closer and closer to our location. He blinked a couple of times before he tossed me his keys. "You drive!"

I caught them and we both turned toward the truck. A crack of lightning struck so close the hairs on my arms stood on end and a bang of thunder quickly followed. We jumped and I shrieked before finally making it inside the truck. I jerked the camera strap off my neck and gently set it down in the space next to me.

Dash instantly rolled down his window as I hit the gas. I swung the truck around too fast and we fishtailed on the road.

"Easy, woman!" he yelled but didn't look at me. His eyes and camera were fixed on the big black spiraling snake cutting through the field. Dirt clods hovered around its base and the pressure from the wind threatened to take control of the truck. I floored it and didn't let off the pedal until we were a couple of miles away. John and Paul had parked and were snapping still shots with their cameras. Dash jumped out of the truck before I could pull the emergency break.

The tornado looked smaller from this distance but equally terrifying. I watched Dash stare it down like he wanted to wrestle with it, and a cold fear seeped into my bones when I thought about how long he would've stayed if I hadn't yanked him away.

Only ten minutes had passed since the tornado touched down, but it felt like hours. Slowly the end of its tail dissipated and the body shortly followed, fading upward in dark gray wisps until nothing was left but a broken nimbostratus cloud—a thick wet gray blanket covering the sky.

Dash finally lowered his camera and capped the lens. A mischievous smile crossed his face and he ran at me.

"What a monster!" He wrapped his arms around me and squeezed me so tight I could feel his rapid heartbeat against mine. I clung to him, too, relishing the sparks that ignited beneath my skin as he held me tight.

We released each other after a few moments, and Dash whooped as he bumped fists with John and Paul. "We got wicked footage for the site. We need to upload it quick. John, did you call the local station and let them know we saw a confirmed tornado on the ground?"

"Yeah, I got the call in right before it touched down."

"Nice!" Dash patted him on the back and handed the camera off to Paul who had his laptop open on the hood of the car.

"What do you think, Meteorologist?" Paul asked.

I jumped at the sound of his adopted nickname for me. My hands shook as I caught my breath, a new addiction dominating my senses. "When's the next storm hitting?"

Dash came over and high-fived me. "Yes! That's my girl! I knew you could handle this."

Heat rushed to my cheeks. Dash never doubted me. The feeling was incredible but completely new. Justin had constantly told me I wouldn't make it in this field because I didn't have the instincts to handle myself under pressure.

I replayed the storm in my head, and it was like a bolt of lightning hit me. I'd never felt more sure of my place in this world than I did in that moment. Dash and I were the same, pulsing with a calling in our blood to stand on the edge of chaos.

He tugged on my hand. "Let's head back to the motel. You can double check if you want, Blake, but Doppler isn't predicting another one until early morning."

"I'm sure Doppler has it right, but thanks," I said and sank into the passenger seat. Sharing this passion with Dash was effortless. I didn't have to battle with him. He understood the feeling, the need. I gazed at him as he drove and another bolt hit me. Fuck. I was in love with him.

***

NO, NO, NO, no. My earlier revelation hadn't eased up on the drive back to the motel.

"You can have the first shower." Dash interrupted my thoughts as we walked into the room.

"Bro, are you serious?" Paul whined. "Just because she's a girl?"

"Because that's the way it is. Learn how to be a gentleman."

"Like you've ever been a gentleman!"

"Thanks," I said softly, grabbing my bag and locking the bathroom door behind me.

The shower was tiny and the hot water setting was more lukewarm, but I was grateful for the privacy. It gave me more time to get my head on straight.

My eight-year relationship had just ended. I didn't even know who I was outside of being Justin's girlfriend. I could *not* already be falling for Dash. I groaned, raking my hands through my hair. Thinking back, I'd had feelings for him long before I'd like to admit, but now that I was free it was beyond clear. I couldn't deny the heat or the sheer *rightness* of me and Dash. We just made sense.

I squeezed my eyes shut and leaned my head underneath the running water. None of that mattered, though. Our friendship did. As did the importance of the storm chasing group we were both a part of. But most of all, I couldn't possibly think about another relationship right now. I needed to figure out my own heart before giving it away again, no matter how easy it would be to give to Dash. And besides the epiphany of my own feelings, it was clear Dash's interest started and ended the night we'd kissed. I focused on that fact to keep my head straight.

I turned the water off and patted dry with a towel that was a relative to sandpaper and slipped on some wonderfully dry and comfortable clothes. I hadn't thought to bring a hair dryer so I pulled my wet hair into a ponytail.

The room was empty except for Dash sprawled out on his back on the bed closest to the door. He'd changed into dry clothes, and the white T-shirt he wore was hiked up slightly, exposing a strip of his skin and defined abs.

A rock lodged itself in my throat and my heart thumped erratically.

"The guys went to grab food after the videos uploaded. You want to check them out while I shower?" he asked, sitting up and opening the laptop on the table.

"Sure." I gulped as images of nothing but water covering him burst involuntarily in my head. What the hell was wrong with me?

I took a deep breath and sat heavily in the chair at the table. Dash leaned over me and clicked a few things on the screen. He smelled like rain and his skin was warm as his arm brushed the back of my neck. A spark rocketed through my middle and I bit my lip.

"Here they are. We've already got a hundred hits."

"That's awesome." I said, genuinely happy for him. I knew the more hits he got the more funds he received.

"Yeah, we do all right, huh?" He straightened and walked toward the bathroom.

"You really do," I said as he shut the bathroom door. Maybe I'd feel better if I talked to him. Surely getting everything out in the air would make the situation much less dramatic. I shook my head and resisted the urge to slap myself.

John and Paul returned a half hour later with burgers and fries from a local mom-and-pop shop down the road. The brown paper bags were half soaked in grease, but I'd never eaten a better burger. We talked over updrafts and rain-wrapped tornadoes between bites and rehashed the F-2 we'd watched.

The footage Dash caught was incredible, as were most of his videos, and the up-close shots offered real perspective on the tendencies of a tornado, which were less erratic than one might think. As Dash put it, "there are patterns to everything, even chaos."

My nerves continued to fray as the night wore on. A constant battle raged inside me. In an attempt to squash the uncontrollable sensations that flared every time Dash spoke to me or even touched my hand softly, I drew upon the many reasons we couldn't cross the line. Best friends. Colleagues. Me, with no clue how to be in a non-toxic relationship.

"Blake," Dash whispered.

I raised my head from where I'd been pinching the bridge of my nose while seated at the table. The room was dark with only the silver light of the moon slipping in from the window and the neon green glow from the alarm clock lighting it. John and Paul had crashed on the bed closest to the bathroom sometime during my mental cold shower.

Dash touched my shoulder and motioned toward the bed. "You take the bed." He kept his voice hushed. "I can sleep in this chair." He eyed the one I sat in, which wasn't any better than a steel folding chair.

"Are you serious?" I asked.

He sighed. "I'm sorry we couldn't get you your own room. You know the videos only pay so much."

"It's all right. I understand. You take the bed."

"No, I want you to be comfortable."

Paul groaned from across the room. "Ugh. Grow up. Both of you sleep in it and shut up."

Dash rolled his eyes.

We stared at each other for a few moments. Dash shrugged and slid underneath the covers. I stood up but hesitated at my side of the bed.

How could I climb in there and *not* touch him? I sighed, the battle raging inside me was beyond ridiculous. A week ago the idea of Dash's skin on mine was a super-secret-locked-up fantasy that only entered my mind in the lonely hours late at night. After knowing what he tasted like, though, it was all I could think about, despite the logical reasons not to.

I contemplated sleeping on the floor, but I was beyond exhausted now that the adrenaline from the chase had left my system. My muscles ached from the tension I'd held during the storm and clung to since we got back. Sleeping anywhere but the bed was just dumb.

"I'm not going to bite you," he whispered and then lifted the covers on my side of the bed.

And with that, all my nerves and worries and doubts slipped away. I climbed under those covers and forced myself to relax. The mattress was horrible, hard and thin, but for some reason I'd never been more comfortable. I fell into a deep sleep listening to the sound of Dash's even breathing.

JUSTIN'S ARM SLIPPED over my hip and pulled me across the bed. He pressed his chest against my back, spooning me. My eyes were heavy with sleep, but I could feel the heat from his body as it radiated onto mine. I sighed as his hand trailed under my shirt and touched the soft skin beneath my ribs. Tingles erupted and raced up and down my body, causing a deep yearning in the pit of my stomach.

I rolled over and hooked my leg around his hip and tugged him closer. His fingers clutched my back and he squeezed me tighter. I took a deep breath, loving the way he touched me, like he savored me as opposed to rushing things like usual. His desire was evident through the thin cover of his shorts, and for the first time in a long time, I wanted him too. I nuzzled his neck, still trying to pry open my eyes. He smelled like rain.

Dash's smell.

Strong enough to remind me Justin and I were no longer together.

Well, if I was dreaming I may as well go with it.

His warm hand slid down my side and gently clutched my hip, pulling me tighter against him. The ache between my legs roared with his agonizing, leisurely movements, but it was more than a want. I *needed* him. My hands moved on their own, reaching down to explore what I desperately wanted inside of me. Every inch of my skin flushed with heat. Either this dream broadcasted on high-def or . . .

My eyes popped open and I jolted. The motion fully woke Dash, who I happened to have my leg wrapped around, my hand resting between our nearly joined hips. His mouth dropped as he took in our tangled mess of a position.

His eyes hooded, mirroring my own in sheer lust factor. He raised an eyebrow, gauging my reaction before pressing his lips to mine. The kiss was gentle, until I relented, and then it escalated to a powerful need. I opened my mouth, letting him in, relishing his taste.

He shifted, encasing me in his strong arms. Still gripping him, I moved my fingers in a come hither motion, loving the groan that tore from his throat.

His breath was ragged as I moved my fingers underneath his shirt, trailing them down his perfect abs. God, I'd never felt muscles like this before, or craved someone so much. Dash slid his hand down my side and pulled his lips away from mine just enough to catch my eyes as he moved lower. He must've found the answer he wanted because he slowly slipped his hand inside my sweats.

He covered my moan with his mouth as he rubbed his fingers against me in a slow circle, drawing out a delicious tingling tension.

"God, Blake." He sighed and slid a finger inside me with perfect ease.

He stroked me with a gentleness I wasn't used to, and the aching within me climbed to an almost unbearable level. Every inch of my insides coiled and pulsed, begging for release. My toes curled as he expertly moved his fingers around my warmth, like he was made to touch me, and I was on the brink of what I knew would be the sweetest release imaginable.

A cell phone from across the room blared Imagine Dragons' "Radioactive" yanking me out the moment.

John grabbed the phone and shut off his alarm. Seconds later he and Paul groaned awake.

Reality crashed over us both. We were so not alone in the motel, and we so shouldn't be doing this.

"I'm sorry!" I whispered, drawing away from him. I covered my face with my hands to try and hide the heat coating my skin.

"It's all right," Dash's voice was coated in early morning husk. He glanced down and quickly yanked the covers up higher.

A new wave of heat rushed over me, and I shoved my face in my hands again.

Dash chuckled, which made me want to punch him.

"This is so not funny!" I glared at him.

He continued to laugh. "It's pretty hilarious if you ask me."

A fierce hungry ache pulsed in the pit of my stomach. I hadn't felt something like this . . . well, since the first time Dash kissed me.

He finally stopped laughing and raked his hands through his hair. He sighed and his eyes turned on me with the serious look he got right before he said something important.

"Blake . . ." He whispered my name, and damn if my heart didn't stutter.

"Whose turn is it to get coffee?" Paul arched his back and stretched his arms.

Dash closed his mouth and swung his feet off the bed. He slipped on a pair of sweats over his basketball shorts before he stood up.

"Mine." I ran to the bathroom to brush my teeth and then bolted out the door. I couldn't be in that room anymore. I needed to get the scent of Dash out of my nose and the sensation of his body against mine out of my system.

The local coffee shop was empty, so they made our drinks entirely too fast. I decided to grab a dozen donuts from the gas station near the motel just to take up more time. Despite dragging my feet, I couldn't make sense of the emotions boiling within me, and as I lugged my haul into the room I assumed I never would.

John grabbed two donuts and his drink. "I like having you around," he said, taking a chomp out of a donut. "These two never think about breakfast." He motioned to where Dash and Paul sat on the edge of the bed, a laptop perched on each of their knees.

Radar filled one screen and Dash's site took up the other.

"How many hits we get?" John asked around his coffee cup.

Dash turned around and startled when he saw me, as if he hadn't heard me come in. He quickly glanced away. "Twenty-four-hundred."

"That's amazing," I said and handed him and Paul their drinks. Dash took his from me timidly, like I could snap at him any second.

My shoulders sank. I didn't want him to feel awkward around me. The constant state of confusion finally hit a breaking point and I gave up my resolve.

"Can I talk to you for a second?" I asked him. He swallowed a gulp of coffee before nodding.

I walked outside the motel room and leaned against the building. Dash followed me a moment later.

"What's up?" he asked, a grin shaping his slightly swollen lips. Had I done that?

"I'm sorry about this morning. Seriously, I didn't mean for it to happen."

Dash shook his head. "Always apologizing. What have I told you about that?"

"Well, I think the situation definitely calls for it."

"No it doesn't. I told you how I felt that night."

"You . . . you still feel that way?"

"Why wouldn't I?"

"Because you've had time to process everything. Realize that we're best friends—"

"That only makes me want you more. Blake, we're a match—"

"Stop, please, Dash. I can't. I just got out of the worst and only relationship I've ever known. Even if I was willing to risk our friendship, I have to figure out who I am before I can give myself to anyone else."

His eyes filled with heat. "You were pretty close to letting me have all of you this morning." He took a step closer, entwining his fingers in my hair.

My lips parted, betraying my brain's plea to not want him. "I swear I'm not trying to lead you on."

Dash shook his head. "I want more from you than that, Blake. I want every piece of you, because I know who you are, and I've never loved anyone as intensely as I do you. But I also understand you need time. Take it. Just know I'll be here waiting."

I shook my head, still unable to believe he could care for me like that. He was too good for me, and way more than I deserved.

Dash moved to go back inside but glanced back at me. "It might be hard to take time for yourself if we keep ending up in each other's arms. Not that I'm complaining, but like I said that night, I want you to choose me when you're completely free. And that means waiting until you've figured out who you are and what you want." He smiled and turned into the room.

I stood outside, shell-shocked, and with an ache pulsing lower than I'd like to admit. My heart threatened to fly out of my chest and present itself to Dash, but I slapped the bitch down, reminding her it was still broken.

CHAPTER

FIFTEEN

"BLAKE, GET TO the truck, now!" Dash screamed, the roaring wind threatening to steal his voice.

"Not without you!" I yelled back, fighting with my hair. It whipped back and forth vigorously, slapping me in the face.

The tornado had touched down faster and closer than we'd calculated. John and Paul luckily hadn't made it to the site when we did and were able to spot it farther away. They'd booked it in the opposite direction and had most likely stopped in a safer spot to catch the massive beast on film.

It wasn't any bigger than the one yesterday, but the muddy brown swirling mass screeched with the sound of a train derailing, and it ripped up the trees beneath it like they were made of matchsticks. A huge branch crunched off the tree trunk, spinning in the tornado's outer flanks and soared over our heads. It landed with a loud crash next to the truck, only missing it by inches.

Dash held his camera steady, the same fiery passion in his eyes as yesterday. He was completely mad. As much as I loved watching storms and experiencing them up close, I wasn't prepared to die for it. And death felt much more real today, like I could reach out and touch it. One wrong move, one shift in course, and . . . lights out.

My heart pounded against my chest and my hands trembled. I should've left like he'd told me, but the need for Dash safely at my side overpowered all of my survival instincts.

Anger flared in my stomach as he cracked a wild grin. I yanked on his arm. "This isn't worth your life!"

He tilted his head, like the thought had never occurred to him. A sharp gust blasted a bunch of leaves at us, their tips nicking the skin on our necks and arms. He held his position for a few moments longer and aimed the video recorder at the monster perfectly. He could've been filming a babbling brook for how effortless he made the job look.

Tiny pebble-sized hail pelted the road around us and the little bastards stung something fierce when they made connection. I flinched but held my ground. The tornado shifted course, thankfully, in the opposite direction. The motion was beautiful, a sky-high twist of brown that swayed back and forth like it was swinging its hips. A calm stole over me with its retreat, and once again the certainty of my place filled me.

Sheer terror leading to pure amazement. Clearly loving the chaos as much as Dash did made me as out of my mind as him.

The tail of the tornado roped out after another two minutes and the rest kind of folded in on itself and drew upward into the afternoon sky. Another few minutes and all the evidence of the beast that was left was the trees ripped up by the roots scattered across the wide opening of land. Dash's shoes crunched on the tiny pieces of hail coating the road as he made his way over to me, his eyebrows drawn.

"What did I tell you about listening to me?" He pointed at me. "I told you to go. You should've gone!" He turned on his heel and stomped toward the truck. He set the camera in its bag and placed it behind the driver's seat.

"You asshole!" Steam could've come out my ears I was so pissed. I shoved him once he turned around. He stumbled back against his truck.

He righted himself. "Excuse me?"

"You heard me!" I pushed him again, but this time he was ready and it barely phased him. "You *told* me to run? And you expected me to just leave you here? You could've gotten hurt or killed! Why? To get the shot for your site? Are you serious?"

"That's the job, Blake! You know it is. Capturing what occurs at the tornado's base where the most damage happens is what we desperately need in order to predict them better. Understanding what happens within that fifty to a hundred-foot range will help us increase warning times. That way people aren't blindsided like we were when I was a kid." He took a deep breath. "We lost so much that day. We were lucky to get away with our lives. Preventing that from happening to others is worth everything."

My stomach shrank, picturing an eight-year-old Dash going through the destroyed remnants of what was once his home. "I want that, too, but it's not worth your life."

"I was fine. I always am. The guys never freak out this much. They just leave me to it."

"They don't care about you the way I do." I blurted out the words and then swallowed the rock in my throat.

Dash locked eyes with me. I could tell he wanted to say something because his lips were tense, but he fought it. Most likely he wanted to tell me to make up my damn mind or to let me know he'd rethought his decision to add me to this group.

Tears threatened at the thought. Why did I have to ruin everything? Why couldn't I just stand quietly by while Dash faced down a tornado like it was a simple dust storm?

"Blake . . ." he whispered, and again my heart stuttered.

"Forget it," I said. I couldn't take hearing the words.

Couldn't face the idea of never chasing again because I'd been too emotional or because Dash and I had an undeniable heat coursing between us. I stomped toward the truck, prepared to climb in and not say another word.

Dash grabbed my arm and spun me around. "Blake, stop. What did you mean by that?"

His eyes held me more than his fingers gently clasping my arm. My breath caught in my throat, the truth stuck somewhere between my heartbeat and the last rumblings of the storm above us.

Dash inched closer, his lips only centimeters away from my own. I froze, unable to meet him despite the aching hunger begging me to. He registered my hesitance and sighed. He drew back and shook his head.

"All that asshole did was emotionally drain you until you were blind to what an incredible, strong woman you are."

Tears welled in my eyes.

He reached out for me, and I fell into his arms, wrapping my own around his waist.

"He ripped you apart, Blake. And I know this sounds horribly . . . *guy* of me, but let me help put you back together." He pushed away to look down at me.

I pulled out of his embrace. "I can't do that. Then *you'd* define me. I need to figure this out on my own. I'm sorry."

DASH ONLY DROVE ten miles over the speed limit on the highway that took us home the following day. I kept my eyes planted on the passing expanses of red dirt, pastures, and small towns. I couldn't look at him, because every time I did a huge bubble of awkward rose in my chest and threatened to burst all over the cab of his truck.

Even though Dash and I had slept in the same bed again last night, we'd hugged the edges like our lives depended on it, and I found the small space between us on the mattress more vast and painful than I'd ever experienced before. I'd barely slept, and I couldn't deny the fierce desire that pulsed within me all night, begging me to cross that line and touch him again. "Dash," I said, still not taking my eyes from the window.

"Yeah?" He sounded hopeful.

"I'm—"

"If the word *sorry* follows that, I swear, woman, I will leave you on the side of the road." He checked his rearview mirror before changing lanes. I gazed at him, finally, and even though it'd only been an hour, hearing his voice refreshed me like a glass of ice water on a hot summer day.

"I wasn't going to say that," I said, though it was a lie.

"Oh really? Then please do go on." He chuckled, which let some air out of the awkward bubble in my chest.

"I was going to say, before you interrupted me that I'm . . ." There were a million things I wanted to say, but my mouth wouldn't form the words. "I'm really glad you brought me." At least that was the absolute truth.

Dash glanced at me for a moment before returning his eyes to the road. He pressed his lips together in a poor reflection of his normal infectious smile.

The truck fell silent for longer than I could stand, not a comfortable silence but one filled with all the things we weren't saying, and it was enough to construct a wall between us.

HAIL'S BUTT WAS extra wiggly when I walked into my apartment. I dropped to my knees, instantly giving in to her more-than-warm welcome. After several good licks from her and more than enough butt pats from me, I stood up and let out a heavy breath. The events of the chase plus what happened with Dash had exhausted me. While I was elated to realize that I could and would chase storms the rest of my life, I was equally disappointed in my heart. Latching onto Dash before I'd even had time to adjust to being out of a relationship wasn't right, but of course, I couldn't stop the feelings I had for him.

Time.

He'd promised me time. And once I figured out who I was outside of the hellish life I'd lived the last eight years, then I'd know what to do with Dash.

I stood up, looking for any kind of distraction for my mind.

All my laundry had been washed and folded or hung up in my closet, and my kitchen was more spotless than when I'd moved in.

Mom.

I shook my head and read the note she'd left me on the fridge.

Made your favorite cookies, they're on the counter. And I picked up a few other things at the store for you. Please text me when you're home safe. Love You. P.S. Hail was an angel.

I opened the fridge. Mom hadn't picked up a few things, she'd fully stocked it. The gesture nearly made me cry.

Instead I popped the lid on the Tupperware on the counter, grabbed three triple chocolate chip cookies, and sank onto my couch. After one bite the taste of home filled me so much I debated calling Mom and begging her to come over. She could hold me and tell me where to go from here, much like when I was little and struggled with the next step in a complicated word problem.

Hail jumped up beside me, her floppy lips in the perfect pout.

"No. I'm sure you've been spoiled enough the past two days," I told her and finished off my cookies. I leaned my head back and stroked her fur. I couldn't put this on Mom. This was my life . . . *finally* mine. I just had to figure out how I wanted to live it.

CHAPTER

SIXTEEN

A WEEK HAD gone by and I still hadn't spoken to Dash. He'd nod to me during classes, but nothing more than that. He was giving me space and time, like I'd asked, to figure out who I was and to sort out my relationship drama. I respected him more for taking me seriously, but I also kind of hated him for it. I missed him on a daily basis—he was the first person I wanted to talk to in the morning and the last person I thought about at night. I knew this meant my feelings for him ran bone deep, but I still wasn't ready. It wouldn't be fair to either of us to dive into a relationship, so I sucked it up and let him stay away from me.

My phone vibrated on the coffee table. I peered over my *Climate Change and Agroecosystems* book and instantly sank back into the couch. Hail snored peacefully next to me, her thick body keeping my feet warm. Justin had called several times a day, every day, since that night at the sorority house. And I still refused to answer. The night I broke it off I'd thought Justin deserved a serious conversation to give us closure, but after seeing him with Lindsay so quickly afterward, I knew I didn't owe him a thing.

I stared at the words on the pages in front of me, but they blurred into a one big blob of white and black. I couldn't stop thinking about him.

Dash.

Justin's loss should be the one I mourned, but I couldn't force the feelings any more than I could force my body to react to him the way it did to Dash.

Every time I closed my eyes our kiss burned behind my lids. I'd never felt more alive or desired in all my life.

My cell beeped with a new text message. I snatched it off the table, hope rising in my chest. I instantly deflated. Justin—he was getting desperate.

We need to talk. You can't ignore me forever.

My fingers shook. I took a deep breath and let it out slowly before texting back.

What's done is done.

I tossed the phone back on the table and heaved myself off the couch. Hail grunted but sprawled out to her full length, taking up the important job of keeping my spot warm. A few minutes later and I sank into a scalding hot bath, completely prepared to soak for an hour before bed. I'd even broken out my special bottle of lavender oil to help me relax, because sleep had been nonexistent lately.

Every time I laid down my mind whirled, mixing the past and present together. Memories of Justin and I in high school battled more recent events, and each time I found myself less and less upset about how things ended. His quick betrayal stung more than losing him, and I knew Dash played a huge part in that.

Thoughts of the future—of what Dash and I could be—consumed all others until I was so worked up and shredded inside that I'd have to abandon the idea of pleasantly drifting off to sleep and instead study until I couldn't hold my eyes open anymore.

Dash's friendship had come effortlessly. Being with him was as easy as opening my eyes. And now, after everything, they truly felt open for the first time. Like I'd spent the last three years of my life in a constant dreamlike state, where everything was shaded in gray, and Dash had been the one to wake me up and show me colors I didn't even know existed.

I sank my head under the water. I'd been so blind. I was mad for him. I think I had been since the moment he walked into my work that first night. Still, I couldn't do anything about it. The timing was off.

Keys rattling in my door startled me to the surface. Hail's bark followed and I hopped out of the tub and dried off as best I could before slipping into my robe and tying it tightly around my waist. I padded barefoot down the hall and peered through the peephole.

Justin grunted outside and pounded on my door, the vibrations making me jump.

"Really? You changed the locks?" he yelled. I took a deep breath. I'd asked the apartment's maintenance crew to change it the day after we'd caught him with Lindsay. *I hadn't wanted any surprise visits, like now.*

"Blake, I know you're home! Open up." Desperation colored his voice and he had a slight slur to his words.

My heart thudded against my chest and a rock lodged in my throat.

"I just want to talk. Just hear me out and I'll leave."

I closed my eyes.

"Lindsay told me Dash's crew had gone on a lot of out of town chases recently. I just need to see that you're okay. Please, Blake," he begged.

Anger boiled in my gut, and I clenched my jaw. I took a deep breath in an attempt to calm down. Perhaps if we got closure we could both move on with our lives and stop dwelling on the past. I raked my fingers through my wet hair and opened the door.

Justin flew past me, and I shut the door with a thud.

Hail gave her usual growl but elected not to move from her position on the couch. I loved her willfulness and understanding that we no longer catered to this man's needs.

Justin looked horrible. His stained jeans were even more grimy than normal and he hadn't shaved in days.

"I'm perfectly fine, Justin. I only went on one overnight chase with the crew anyway," I said, trying not to let the disappointment ring in my voice. I knew they'd continue chasing while Dash gave me space, but I missed the action almost as much as I missed him.

"Why haven't you answered your phone?" he asked, coming closer.

The sour smell of tequila coated his breath, and I backed up toward the kitchen.

"Do you seriously want me to answer that?"

"No." His head dropped. "Blake, I'm so sorry. I don't want to lose you. Please, give me another chance."

I shook my head, astounded that he launched into one of his standard cut-and-paste apologies. "Justin, what you did . . ." There was no fight to my voice. "I understand why you did it. We've been broken for a long time. It's not your fault. It's just . . . it's over. All right?"

"Just like that?"

"No. Not just like that. We've been growing apart. You know that."

"No we haven't!" He slammed his fist onto the counter, and I retreated farther into the kitchen.

Noticing the sheen over his eyes and the clench in his jaw, I kept my tone calm. "We'd been together so long, it was bound to happen. People change. I grew up."

"You can't say we're over. I don't want to live if you're not with me."

I swallowed hard. I'd prepared for this, but I didn't believe him. Not anymore. I couldn't. Not after he'd so quickly hopped into another woman's bed after we'd ended things. The act had brought to light all the ways in which he'd manipulated me over the years and isolated me from friends. "You said yourself that was just a ploy to keep me. It won't work anymore."

Justin hadn't wanted me to know anything outside of us. Maybe he knew if I did, then I'd wise up and realize the way he treated me wasn't how real love worked. It had taken finding myself—through chasing storms and becoming friends with Dash—to realize that.

"We aren't right for each other," I continued. "We don't fit. Maybe we used to, when we were younger, but not anymore. You need someone different than me, and that's all right. Someone else can make you happier. Maybe Lindsay can, because I know I haven't been."

And in my heart, behind the massive hole of realization of all that he'd done to me over the years, I really wanted that for him. I didn't want him to suffer. I could still see the potential of the boy I'd fallen for long ago becoming the man I knew he could be, but I wasn't the one to make him find that man inside. I hoped someone else could.

Justin looked back up at me after a few moments, his dark eyes slits. "You aren't the girl I fell in love with."

"I'm not. I grew up, Justin."

He scoffed. "You didn't grow up! You're still an immature little girl playing at the real world. You want to know the real reason I went to Lindsay? Because you could never give me anything in bed. You know how hard it was, getting it up for you time after time?" His voice heightened, and he stalked toward me. I backed up as far as I could against the kitchen counter, until he towered over me. "You couldn't even come with me, Blake! You know how messed up that is? You're so fucked-up you couldn't even get yourself off. It was disgusting, knowing that every time I was inside you, you were going to be as dry as the fucking desert!"

With each stinging word, the memory of all the painful, foreplay-less sex flashed in my head. All the times he'd told me it was my fault or denied my suggestions for alternate positions. All the times he'd laughed at me for wincing. It pierced me until I couldn't take it anymore. "I'm perfectly capable of getting wet. Just not with you."

He flinched as if I'd hit him and grabbed my shoulders. "Oh yeah? Who with then? That tool, Dash?"

His fingers cut into the soft fabric of my robe, and I suddenly felt extremely vulnerable with nothing underneath. When I'd let Justin in, I hadn't even thought about it, we'd been together so long he'd seen me in every manner of dress. Now, with him towering over me, the smell of alcohol on his breath, and the anger coming off him in waves, I felt terribly exposed.

Justin took my silence as confirmation, and his mouth dropped. "Wow. I fucking thought so! I knew the second I met that douche bag he'd weaseled his way into your pants."

"It's not like that," I said, but my voice came out a whisper. His hold on me bordered on a death grip, and I tugged at his hands. "Justin, let go. You're hurting me."

His focus sharpened through the glaze in his eyes. "I couldn't hurt you as much as you've hurt me! You're throwing us away for some blond douchebag!"

I pulled harder on his wrists.

"No!" he yelled. "I won't let you! I'll make you love me again!" He released his grip and the blood rushed back to my shoulders so fast it stung. His fingers yanked at the fabric of my robe.

I pushed him backward. "Stop it!"

Justin came at me again, this time pressing his full body against mine so hard my back snapped against the counter. A white-hot wallop of pain erupted on my spine. I sucked in air through my teeth and shoved him harder. He barely stumbled backward this time.

He ripped part of my robe open, exposing the top left half of my body. He grabbed my breast and bit at my neck. "You'll understand again . . ." he slurred against my skin. "How it feels to be with a real man." He dragged his tongue across my ear and shoved his hand lower. "Is this what Dash did? Huh? Did you give it up to him on that first night?"

I trembled, the cold hand of fear clutching my heart. "Justin, please!" I yelled and pounded on his chest with my fists.

A loud growl broke through my plea and Justin flinched.

"The fuck?" He whipped his head back and looked down.

Hail jumped up, pushing her front paws against Justin's thigh. She lost her balance and stood on all fours again, barring her teeth and growling like I'd never seen before. The fur on her back stood on end. I took advantage of Justin's distraction and quickly slipped to the left, holding my robe closed with my hands, my heart pounding furiously against my chest.

Hail growled, a low snarling sound. Justin sucked his teeth and swung his right leg out. The connection his foot made with Hail's side was sickening, but her loud yelp was worse. She instantly fell to her side, whimpering.

Something snapped inside me. Broke completely the fuck off.

I reached for the first thing I could grab—an empty long-neck of Dash's from last week I hadn't been able to throw away—and hit Justin over the head with it. The bottle didn't smash into pieces like I'd always seen in the movies. Instead, it made a horrible thunk sound and the vibrations from the action reverberated through the glass and into my fingers.

Justin stumbled backward with his head in his hands. My chest heaved and I held the bottle over my head, ready to hit him again.

"Get out!" I screamed.

Justin dropped his hands, revealing a red lump already rising on his forehead. I took a step toward him with the bottle and he moved to the side, until finally he stumbled out of my door. I slammed and bolted it behind him and grabbed my cell.

My knees hit the hard kitchen tile, shocking my already frayed nerves. I used one shaking hand to dial the only number I could remember at the moment and the other to stroke Hail, who lay whimpering on the floor.

She kept raising her head as if to try to get up, but would yelp and lay it back down. Hot tears welled in my eyes and I trembled as I ran my free hand over her side. A knife pierced my heart when I felt a distortion in her ribs.

"Please, please, pick up . . ." I keened, unable to control my sobs.

"Hello?" A gruff voice finally answered.

"Dash! Look, I know things are weird between us right now, but please come as fast as you can!" I stuttered through my plea, sobbing and out of breath.

"Blake, what's wrong?" he asked and I heard his truck door slam.

"Please, Dash. Just get here."

"Already halfway there."

Thank you, God. I glanced at the ceiling and hung up. He must've been at Bailey's.

I put my face close to Hail's. "It's going to be all right, baby," I whispered, sniffing loudly in an attempt to pull myself together. She rolled her eyes toward my face and looked at me like she wished she could move to comfort me. I shook my head.

By the time Dash knocked on my door, Hail's breathing had grown ragged.

He walked in, looked me up and down, saw Hail, and sprinted into action.

"Get dressed faster than you can think. And grab a blanket while you're at it," he ordered, sliding next to Hail and running his hands over her fur. Her tiny tail wiggled, but she whimpered again, and I ran down the hallway so fast my feet barely touched the floor.

Dressed in who knew what, I hopped to Dash's truck while yanking on my shoes. He carefully loaded a blanket-wrapped Hail into the center seat and flew down the street before I'd buckled in.

"There's an emergency vet clinic not far," he said, making a quick right turn.

"Thank—"

"Don't thank me yet," After a short ride, Dash slammed on his breaks in front of a building with a bright red neon sign that read "Moore Emergency Vet Clinic."

I silently thanked God again, because Hail's normal vet wasn't an all-hours and I'd had no idea about this place. Dash carried her in with strong steady arms, and they rushed her to the back before I could squeeze out the words "she got kicked in the side."

We weren't allowed to go with her, despite my desperate pleas, so I reluctantly took up a seat in the waiting room, my knees bouncing anxiously. Dash gripped the arms of the chair he sat in and swallowed hard.

"Now, tell me," he said.

Tears welled up in my eyes again, and his arm instantly wrapped around my shoulders. I winced, a sharp pain pinching the area he touched. He lifted his arm and gently moved my shirt to the side. I glanced down when his eyes turned to slits.

Fingernail marks and the dusting of red and purple sat on each shoulder from where Justin had clung to me.

"Explain," he said, his voice tense.

I leaned further into him, pulling his arm down around me, ignoring the pain. He smelled like rain and comfort, and I spilled the night's events into his shirt along with some more tears.

"If anything happens to Hail, I'm going to kill him," I said, finally reeling in my sobs.

Dash clenched his jaw and stood up, pacing the area in front of me. "I'm going to kill him for touching you."

The scene replayed in my head and I shuddered. I wondered if I could've done anything differently to avoid the outcome. Maybe if I'd just let him do what he wanted, then Hail wouldn't have needed to intervene, and she wouldn't have gotten hurt.

"Don't." Dash sank to his knees in front of me and placed his hands on either side of my face.

"What?" I asked.

"You're blaming yourself. I can tell. Put this blame where it belongs. On that asshole."

"I already did." The sound the bottle made as it hit Justin's head rang in my ears. I didn't feel bad about doing it, and anger seethed below my worries for Hail, threatening to burst out, and track him down, and bash him over the head some more.

"I'm proud of you for that, but you shouldn't have had to." Dash raked his hands through his hair.

After a few deep breaths I realized we were alone in the waiting room. The only attendant behind the massive counter had gone to the back to check on Hail. The place smelled heavily of fur, disinfectant, and urine.

Dash looked at me, his eyes softening.

"Thank you for coming," I whispered.

"Blake . . ." He sighed. "Look—"

"Ms. Caster?" A tall woman in a white coat stepped out of the swinging door that lead to the back.

"Yes." I bolted to her and Dash quickly followed.

"Hail is going to be fine . . ."

I let out the breath I'd been holding since Justin had knocked on my door.

CHAPTER

SEVENTEEN

D ASH CARRIED HAIL inside and set her gently on her oversized pillow in the corner of the living room. She normally never used the thing, electing to dominate the couch, but she wasn't allowed to jump up and down for at least two weeks. Her eyes were heavy from the painkillers they'd given her at the vet clinic, but she still managed to give Dash's hand a slow lick as he pulled away.

"I'm so sorry about all of this," I said again, setting Hail's three prescription bottles on the kitchen counter. She had a broken rib, and the doctor had given me anti-inflammatories and antibiotics to stave off infection, just as a precaution. I knelt to pick up the beer bottle I'd left on the floor and rolled it between my hands. I heard Hail sigh from the other side of the room and I clutched the bottle with a fierce grip.

Dash uncurled my fingers from around the neck and slowly set it down. He didn't let go of my hand, and warmth radiated from his body so close to mine. He tilted my chin up so I had to meet his eyes, which were as green and intense as ever. I swallowed hard, my heart racing.

"I'm getting sick of you saying that, woman," he said and slipped his hand around my hip to the small of my back. Tingles erupted under his touch, and he pulled me to him. He pressed his cheek against the top of my head. "None of this is your fault," he whispered.

I melted into him, hugging him close to me. "You're wrong," I said, and it was probably the first time in Dash's life that he was.

"None of this would've happened if I hadn't let Justin in my apartment. None of this would've happened if I would've listened to my heart that summer before my freshman year of college when he'd made me choose between him and my dream school." I sighed. But if Justin hadn't, I wouldn't have met Dash. I made to step out of his embrace, but he stopped me.

"Don't," he whispered, and then his lips were on mine.

I opened my mouth willingly under his, my eyes closing automatically. He massaged my tongue with his own, and with each caress my heart beat faster. I grabbed his hair and kissed him deeper, suddenly needing to close the tiny space that separated our bodies. He ran his hands up and down my back and sides, every graze igniting a trail of internal fire that made me weak. His breath was ragged against mine, and he gently pushed me backward.

My back tapped the kitchen counter, enough to make me wince. I flinched out of the kiss, and the scene from earlier tonight filled my eyes so quickly I had to squeeze them shut. The icy fingers of fear gripped my heart again, as if I were reliving the moment, and the cold froze the fire within me.

Dash stepped back. "Did I hurt you?"

I shook my head, realizing for the second time he'd had to ask me that after kissing me. And he hadn't done anything wrong. Justin had. Again.

The shock of the situation returned, and I trembled despite

my efforts to take a deep breath and push past it. I would never know how far Justin would've taken it, thanks to Hail. If she hadn't intervened . . . I clenched my eyes shut again and refused to think about it.

"I'm so—"

Dash put his finger on my lips.

I saw the tension in his eyes, the confusion, and all the space we'd put between us crashed down on me like a tidal wave. I wanted to curl up in bed with Dash's protective arms around me, but I couldn't ignore the exhaustion settling into my bones. The adrenaline slowly crept from my body, and the reality of tonight punched me in the face. No matter what my body wanted—which was all of Dash's—I couldn't jump into bed with him. I couldn't jump into anything with him. Not with everything so fresh.

He must have seen the hesitance in my eyes because he put what felt like an ocean of space between us.

"Dash . . ."

"You don't have to explain, Blake." He shrugged and walked toward the door. "I get it. You still need time. "

"After everything tonight . . . I can't even think straight," I said.

Dash had his hand on the doorknob and I put mine on top of his, stopping him.

He stared at the floor for a few moments before glancing back at Hail, who snored loudly in the corner. "I'm glad she's all right. I'm glad you both are."

I pressed my lips together, wanting to say a million things, but coming up blank.

"Do you think he'll come back?" he asked, his eyes hard.

I shuddered. "I really hope not."

Dash turned toward me and took his hand off the knob. "I could stay."

Heat simmered low in my belly with the thought of lying

in bed next to him again. It would be so easy to let Dash put me back together.

"Would you?" I was still resolved to fix my issues on my own, but that didn't mean I couldn't take him up on his offer to make me feel safe. "Even if I'm not ready to—"

"Of course," he said and slid his fingers in my hair, gently stroking. "I'm not him, Blake. I'd never force you into anything. Ever."

I bit my lip, wondering how on earth I could possibly deserve Dash's kindness. "Thank you." I sighed, the tension leaving my body knowing Dash was there for me in whatever way I needed. That kind of stability was new and refreshing and put another kink in my stay-away armor.

I showered, despite having taken a bath earlier in the night. I pressed my loofa so hard against my skin I was rubbed raw by the time I got out, but I couldn't help it. I'd felt the intense need to scrape away all traces of Justin, all eight years' worth. Patting dry, I looked at myself in the mirror and realized that I'd never really be rid of him . . . not unless I shut him down completely, once and for all.

Walking into my bedroom, I sighed. Dash lay sprawled out, taking up more than half the bed. He'd argued with me earlier, saying he'd take the couch, but I didn't want him there. I wanted him in my bed, next to me, where I could smell him and hear his breathing, even if we'd agreed not to have sex.

I tried to climb in as gently as possible, but he shifted regardless.

"You were in there a long time," he said, his voice soft with sleep.

"I had a lot to think about," I said, slipping underneath the covers he held up for me.

"Did you figure it out?" he asked as I sank into the crook of his arm, resting my head against his chest.

"Not everything, but, yes, I figured something important

out."

"What was that?"

"Something vital in order for me to be free."

"Want to clue me in?" He traced his fingertips lightly against my arm. The sensation gave me chills and made my heart beat faster.

"Not tonight," I said, taking a deep breath. The scent of rain filled the bed, and my muscles turned to jelly.

I glanced up at him, his eyes barely held open, and smiled softly. This felt too natural to ignore. We fit. Effortlessly.

"I gave Hail her last dose before coming in here," he said, stretching. The motion forced more of his body to graze mine and the fire in my veins had me wishing I'd opted for shorts over sweats.

"Thank you," I said as he settled himself again.

"Always, Blake."

The touches he gave me were featherlike and completely innocent, but each time his fingers met my skin or his leg slid against mine, I melted. And yearned.

I slid my arm across the hardness of his abs, holding myself to him. A steady electric current buzzed between us, a low pulse aching with need. It would be so easy to let go and give in to the urges consuming me. To take things with Dash to the next level. To be *that* girl. His girl.

I sighed. That would leave me being defined by nothing but a relationship for as long as I could remember. No. I would figure out who I was first, then I would ask him to be mine. And tomorrow I would take the first step to reclaiming my identity—but Dash wouldn't like it.

MY FINGERS TREMBLED as I gripped the keys in my purse with one hand and my cell in my jeans pocket with the other. Ice-cold dread settled in my stomach, despite the warm air and gentle breeze blowing on campus.

It had taken me two whole days to work up the courage to ask Justin to meet me. I wanted to close the door on him for good, but on my terms.

Public place. Campus quad.

Dash hadn't slept over again after that first night, but I had my thumb hovering over the call button on my cell, his number already up. I'd told him what I planned to do. He'd nearly talked me out of it; he was so against me going through with this. Asked me to simply never speak to Justin again. But I didn't budge. If I didn't see an end to this, then there would never be closure, and Justin would harass me for the rest of my life.

My teeth threatened to chatter with the adrenaline coursing through my veins. My heart plummeted to my stomach when I saw Justin crossing campus toward where I sat on a bench. Seriously? I'd faced down tornadoes from a hundred yards away without this much fear. I needed to suck it up and fast. This was nothing compared to chasing one of God's most deadly creations. I could do this.

"Blake," Justin said when he'd reached me. His face was a purple and blue mess, a black eye, swollen cheek, and busted lip all accented the noticeable lump I'd given him two nights ago.

"What happened?" I blurted out, but instantly regretted it. I could easily guess who'd given Justin the beat down and suddenly understood why Dash hadn't checked on me or Hail in person in two days.

"That's not really any of your business anymore, is it?" Justin took a seat on the bench, and I instinctively moved as far away from him as possible. He noted the action and ducked his head, like a beaten animal. The thought made my blood turn to fire, picturing Hail at home, nursing her wounds. Good, the fire was better. I could cling to that with a stronger grip than the stupid icy fear.

"You're absolutely right, Justin. You're no longer a worry for me."

He huffed. "I don't remember everything," he said after a few moments. "But I've been told it wasn't good."

Hot tears welled in the back of my throat, the night replaying in my mind. "Wasn't good? Are you kidding me? Justin, you nearly . . . *raped* me." I whispered the last two words, weary of the students walking by.

His eyes popped wider and then he looked up, as if trying to recall the worst night of my life.

"And you broke Hail's rib. You're lucky only a beer bottle was within my reach and not a knife because I swear to God I would've stabbed you." He opened his mouth, but I cut him off. "Don't you dare say you're sorry. I don't want to hear it. I only came here to see to it that you knew what you'd done to me. To *me*, the girl who stood by your side for years. I can't believe you took things that far. It proves how toxic I am for you, and you for me. But no more. I'm done. And after what you did, I don't ever want to speak to you again."

"I *am* sorry. Not that it counts for anything. I got wasted, listened to Lindsay go on and on about how she thought you and Dash were together now, and I fucking lost it. I didn't go over to your place with an idea in mind, it just happened. I don't even remember driving there. And, for the record, in my mind, you were still mine. You've always belonged to me."

I jerked my head to the side. "No. That isn't how relationships are supposed to work. One doesn't *own* the other. And Dash and I aren't together." Not in any sense he needed to know about. My personal life was no longer his concern.

"I never thought I'd be this guy." Justin he stared at his scuffed work boots. "I really didn't, Blake. But I'm pretty sure it's your fault."

I shot to my feet, clutching my keys so hard I felt them nick my skin. "Excuse me?"

"You've driven me crazy for years. In love and lust, and sometimes I hated you because I knew I was never the man you wanted . . . the man you deserved. Who could live up to your standards?"

"My standards? I stayed with you after all the hell you put me through. The selfish sex, the suicide threats, everything. I didn't have any standards until I realized how a real man treats a woman." I practically spat the words. There was no more fight filter in me. I was free and would not spare him any ounce of pain.

"You mean Dash." Justin stood, too, but kept his distance.

"Yes. He's shown me more kindness in the short time I've known him than you have your entire life. Don't you get it, Justin? We only brought out the worst in each other."

"He's only trying to get into your pants."

I glared at him, not bothering to respond.

He put his hands up in defense. "Not that I blame him. Not that it matters anymore. You're right. I hated the person I was with you. Every day, I hated him. I still do. I don't know if I can come out of it, but now that we're done, I'll try." Well, finally, an instance of brutal honesty. For once he wasn't spouting bullshit.

"We *are* done. I mean it. Really done. I don't want one text, one call, or so much as a drive-by from you. Do you understand? I'll call the police and bring up charges. I should've done that already, but the only thing that stopped me is our years' worth of history. I can easily forget that if you bother me again." My voice didn't waiver like I thought it would with my heart pounding against my chest so hard.

"Understood," he said, not bothering to look me in the eye.

With each word, I took a sledgehammer to the chain he'd had wrapped around my heart for years. "Goodbye, Justin."

Crack, I'd given the final blow and was absolutely, finally free.

CHAPTER

EIGHTEEN

"HOW IS HAIL?" Mom asked, sliding a third home-made cinnamon roll on the plate in front of me. I sat at her dining room table, spilling my heart out between bites.

"She's almost completely healed," I said, smearing the bite on my fork in the melted icing on the plate. It'd taken three weeks, but Hail was back to the normal lazy and loving dog she'd always been.

"That's good, honey." Mom took a seat next to me, squeezing my wrist. "I'm so sorry about what you had to endure. I wish you would've talked to me. The way he treated you wasn't right, and sex shouldn't be like that. It should be about mutual satisfaction. It can be incredible . . . mind-blowing with the right person. I can give you some pointers, so you can tell the next man in your life how to move to get you—"

I jerked my hand up to stop her, color rushing to my cheeks. "No! Please don't." Obviously I knew my mother had sex before, but I did *not* need the visual, or the embarrassment that she knew infinitely much more about the subject than me.

"All right, honey, but I'll be here if you want to talk about it. I'm always here for you." Her eyes shot down to the table, and the slight hurt in them registered in my heart.

"I know I should've come to you. I honestly didn't even realize how toxic our relationship was until I met Dash." I'd been blind. Or in denial. I couldn't decide which was worse—my utter cluelessness on how healthy relationships functioned or the fact that I'd never once questioned if I deserved better.

She squeezed my wrist again before she pulled back and took a sip of her iced tea. "Have you heard from Justin?" She said his name through clenched teeth.

"Not since I shut the door on him forever. Not to mention I threatened to call the cops. We've heard the last from him." I shoved another gooey bite in my mouth.

"I'm so proud of you. You're finally embracing the strong woman I've always known you were."

She was right; I was strong. And I had a passion that burned hotter than the sun for storms. I hadn't been able to acknowledge either of those aspects when I'd been blinded and buried in my relationship with Justin. I knew myself better now. The last three weeks had been a revelation where I relished in the freedom and took the time to figure out what I really wanted.

And I knew what that was now. But I couldn't deny that I'd have baggage for a long time. I couldn't just blink the past eight years away, or that awful night Hail got hurt, no matter how badly I wanted to. I'd actually contemplated seeing someone to help me work through it, but as of right now I wasn't ready to dive that deep. If the time came where I needed even more clarity on why I'd stayed with him so long then I wouldn't hesitate, but for now I was just happy to be . . . me. Really me, with no chains, no expectations, and most of all, no disappointments.

Well, maybe one. I still hadn't been able to bring myself to cross the line with Dash. I knew I wanted to. Knew my life without him wasn't nearly as bright as it was with him in it, but he'd given me my space like I'd wanted, and I hadn't pressed unpause on that yet.

"How is Dash?" Mom asked, as if reading my mind.

I snapped to attention before quickly returning my focus to the plate. I hadn't told her about what had happened between us.

"He's fine." I thought. I'd only heard from him a couple times since I broke things off with Justin.

Once when he called a few days after the incident to check on me and Hail. He'd asked if I needed anything, offering to bring me food or chocolate or whatever would make me happy. I'd wanted to say, *you . . . I need you*, but I couldn't shape the words with my tongue. Regardless of his acceptance of my need for time, I couldn't get past all the drama I'd caused him. I didn't even know how to begin to apologize for it. And when I returned to classes, we kept our distance there as well.

The second time we spoke I'd called to give him my new cell number—I'd changed it for a new start. He hadn't bothered using it in the days since and really I'couldn't blame him. I'd brought so much drama to his world, he probably needed an infinite vacation.

"Some coincidence, huh?" Mom's voice cut into my thoughts as she rose from the table and took my cleared plate to the kitchen sink.

I followed her, leaning against the counter with my arms crossed. "What is?"

She scrubbed the plate with a washrag. "That the two of you broke up with your partners in the same month." Mom arched an eyebrow at me while she grabbed a towel to dry with.

My lips parted and heat rushed to my cheeks, the images of all I wanted to do with Dash pulsing behind my eyes. I clenched them shut, but that only made his body pressing against mine play on HD in my mind. "He's my best friend,

Mom . . ."

She put the dish up and reached for me. I hugged her, sighing into her shoulder. "You know what they say the definition of true love is, honey?" she asked, placing her hands on either side of my face.

I shrugged.

"True love is friendship set on fire." Mom pushed some hair out of my face and gave me a too-knowing grin. I hadn't told her everything, but she'd understood regardless.

CHAPTER

NINETEEN

I STRAIGHTENED UP at my register trying to focus on the task instead of analyzing the events that occurred since the start of last semester. In that time I had rid myself of the heavy weight of Justin and I could finally do whatever it was I wanted without fear. And yet, his absence wasn't what left a hole in my chest. It was Dash's.

I'd grown used to all the time we spent together, and these last three weeks where he'd given me more than enough space, I missed those times more than I missed any moment with Justin over our entire relationship.

The kisses Dash and I had shared burned the back of my eyelids and a flush raked over me. I tried to hide it with my hair as my next customer approached, a young man with brown hair and evidence of a five o'clock shadow. He had pretty blue eyes and was handsome enough. I was a single woman for the first time in . . . well, ever, but no urge to flirt tickled my insides. No curiosity on how his skin would feel against mine.

I handed him his bag of video games and sighed. How

could I be newly single and already completely in love with someone else? And why did it have to be Dash? My heart was twisted, locking on to the only person in the world I'd ever considered my best friend—human wise anyway.

Despite my best efforts and all the space and time I'd taken, I'd still come to the conclusion that I loved him. Loved him with every piece of who I really was, and I couldn't deny that I'd learned more about myself through our friendship than I had any other time in my life. He pulled the best out of me, encouraged me, supported me, and believed in me. And he did this without asking for anything in return, except for a chance at my heart.

I sighed, looking at the clock. The second I got off I would call him and see if he'd meet me. See if he still wanted to take a chance on us. Part of me feared he'd changed his mind, that our time apart had let him realize how damaged I was, or that we were better as friends. I swallowed the fear and reminded myself that I wasn't that girl anymore, the one who let fear control her life. I was a girl who went after what she wanted, whether that be a tornado or a man.

"Blake!" John called, snapping me out of myself. He walked into the store, his laptop tucked under his arm and his brick red faux-hawk clashing terribly with his bright yellow T-shirt. Paul jogged after him, catching up to him with a strained look on his face.

My excitement over seeing the pair almost hurt. I shook my head, not realizing how much I'd missed my friends. "Hey," I said as they stopped in front of my register. "What are you two here for? Music or video games?"

"Neither. I've tried calling you, but the line said your number was disconnected." John squinted his dark eyes.

"Long story. I thought Dash would've passed the new one on to you guys." I studied his and Paul's expressions, and it was like a punch in the stomach. "What's wrong?"

"It's Dash—"

"Don't, man." Paul cut him off, shaking his head.

All the air around me disappeared and my stomach hit the floor. "What happened?"

John glared at Paul before returning his eyes to me. "Nothing, yet."

"What do you mean, *yet*?"

Paul grabbed John's arm like he could hold his words back with the motion. "I'm telling you, man. Don't."

"She's the only one who can help us." John jerked his arm away. "All right, look, Blake, he said he'd kill me if I told you. In fact, he made me promise not to, but he took off earlier today for a storm near Broken Arrow."

Paul groaned and shoved his hands in his pockets.

I sighed, relieved at first and then it quickly turned to aggravation. "So what? That's what Dash does. Damn it, John, you made me think he'd been in an accident or something."

"No, you don't get it. No *one* is going after this storm." He set his laptop on my counter and opened it. "Doppler has been tracking it for hours, and it's going to drop something so nasty tonight, we were all warned off it. The locals are already preparing."

I swallowed hard, glancing at the radar images aligned next to the weather map that filled John's screen. My heart kicked up in speed, I didn't even need to be good at compiling this data to see it would produce something awful. "Dash knew all this?" I asked, returning my focus to the boys.

John shrugged. "'Course he did."

"And he went anyway?"

"He's been acting weird the past few weeks. Distant, but more reckless than normal. He almost totaled his truck last weekend when we tracked a mesocyclone in Shawnee. He snagged an incredible shot, but the hail damage was ridiculous."

He must've registered the hurt in my eyes because he sighed. "I wanted to call you for the chase, but Dash told me you needed a break."

I nodded, knowing it was my fault for pushing him away.

"Damn, bro, why don't you go ahead and tell her everything," Paul snapped.

"There's more?" I asked.

"Yeah," John said. "A few weeks ago he showed up to the lab with a black eye and scraped-to-hell knuckles after a fight with J—"

"Shut up, John!" Paul cut him off and punched him in the shoulder.

John flinched. "What the hell? She's one of us; she needs to know."

My stomach sank, the visual of Justin's beaten face the last time we spoke clear in my head. I'd assumed as much but had never confirmed it since I'd known from the two times we'd spoken that Dash was fine as opposed to hospitalized. I shuddered and piled on another load of guilt.

"Anyway," John continued, "you're the only one who has ever been able to pull him off a storm. I've never seen anything like it. We've both tried for years when he's gotten too close, and he never once left when we did. You join the team and the man finally listens."

I took a deep breath. I hadn't gotten Dash to leave as early as them, but apparently it had still been earlier than he normally would have. Dash had always lived on the edge with storms, but I never believed he'd be this careless. "Has he left already?"

"About an hour ago. But it's a three-hour drive and then the storm isn't predicted to hit until late tonight, between ten and midnight. We could make it and you could call him off, at the very least keep him from getting too close. Paul and I would go alone, but like I said, he's never listened to us before."

It was only two o'clock. I could get there before nightfall. I flipped off the bright yellow number above my register and practically sprinted to my manager's door. I pounded on it till he opened.

"Dustin, I've got to go. Emergency," I said and whipped around, rushing to my car.

John stopped me before I opened my car door. "Blake, I hate to do this to you. I never would put you in this kind of danger if I wasn't honestly worried about Dash. You know how rare and ugly cells like this can get, especially after dark."

"I know." I held my cell to my ear willing Dash to answer, hoping I could talk some sense into him sooner rather than later. I pocketed the phone after two more attempts. "How are we going to find him?" I glanced at Paul climbing into the passenger seat of the Tracker Jacker across the lot.

"Just follow us," John said, reaching in his back pocket and handing me a walkie-talkie. "We're all linked to the same hot spot for our laptops, so when we get within a five-mile radius, we'll know his exact location."

I gripped the radio and arched an eyebrow. "What if we don't get in that radius?"

He set his laptop on the trunk of my car. "He'll most likely be near where the storm is predicted to drop down. You'll probably be able to predict the location better than me at this point."

I eyed the data carefully. After a few moments I had a better handle on the storm. "Everything points to a section off of 51," I said.

He quickly clicked the data to the side and pulled up his go-to site for maps. "Got the routes. We'll check the back roads surrounding that area. 209 E Ave is the where I would've taken him if I'd been tracking, so you can start there while we try to get a hit on the network." He eyed the radio in my hand. "We'll have ours on. Stay in touch."

I gave him a firm nod and opened my car door. John held it as I sank inside.

"And Blake?" He looked down at me.

"Yeah?"

"Be safe." He shut the door and jogged to the Tracker Jacker.

***

LUCKILY I HAD a packed bag in my trunk. I'd stuffed a duffle with a couple sets of clothes, a pair of flat leather boots, and a disposable toothbrush in my trunk after the last chase. I'd wanted to be ready at a moment's notice if Dash ever asked me to go again—knowing that he kept the same stocked bag in his truck, too. Of course, he hadn't asked me to tag along on this one, and with good reason. He knew I would've tried to stop him.

I changed out of my work clothes quickly when we all stopped at the halfway point to fill up our tanks. I'd ridden John's taillights the entire way. I had called my mom on the road and asked her to take care of Hail. I'd never been so thankful that I'd given her the new key when I'd had my locks changed. Guilt bit my insides over not telling her the exact storm I was chasing, but she would've flipped.

My knuckles were white I gripped the steering wheel so hard. I broke the speed limits, as John did, but neither of us was bold enough to push it as fast as Dash would've. He'd probably made the three-hour drive in an hour and a half. I could clearly picture him already set up on the side of some back road, sitting on his truck bed, camera in hand, just waiting to catch the biggest storm predicted in years.

I knew we were close before John radioed saying we were only a couple miles outside of the storm. The color of the sky told me everything I needed to know. Night hadn't taken over yet, but the sky was a dark gray, almost black, and had a green sheen to it. It stretched for over a mile before running into the lighter evening tones of blue in the distance. The contrast settled eerily over the small town, casting the buildings and homes in an odd mish-mash of dark and light. The streets were deserted and stores had closed early. This town knew what headed toward them and smartly took cover.

"This is where we split up," John said over the walkie-talkie. "We're going northwest to see if we can get a signal. You go southeast to the area you predicted. Keep your cell on in case we get too far apart for the radios, all right?"

I clicked the button down. "Got it. If you find him before I do . . ." I took a deep breath. "Just tell him I'm here."

"I will."

I set the radio in my empty front seat and a few miles later took a hard right on the road John had suggested. It was a lonely road bordered by farmland and rolling green pastures with tall grass that buffeted back and forth in the steady wind. A chill crept across my skin as the sky grew darker the farther I drove. Normally I would've seen at least a few other chasers setting up their gear on the sides of the road, but no one was here. Not for this one.

After a mile a sliver of hope slipped into my chest. I hadn't spotted Dash's truck. Maybe he'd thought better of it and had turned back. I pulled over and grabbed my cell, hoping he'd answer this time. He'd already ignored four of my attempts, but reception out here was finicky, and this time the call cut off after only two rings. I stared at the one lonely bar on my screen before looking at the road ahead. I couldn't spot anything, no sign of a truck in either direction as far as I could see.

I shoved my phone back in my pocket and a cold sweat popped from my forehead. The sky moved now. The black wall cloud stretched over a mile wide and had a wicked updraft that slowly churned its way into what would be a terrible beast of a tornado. Two small funnel clouds peeked out of the bottom of the cloud, and their rotation was like two ominous dentist drills preparing to split open someone's teeth.

I swallowed hard and threw my car in reverse. This storm would hit earlier than predicted, though when had storms ever really been predictable?

Dash was here somewhere. I could almost sense it—the passion building in him as he watched the sky with hawk-like green eyes. The wild excitement as he planted his feet on the trembling ground and pointed the camera toward the production. He wouldn't miss the opportunity to be the only one with real footage of a monster like this, not even if it cost him his life. The data collected would be invaluable to him—and I knew people would benefit from his in-depth research in the field—but I couldn't justify that as a reason to try to capture a supercell like this. It was too risky. Too much at stake.

I swung my car around and scanned the area surrounding the fields. Another road led southeast and would allow him to get ahead of the storm. It definitely would be the better vantage point to film, though it was a dirt road and therefore the more dangerous choice. If it rained, which it almost always did, then even a truck like Dash's could get stuck. And without a vehicle to get him out, he'd just be more potential debris for the tornado to project.

As much as I prayed he didn't pick that road, I turned and drove down it.

A strip of sky lit by the sunset peeked below the pitch-black wall clouds that stretched farther than I could see. It hovered over the massive field like a slowly lowering velvet curtain, but this wasn't the end of an act . . . no, the show was about to begin, and way ahead of schedule.

Just as I made out a black truck a mile down the road, a loud crash of thunder boomed and rain fell in sheets as if the thunder had burst the massive balloon holding it. I turned my wipers on to full blast and stupidly kept my speed. I grabbed the walkie-talkie. "I found him!" I shouted into it.

"What's your . . . cation?" Static crackled over the line, causing John's voice to cut in and out. I repeated my location twice while gaining ground on Dash. The static grew louder, so I tossed the thing aside.

Dash stood on his truck bed, pointing the camera toward the wall cloud. His chest puffed out slightly as if he taunted the storm. His gray T-shirt clung to his carved abs like a second skin and his jeans were so soaked they looked black.

I skidded to a stop next to his truck. He glanced in my direction and instantly threw his head back, eyes clenched. He stomped his foot before leaping off his truck. I'd barely made it out of the car before he was within inches of my face, his green eyes practically on fire.

"What the hell are you doing here?" he screamed. "I'm going to kill John!" Dash darted his eyes around the area behind me, like he was searching for the Tracker Jacker. I spared a second to hope they'd heard my location before anger flared in my stomach.

I shoved him backward and flung the wet strips of hair out of my face. "What the hell are *you* doing here, Dash?"

"This is what I do!" He jerked an arm in the air, the camera steady in the other and still pointed expertly at the clouds, like it wasn't even a thought.

"No, Dash, this is what *we* do, and even I'm not this stupid!"

He scrunched his eyebrows together. "Did you just call me stupid?"

I smacked his chest. "Yeah! I did! This is the dumbest thing you've ever done!"

Dash didn't try to fend off my attack. "Have you ever seen an entire town wiped out, Blake? Homes destroyed, sucked into the sky and spit back out like shredded junk mail? This needs to be studied. You've got to understand that. No one has captured a storm like this. It will help!"

"It's not worth your life!"

"How many times do I have to tell you? I know these storms and how to handle them."

"You can never know storms, Dash. And the minute you think you do, it'll turn on you."

"Well, I'm used to that, aren't I?"

"What the hell is that supposed to mean?" I yelled at his back as he walked toward his truck.

"Nothing," he said and flung his truck door open, leaning over an opened laptop.

The rain continued to dump buckets on us, and it thundered so loud I flinched every time. I gripped his shoulder and forced him to look at me. "What did you mean?"

His shoulders dropped. "You! I know I said I'd give you time, and I still will, but it took me all of five minutes to realize I was crazy about you. That's why I can't be around you until you've made up your mind. It physically hurts to be near you and not touch you." He grabbed at his chest like the lightning cracking the sky had hit him.

I looked toward the sky and raked my hands through my soaked hair. "I'm so sorry. But I couldn't be *that* girl."

"What girl?"

"The relationship girl or the broken girl. I had to figure out who I was outside of him before I could even think of giving myself to someone else."

"I know that. Did you figure it out?"

I took a step forward, the rain drenching my entire body. The move felt like a leap. No going back. "I'm the girl you saw, even before I could see her myself. I'm the girl who always eats three cookies instead of one and who thinks Nutella belongs in the dairy food group. I'm the girl who chases tornadoes, interprets weather maps on the fly, and senses when it'll downpour." I glanced up, my eyes stinging with the rain. "I want to save lives someday, and I want to be an asset in weather reporting and tracking. So, which girl am I?" I took a deep breath, my revelation pouring out of me harder than the rain. "Yours."

Dash's eyes widened. "Truly?"

"If you'll have me as is. Baggage and all."

"Took you long enough, woman." He lunged at me, pinning my back against his truck, his lips crushing mine.

I opened my mouth, letting him in, relishing the feel of his warm tongue mixed with the cold rain that drenched us both. We were only getting wetter, but I didn't push him away; instead I yanked him closer, our hips pressing against each other. He explored my body everywhere his hands could reach—and with total abandon. I'd finally lifted the restraints on the passion we'd bottled up for way too long. I felt like I was about to burst like the storm that had gathered around us to shake the world.

I shook now, trembled with delight as I sucked Dash's tongue into my mouth. His fingers slipped into my jeans, and he pressed against my warmth with his rain-soaked fingers. I gasped, his mouth still on mine as he rubbed against me, drawing out a delicious tension that made my thighs quiver. A deep pulse throbbed low in my belly, and all I wanted to do was drop to the ground and have Dash on me, in me, consuming me.

Dash jerked his head back, his green eyes sparking with matched lust. We were on the same page as usual. I tucked my hand low between us, exploring the length of him, and smiled when he growled. He moved to my mouth again, an inch from my lips, and then the sky screamed.

Thunder clapped so loud and close it shook my chest like a hit with a sledgehammer.

Reality crashed down all around us, harder than the downpour.

We'd been careless getting caught up in the moment like

that.

Dangerous.

The storm had arrived, on top of us like I ached for Dash to be on me.

And it was show time.

The funnel clouds I'd spotted earlier had dropped lower and combined sometime in our distraction. In seconds it met the ground, forming a tornado, at least one hundred and fifty yards wide. It quickly churned up a massive amount of earth. The horrible roaring sound of a freight train screeched through the sky.

My heart jumped into my throat. I'd never seen a tornado so big or so beautiful. Even over five hundred yards away, the wind soared past Dash and I, flapping my hair back and forth wildly. I glanced at Dash, shocked he'd had the presence to get his camera out when I could only stand in awe.

The tornado moved with an elegant fierceness that both mesmerized and terrified me. Adrenaline coursed through my veins, pumping my heart against my chest so hard I thought it would bust. My limbs shook—the fight or flight instinct battling within—and my brain called me an idiot for not taking cover.

It was spectacular the way the beast snaked from the clouds in the sky and pierced the ground beneath it. And in that moment I understood why Dash was here, why he didn't want to miss this. I clutched his free hand.

Dash went rigid and jerked his hand away. He tossed the camera in his truck and grabbed my waist, pulling me around to the other side of it.

"It's changing course!" he yelled and shoved me into the passenger seat.

My fingers trembled as I fumbled with the seatbelt, all the giddy sensations leaving my body quicker than a blink. As I looked out of the windshield at the massive monster headed toward us, I remembered the *stupidity* of being out here.

Dash slammed the door, buckled up, and spun his truck around. The tires splayed mud all over my car, and I only spared half a thought as to what would become of it. He peeled out, speeding down the way I'd come in, but not fast enough. The wet earth sucked on the truck's motion and threatened to stop our retreat all together.

The back end of the truck jerked suddenly, as if the Hulk had grabbed ahold of Dash's tailgate. The force slammed us against our locked seatbelts. A wallop of heat burst in my chest from the abrupt halt. The back wheels squealed, Dash's foot placed firmly on the gas. We looked at each other and then backward.

We were entirely too close. The massive churning beast stalked right behind us, stretching across the road and field. The truck's back end was caught in the outer suction vortex of the tornado, but the primary would swallow us whole in seconds.

I grabbed Dash's hand, which gripped the steering wheel. "What's your real name?" I shouted and clenched my eyes shut.

"What?"

"We're about to die, Dash! I love you and want to know your real name!" I screamed over the rushing sound of the wind threatening to consume us. I thought of my mother and Hail. I hoped they knew how much I loved them.

"No! We're not going to die!" he shouted back.

The tires screeched and the smell of hot rubber filled the cab before the truck suddenly took off. I popped my eyes open, shocked that Dash gained speed and fishtailed all over the dirt road.

I spun in my seat and scanned the area behind us. The tornado let us go, but kept chasing *us* in a terrifying role reversal. Dash sped down the road, taking a hard turn onto the paved road that led toward the town. We gained a tiny bit of distance, but the beast took up the entire back view of Dash's truck. I couldn't tear my eyes away, and once I separated sheer terror from duty, I reached down for Dash's camera.

I'd barely pressed the record button before Dash took another fast turn.

"Fuck!" he screamed, the tires squelching in the background, Dash losing control of the truck as he tried to slow our momentum.

I whipped my head around just in time to see us crash head on into a telephone pole. The sound of metal and glass crunching broke through the roaring wind and pouring rain, and I was jerked so hard forward and back my head slammed into the back of the seat.

Stars burst behind my eyes, but the adrenaline quickly cleared the stun of the crash.

"Are you all right?" Dash already had his seatbelt unbuckled and reached over to me.

"I'm fine," I assured him with a gasping breath, my heart racing.

He turned the key over and over, but the truck was dead. He glanced behind him. "We've got no time. I was heading to that gas station." He pointed to where a gas station sat empty only a parking lot length away. "Run. Now!"

He didn't leave room for a discussion. Neither did the screeching beast behind us. I bolted out of the door, my feet shaking with adrenaline as they hit the pavement. Dash stuck close behind me as the wind whipped my hair back and forth, suctioning my clothes to my body. It was like running against an ocean current, and the short distance to the station became an Olympic event. Dash pushed at my back the entire time, forcing me to go faster, until we finally made it.

The lights were off inside and the doors wouldn't budge.

"Damn it!" I screamed, yanking on the handle as if my

strength and determination could break the locks.

Dash was two steps ahead of me, grabbing a huge rock that held down a fat, three-foot-high stack of newspapers left out for what I assumed was recycling, and smashed the glass door. He kicked the rest of it in, and we clambered through, rushing toward the back of the store where the access to the large cooler stood.

I jerked open the door, chills instantly covering my wet skin as we entered the cooler. Dash slammed the door shut, pushing me to the farthest back wall, the only spot in the station that could be considered the most interior.

I dropped to my knees in the corner, Dash kneeling next to me, and hoped the three walls made of strong metal would withstand the tornado. The wide variety of soda bottles rattled in their cases, the doors on the outside opening and closing frantically. The energy pumping through my veins made my entire body tremble, and I locked eyes with Dash, an apology on my lips.

He shook his head, opening his mouth to speak, but was cut off when the roaring sound outside reached an epic high.

It was here.

And it would swallow this place.

The heavy weight of Dash's body fell on top of me then, pinning me to the ground as I heard the glass from the cooler doors break, and the thunking sound of hundreds of plastic bottles hitting the ground. I felt Dash jerk above me, but couldn't hear if he said anything. I could only lay there, praying for the sound of the wind to go silent.

After an eternity—or a few minutes—it finally did. Dash rolled off me, and hissed as he grabbed his leg.

I quickly jumped up as he yanked a four-inch piece of glass out of the back of his thigh with a yelp.

"Dash!" I instantly covered the wound with my hands. His blood pooled beneath my fingers, warm and sticky.

"It's fine, Blake."

"No it's not! You're hurt. Because of me!" Damn it, he wouldn't be hurt if he didn't feel the need to protect me.

"It's not your fault I chose to take shelter in a fucking glass box."

I shook my head, pressing harder on the wound. "You wouldn't have even chased this storm if I hadn't pushed you away." Tears filled my eyes, knowing his more-than-reckless behavior had been a direct result of me.

He cupped my cheek, forcing me to look him in the eye. "Stop. You can't keep taking the blame for everything, woman. You know I would've chased this every time."

I sighed. Maybe. We'd never know, because I'd do every-thing in my power to talk him off monsters like these. Or at least get him to compromise to chasing from a safer distance. Fuck we'd been too close. I peeled my hand away from the wound to look closer. If this had been the same spot on the front of his thigh, instead of the back, Dash could've bled out in my arms.

The injury wasn't life threatening, but the danger was real. We'd been lucky.

I couldn't lose him. Not now. Not ever. And I knew that didn't make a difference because we would never stop chasing and the storms would never stop chasing us back.

I yanked off my T-shirt, leaving me in the spaghetti-strap tank top I wore beneath it, and twisted and wrapped it tightly around the wound. Dash flinched as I secured it, but then he reached for me.

"Blake." He sighed my name like it was a prayer. Like after nearly being eaten by a tornado it was the only word he ever wanted to say again. And I melted. Fell into his open arms, pressing my chest against his, and kissing the hell out of him.

I kissed him hard enough to convey my love, hard enough to show him my anger at his recklessness, and hard enough to take the blame for not being able to talk him out of this storm. He tugged on my hair, yanking me closer, and I gasped against his lips.

The heat between my thighs had me aching to let him in, let him be as close as humanly possible, but the realization of where we were stopped me. I slowly pulled back, my chest heaving.

Dash gave me a look that was both disappointment and understanding. "We have to search the damage. See if there are any victims."

"Can you walk?" I asked, standing up and offering him a hand.

He took it and stood, wincing but able to walk with a limp.

I forced his arm across my shoulder, bearing as much of his weight as I could. Together we walked out of the cooler—careful not to trip on the hundreds of soda bottles littering the floor—into the gas station, which no longer had an entrance. The tiled floor, covered in candy, napkins, boxes, drinks, and broken glass, simply gave way to the parking lot outside, the glass and metal front of the building had been completely wiped out.

CHAPTER

TWENTY

WE STOPPED AT his truck first, shocked it still stood, if not crashed against the telephone pole. Dash reached underneath the driver's seat, pulling out a small first-aid kit.

"There's one on the other side, too," he said, motioning with his head for me to go grab it. I did and forced Dash to stand still as I ripped open the tear in his jeans a bit more, giving me room to swipe the cut with an alcohol wipe and seal it with a butterfly bandage. I forced myself not to linger, holding his muscled thigh in my hand, and he gave me a small smirk when he saw the heat in my eyes. I tossed my now ruined bloody T-shirt in the cab of his truck and then we slowly made our way into the residential part of the town, which wasn't far from the gas station where we'd desperately taken shelter.

It was almost too quiet after the thunderous noise the storm had made. Now the only sounds that broke the calm settling in the sky were distant sirens, wood snapping, and the occasional bark of a dog. I'd expected screaming or cries for help. This was worse. I scanned the area for the Tracker Jacker, coming up empty.

I punched John's number again on my cell, cursing the busy signal I received. "That's the fourth time. Same damn signal."

"They're smart. Probably on the other side of town already helping with the search," Dash said, reading my worried gaze. "If we get separated, we meet back here, all right?" He pointed to his truck. "You have your cell," he eyed me clutching it. "Who knows if you'll get through, but if we find anyone hurt we'll need to notify emergency personnel. And watch for fallen power lines."

I nodded. "All right."

A toppled tree blocked our path to the first group of residential houses. The roots twisted out in all directions and black dirt clods clung to them like the remnants of torn flesh. Dash placed a palm on the thick trunk and climbed over it, trying to hide his wince when his feet hit the ground on the other side.

I followed suit, climbing over it before Dash could turn around to offer me help. He surveyed the area with sharp eyes. I was jealous of his stoic calm demeanor and made a mental note to take the same first-responder courses he had as soon as possible. My hands trembled while holding the first-aid kit to my chest. He must have done this dozens of times, but this was completely new territory for me.

He pointed toward a group of homes that had been hit to our right. Some of the structures were still easily identifiable, but the insides were gutted. What had once made these buildings homes were scattered about the area, spilling out like someone had reached in and ripped out a handful of organs.

"We start there and spread out to cover more ground," he said as he limped in that direction. I kept pace with him, my heart racing. "Be careful where you step. People may be covered with debris."

I swallowed the lump in my throat and slowed several yards past where Dash stopped.

I approached the walls of a concrete basement, which without the house sitting on top of it, looked like a giant trap for a massive animal. Broken wood with wickedly jagged edges covered the surrounding area, some long pieces sticking up out of the basement as if someone were about to light the biggest bonfire ever known.

Careful where I stepped, I tried to find the ground between the debris and make myself lighter than air. I navigated my way over dirty dish towels, a broken dog bowl, and a mangled bed frame. Ripped-up magazines, busted baby-blue dishes, and dirt-covered pillows also littered the area. I scanned past these items, so out of place in the shredded pieces of this home, and searched for movement.

I glanced back at Dash, his eyes trained on the ground as well. A low whine snapped me to attention and I whirled my head toward the noise. Behind an upturned cedar hutch I found a shaggy dog with soaking wet brown fur. Its back leg was caught underneath a chunk of wood that looked like it could've been an attic beam.

Tiptoeing to it, I gently shimmied the wood until its leg came free. The dog instantly headed a few feet away, limping across two couch cushions with the stuffing spewing out of them. He stopped next to what I could now see was a toilet, though broken bits of wood half covered it as well. I made my way over quickly.

The dog pushed its nose deep into the pile of wood, whimpering more than when I had freed its leg. I gently nudged him away and my heart leapt into my throat.

A dirt-covered hand clung to one side of the toilet. Adrenaline filled my veins and I hurried to scoot the wood off the person, checking the surrounding areas for other people before I let the beams fall in the other direction.

Pitch-black hair plastered to the woman's forehead and she wore a pair of gray sweatpants and a purple hoodie. Blood streamed down the right side of her face.

I lifted the final beam off the toilet and stepped closer to where she lay curled up with her arms around the base. Glancing down as my boots crunched on glass, I noticed at least a dozen picture frames of various sizes. Half were broken and their pictures ripped, others remained intact. I knelt down and carefully placed my hand on the woman's neck and breathed a sigh of relief when a steady thumping met my fingers.

The dog limped around to the other side and licked the woman's face furiously before I could stop him. She jerked hard and her eyes popped open. The panic in them was evident, but when she took in her surroundings, pain filled them enough to break my heart. She tried to move, but I stopped her with a gentle hand on her shoulder.

"Ma'am, you shouldn't move." I flipped open the lid of the first-aid kit and rummaging through it. "Everything is going to be all right," I assured her, though I knew that was stupid to say when her entire house was a pile of broken pieces that couldn't possibly ever fit together in the same way again.

"I waited too long," she moaned.

I shook my head and ripped open a disinfectant wipe and cleaned the blood off her face. "You got to the bathroom. That was smart." I found the source of the blood. An inch-long gash near her hairline. The cut was clean so I assumed a shard of glass from one of the picture frames had been the culprit. I dabbed at the wound and sealed it as best I could with a butterfly bandage from the kit.

"No." She sighed. "I should've been in the basement. I'd gotten everything down there me and my dog would need. Food, water, flashlights, and radio . . . but I forgot my pictures." She clenched her eyes shut. "Stupid. I thought I had enough time to grab them and get back downstairs. I told George to stay down there, that I'd be right back." Her eyes landed on the dog dutifully sitting by her side despite the pain I imagined it caused his leg. "You should've minded me."

From where I'd found him he was only a few feet away from getting to her in the bathroom before the tornado hit. Amazing he'd survived at all. I lifted the woman's hand and placed it on his back. "Thank you," she said. "Did my pictures make it?"

I looked down and tried not to crunch any more glass as I searched for one. I found a small unbroken frame with a picture of two little blond girls who couldn't be over the age of three. Their faces filled the frame, both grinning widely. I held it above her face. "Looks like most of them survived."

The woman's eyes lit up with hope as she gazed at the picture. "Those are my grandbabies."

I set the picture gently on her chest. "You keep them close while I try to get ahold of an ambulance, all right?"

"My legs are tingling," she said, "is that normal?" She gulped hard and her chest rose and fell faster than it had seconds before.

I patted her shoulder and held my cell to my ear. Nothing but a repetitive beeping—either bad reception or busy circuits. I tried again without any luck and whipped my head around.

"Dash!" I hollered across the distance. He jerked his head up from searching. I waved my arms at him and pointed toward the woman. "I can't get through on my cell!" He hobbled as fast as he could down the road we'd come from. I was glad he knew I needed an ambulance without me shouting it in front of the already scared woman.

I scanned the surrounding area until I spotted a half-crushed cardboard box a few feet away. I tiptoed to it, scooped it up, and hurried back to the woman. "Were you here all by yourself?" I asked while brushing some dirt out of the box. It was half-soaked, but it would have to do.

"Just me and George. Thankfully I didn't have my

grandbabies this weekend." A shudder ran through her, and I almost cried in relief when the action twitched her legs.

"I'm going to put as many of these as I can find in this box, all right?" I said, holding up another picture frame. This one had a photo of what looked like a much younger version of the woman holding an infant.

"Thank you," she said, and George went to licking at her face again.

I picked up as many frames as I could, scraping my hands slightly on the shards of glass scattered around. The action gave me something to do when I felt helpless. I wished Dash would get back with help faster. Putting the last picture I could find in the box with the others, I smiled at the woman with what I hoped was a reassuring look. "There. Now you don't have to worry about them getting lost."

"Blake!" Dash yelled, and I snapped my eyes to him.

He jogged—a kind of skip-like run that favored his good leg—toward me with two men on his heels, each one wore a light blue button-up and black pants. The two carried an orange gurney with thick black straps and large square zip-up bags hung over their shoulders.

Dash touched my shoulder when he reached me, and I glanced down at the woman. "Help is here," I said, and Dash and I took a step back to let the men do their work.

After assessing her vitals, they strapped her to the portable gurney, all the while poor George whimpered and worried at her side. One of the EMTs looked up at Dash.

"You think you could help us carry her back to the ambulance?" he asked, positioning himself on one side of the gurney.

"Absolutely," Dash answered without hesitation and no mention of his wounded leg.

The EMT nodded and, once Dash had gotten his hands underneath the gurney, counted to three. They hefted her up and made it look easy.

"George," she called, and cut her eyes toward him since she couldn't move her head.

"I'll bring him," I said and lifted the box of pictures. "And these, too."

AFTER WE MANAGED to get the woman, George, and her pictures to the safety of the ambulances stationed just outside the main road, Dash and I split up again and went right back to searching.

As the hours passed, we found more and more people. Some crawled out of shelters unscathed and took up in the search for those who weren't so lucky—using flashlights and lanterns and whatever else we could scrounge up. The people who could help did so without question, and an instant trust formed between us, a cosmic understanding that we were needed and could count on each other for anything.

We didn't stop until dawn broke the night sky. I stood next to Dash after helping a teenager find his mom where all the EMTs had set up. My feet screamed at me, my muscles seared, and my lungs threatened to burst from the constant running back and forth and lifting, but I still felt it wasn't enough.

I took a long gulp from the water bottle Dash offered me and watched as the sun broke through a section of puffy white stratocumulus clouds and shook my head as its rays shed new light on the wreckage the storm had left in its wake. Crumbled houses, broken support beams, and every manner of debris from teddy bears to boxes of cereal to sheets of house-siding wrapped around half crushed cars.

And yet, in the middle of all of this chaos, were *people*.

They stood in groups, comforting one another or walked out in teams to continue searching. EMTs bandaged up the wounded and medevac'd the seriously injured. Young children handed out water bottles and strangers wrapped blankets around shocked neighbors. The camaraderie was infectious and awe-inspiring. I never thought I'd see anything more devastatingly beautiful in all my life.

John and Paul found us shortly after the sun had fully risen. The relief I felt was so strong it nearly robbed me of what little energy I had left.

"We've been helping the other side of town, there is total damage over there," John explained, wrapping me in a hug.

Paul's mouth dropped as he took in the scene. "You two all right?"

I glanced at Dash and we both nodded. We were lucky. We'd been so close to the tornado and got off scott-free, where others hadn't.

"You got a joke for me, Paul?" I asked with a soft voice.

"Not today," he said, shaking his head. "I'm glad you're both all right. You look like hell though. Go get some rest. We'll take your spots."

I opened my mouth to protest, but John shook his head. "No arguing, Blake. You won't be able to help anyone when your body starts to crash."

They were right. The adrenaline slowly left my body and a sinking sensation took its place. I'd never been more tired and yet the thought of going to sleep seemed selfish.

"My truck is dead against a telephone pole," Dash said, glancing at John. "Can we borrow the Tracker Jacker?"

John instantly handed Dash the keys. "It's parked a few blocks back that way," he said, pointing behind a line of ambulances.

"Thank you, guys," Dash said. He placed his hand on the small of my back and guided me to the Tracker Jacker.

John and Paul were already coordinating with a police officer before we'd even got the truck started. At least they weren't losing numbers with us leaving.

After about fifteen minutes, Dash pulled the truck off the road and onto a flat patch of grass just outside of a massive pasture. Tall green grass rolled in the light breeze and cows grazed a few miles away. The scene was so normal. The storm had left this area untouched and pristine when only miles away a town had been turned upside down.

"Nearly the whole town is without power and I doubt the motel is even open. Almost everyone is out searching or clearing debris. Sorry," Dash said and turned off the engine truck. "This is the best we have."

I shook my head. "It's all right. I want to get back soon anyway."

He gave me a soft smile, and I noticed the purple bags under his eyes. I wondered if I looked as drained as he did. We'd been so lucky. He'd been hurt, but it could've been so much worse.

He shifted his back against the driver's side door and I scooted up so he could stretch his good leg out behind me. I leaned back against the seat once he'd gotten situated and tried not to think about how his shin dug into my back.

Dash sucked his teeth and I glanced at him. He opened his arms and flicked one of his hands in a come-hither motion. My heart galloped and I swallowed hard as I moved to lay my head on his chest. His arms encased me instantly and I breathed him in, his scent rushing to each of my nerve endings and mending them.

I absently traced my fingers over the back of his hand, my attention awakening when I felt a line of scuffed, newly healed skin. I turned my head to meet his eyes, darting them from his, to his hand, and back again.

Dash sighed. "You don't want to know."

"I already do, and again I'm sorry," I said, remembering the fight Paul had mentioned. "Especially because that's my fault, too."

"You've got to *stop* taking the blame for everything, woman."

I knew Dash was right. I'd learned more about myself in the past couple months than I had in years, thanks to him and the storms, but it was hard to let go of the responsibility for every bad thing Justin did after years of holding on to it.

"I sought him out," he explained.

"The day after Hail got hurt?"

He tensed for a moment before relaxing underneath me. "Yes. He won't bother you again."

"You didn't have to do that. You may have gotten to him before me, but I ended it with him for good. I wanted to handle it on my own."

"I know and for that I apologize. But I couldn't think straight. I'd held you the entire night and listened to you whimper in your sleep. Every time you moved your shoulders, you cried out. And then Hail was hurting in the next room . . . I had to find him and make him pay for what he'd done."

A shudder ran through me. I hadn't remembered crying out, but I did remember the pain and the overwhelming desire to dole out some of my own to Justin. I sighed, such drama I was so happy to be rid of. "I understand, but from now on, if I say I want to handle something on my own, let me, all right?"

Dash ran his fingers through my hair. "Deal."

I relaxed against him.

"It's time for you to stop worrying," he said and held me tighter.

CHAPTER

TWENTY-ONE

THE TORNADO TOOK three people when it left this earth and injured dozens of others. Despite the town's efforts to prepare for it, the storm had surprised them with its sheer ferocity. Dash and I had stayed for three days helping with the cleanup and took damage measurements. During that time I learned the harsh reality of the true reason for chasing storms.

Study.

Not for the thrill. Not because reading weather maps and interpreting data came so naturally to me. Not for the awe factor and not because being so close to them made me feel complete.

The incredibly close images Dash captured on film of the tornado's mannerisms provided us with invaluable information regarding its habits, wind speeds, velocity, tenacity, and offered insight into its construction. Studying the data collected on each chase allowed us a better perspective into the tornado's process from cloud to ground, and the more we understood about them, the better we could predict them, and hopefully prepare people more adequately, too.

It had been a month since that devastating storm—I'd just gotten my car back from the shop after it had been thoroughly roughed up when we left it on that dirt road—and still reports aired on the news about the reconstruction of the town. It would take a long time to rebuild all that they'd lost and I wished we would've been able to do more, but we had to come home. We had classes and work and the world had to continue spinning.

I looked at the sky outside of my window now and marveled at its gorgeous slate-gray. Radar predicted a light thunderstorm tonight, but nothing serious enough to merit a chase.

Hail wiggled her butt furiously as my front door opened after a quick knock.

"How are my girls?" Dash asked as he let himself in.

Hail ran over to him so fast her lips flapped up and down. He knelt to pet her and had to dodge her massive tongue aiming for his face.

How I looked at storms wasn't the only thing that changed the night of the biggest tornado to hit in years. The morning I'd woken in Dash's arms, in the terribly uncomfortable cab of the Tracker Jacker, I realized I was home. He was my safe haven. And despite that one night of sleep, Dash and I hadn't spent the night together since.

The pace didn't bother me so much as the anticipation. If sex was anywhere near as much fun as kissing him, I knew I was in for a wickedly delicious treat, but he'd insisted from the get-go we take it slow. He wanted to show me how much he cared by waiting for the right moment, and all I wanted to do since he'd asked me to officially be his girlfriend was tie him to my bed.

"Nice out, isn't it?" I asked as he gave me a quick kiss.

He glanced out my opened window. "Glad you think so.

We're going out."

I glanced down at my jeans and T-shirt combo. "Do I need to change?"

"You're perfect." He kissed me again. Butterflies flapped in my stomach each time his lips met mine, and I knew I'd never tire of it. I shook my head, heat rushing to my cheeks. I didn't think I'd ever get used to the compliments, either.

"Don't think about arguing, woman," he said and turned around, tugging me toward the door.

"Please, you wouldn't know what to do with me if I ever disagreed with you." I followed him.

Dash stopped short with his free hand on the doorknob. He craned his head around, flashing me a devious gaze. "Blake, *you* have no idea what I'd do to you if you did."

"I wouldn't mind a bit if you wanted to punish me for it." I arched an eyebrow at him.

"You want to be punished?" He grabbed ahold of my butt with two strong hands and lifted me to his level with ease. My heart raced, pressed against him, and the intensity in his eyes nearly stopped it. He crushed his lips on mine, kissing me so deeply I forgot everything outside the boundaries of his mouth.

He pulled away sooner than I wanted. "That's me going easy on you."

Twenty-five minutes later Dash pulled his new truck—insurance had ruled his old one totaled—off onto a dirt road and parked underneath a huge oak tree near the lake. The tree's branches stretched out over the calm water's surface like they reached for something just outside their grasp. The sky was still a smooth gray and a soft breeze whispered through the air.

"This is one of my favorite spots," Dash said, hopping out of his truck and grabbing a stuffed duffle from behind his seat. "I sometimes bring my gear out here and plot our courses or do research in preparation. Somehow I can think clearer here than in the weather lab on campus."

I gazed at the lake. "I understand that." The place was beautiful and secluded despite the openness of the area. The water stretched over a mile wide and more trees bordered the opposite side. Without any other cars or people around, it appeared to be a private and wonderfully untouched slice of land. No distractions other than the occasional chirp of a bird or the steady lull of crickets.

Drawing my attention from the lake and back to Dash, I found him laying out the last of what looked like at least three huge blankets in the bed of his truck. He returned to the cab and came back with two Native Amber longnecks. I took the offered bottle and sat on the edge of the truck bed, the blankets offering a nice cushion.

"I brought you out here to ask you something, Blake."

My eyes widened and I swallowed hard. "Yeah?"

Dash raked his hands through his hair. "I know it's a little soon in our relationship . . ."

Holy shit. "What is it, Dash?"

He sighed. "Would you like to come with me down Tornado Alley?"

I let out my held breath in a gasp. "Of course!"

A smile spread across his lips. "Are you sure? Because we've been incredibly lucky so far. This is our end of the season blitz. A three-week trip filled with a ton of driving—and usually more misses than catches. And you know the funds we have, so it'll mostly be cheap motels and fast food."

"What about classes?" I asked.

"As long as we do the make-up work and have it in by the end of the semester, the professors don't care. They understand that there is only a small window of opportunity to catch these things." Dash dropped his eyes for a moment before returning them to me. "You think you can stand me for three weeks straight? No breaks? I understand if you think it's too soon—"

"Stop it," I cut him off, knowing full well I wouldn't tire of him that easily. I doubted I ever would. The thought of sharing the same bed with Dash every night sent tremors rocketing through my core. "I'd love to."

He clanked his bottle against mine. "Can't wait," he toasted and we each took a drink.

I studied the label on the longneck.

"What?" he asked after taking a swallow.

"This was the first drink you ever bought me," I said.

He tilted his head.

"That first night at Bailey's." That night seemed ages away instead of months. So much had changed. *I* had changed.

"Right. The night you thought I was trying to pick you up."

Heat filled my cheeks at the memory. "Crazy, I know."

Dash focused his signature look on me—the one where he thought I was being ridiculous. He set his bottle down on the grass and took mine, too.

He cupped my face and softly kissed the corner of my mouth, then the space underneath my jaw. He worked his way down my neck before returning to my lips. "Does that feel crazy to you?" he whispered.

I let out the breath that had caught in my throat. "No, it feels ama—"

Dash cut me off with his lips, crushing down on mine with a sweet force. He slipped his tongue in and gently massaged my own. My heart raced as I wrapped my arms around his neck, pulling him closer.

He wound his fingers in my hair with one hand and held the small of my back with his other. He slowly navigated us further into the truck bed, laying me on my back without ever breaking our kiss. He hooked my leg around his hip and ran his hand up and down my thigh.

The fire only Dash could ignite inside me flared to a roar and I shoved my hands underneath his shirt, tracing my fingers along his rigid abs before pulling his shirt off altogether. Lord, he was glorious to look at, and the gray sky that filled the backdrop made him look more like a Greek warrior than my storm-chaser boyfriend. He arched up enough to grab the ends of my top and slipped it over my head. I'd never been so glad I'd passed up my usual beige bra that morning for my black bra and panty set.

His emerald eyes lit up like lightning when I reached around and unhooked it, letting it fall to the side. Butterflies flapped in my stomach and heat rushed to my cheeks—Dash had never seen me naked and there was no light switch to flip out here. I was completely exposed and yet, somehow, I felt a level of intimacy I'd never experienced before.

Dash kissed me again, deep and long, and the feel of his bare chest rubbing against my breasts uncurled delicious warm tendrils throughout my body. He drew back, his breath as ragged as my own, and grinned deviously at me before leaning down to kiss my breasts. I closed my eyes and moaned when he lightly bit my nipple.

He worked his way lower, trailing his lips down the length of my stomach until he reached my jeans. He unbuttoned them, and I lifted my butt up so he could easily slide them off. I waited in terrible anticipation for him to take my panties off, too, but he stalled. He pressed his lips against my hips before slowly bringing his mouth to hover a centimeter above my underwear, the heat from his breath fueling the aching pulse between my thighs.

Dash lightly kissed the fabric, from the hem of the thin cloth to my center, before returning. I gripped a handful of his hair, wanting to scream at him to take them off already. He unhooked himself from my grasp long enough to rip off his pants.

"Oh, finally," I said with a sigh, about to burst with the need for his skin on mine.

Dash smirked and shook his head. "Not yet," he whispered and gently inched my underwear down my legs.

I half expected him to flip me over and I hated myself for the breech in my mind. Luckily Dash trailed his tongue across a small bundle of nerves and I completely forgot . . . everything. My eyes rolled back in my head and I thought of nothing but his tongue, working its way up and down, slipping inside me quickly and then out, repeating in agonizing circles until I was sure the sparks erupting underneath my skin would consume us both.

"Oh, God, Blake," he practically growled as he worked his way back up to my face.

The sound of my name from his mouth curled the pleasure throbbing inside me and I knew I couldn't handle much more. I gripped the sides of his briefs and yanked them down. He quickly shimmied them off.

His body fit perfectly between my legs, and he brought his mouth down on mine while rubbing his tip between my thighs. "Mmm," he moaned. "Blake . . . you feel so incredible."

The freaking Amazon could have been running through my thighs I wanted him so badly, but he continued to tease me, pulling away from my attempts at lifting my hips and taking him in. I kissed him harder and clutched at his strong back with desperate fingers.

"Dash," I begged. "Please."

His eyes caught mine and they were molten green. "Say it," he commanded.

My heart leaped into my throat, but my need for all of him overpowered my shyness. "I want you."

He groaned and put his tip inside a fraction before bringing it back to the outer edges. "Say it again."

"God, Dash, I want you," I complied.

He kissed me before slowly slipping inside. The motion drew a loud moan from my lips and sparkling tingles brushed every inch of my body. I bucked my hips and squeezed my legs around his, rocking back and forth to the speed Dash controlled until the pleasure mounting within me hit a crescendo.

He broke our kiss to catch my eyes again, and his lips moved against my own as he groaned, "Come with me, Blake." And he pushed himself further and harder against me until my eyes rolled back in my head and my toes curled.

I gasped with the sweet release of a thousand tiny explosions erupting and didn't stop bursting for what felt like an hour. My body trembled underneath his as the pulsing ache slowed to a sweet and steady speed like a heartbeat. Dash moaned and clutched me closer before he slackened slightly.

Our chests heaved against each other as he brushed some hair out of my face and kissed me lightly before resting his head against my shoulder. I smiled, unable to contain the giddiness soaring through me. The sky had darkened and gray wisps of clouds only allowed a few stars to shine. A crack of lightning lit up the sky and twenty seconds later we heard the distant rumble of thunder from the north.

Being outside, with Dash still inside me, was more perfect than I could've ever imagined, and for the first time ever, I instantly wanted to make love again.

I turned my head and nibbled at his ear.

He lifted himself, his rippling arms on either side of my head.

I rubbed my hands up and down his back. "More," I whispered before slipping my tongue between his lips.

Dash kissed me, then chuckled as he drew back an inch. "Don't you hear that storm coming, woman?"

I wiggled underneath him, satisfied when he arched his head back and his eyes hooded. "You're the only thing worth capturing tonight," I whispered.

"Then I better give you one hell of a chase," he said and gently slipped out of me. His lips trailed to my breasts and the teasing torture started again.

Another white spark of lightning lit the sky above us, bathing Dash's incredible naked body in light for three glorious seconds before returning us to darkness. Thunder clapped, closer than before. I tugged Dash's head up, squeezed my legs, and rocked to the side until I straddled him.

I flipped my hair over my shoulder and glanced upward before leaning over to kiss him. "You've gotta see this," I whispered against his lips and motioned my head upward.

The next lightning strike illuminated Dash's green eyes, and the passion in them usually reserved for chasing storms doubled. I reveled being the object of that much desire.

I ground against him until he was so hard I had to take him inside me. I rode him slowly, the sounds of thunder accompanying our moans. He made me come again and again, and I knew without a doubt I'd let Dash catch me whenever he wanted.

After another hour of sheer pleasure bordering on torture, I snuggled up under his chin. I had everything I'd ever wanted . . . almost.

"What's your real name, Dash?" I asked, knowing he'd never tell. A tornado nearly swallowed us whole and he hadn't told me.

"Alfred," he said, interrupting my thoughts.

"What?"

"I won't say it again." His arms tightened around me.

"Like . . ."

"Yes, like from Batman, and if you tell anyone outside of Hail—"

My laughter cut him off as I thought about how starkly different he was from the old butler. "Why now? The tornado had us and you didn't . . ."

Dash shifted so he could meet my eyes. "Giving you my heart is the most dangerous thing I've ever done, Blake," he said and then parted my lips with his tongue.

The sky trembled again, but I ignored the call. Thunder and chaos could remain within the chase. The only thing I needed were the sparks between Dash and I, which crackled brighter than a lightning bolt, and the home we'd built between us, strong enough to withstand any storm.

ACKNOWLEDGMENTS

THERE ARE SO many people I have to thank for helping me with this journey, but first, I want to thank *you*. Thank you for taking a chance on this book. You are what fuels the lifeblood in my characters and make the story possible. So thanks for that, dear readers!

Thank you, Daren, for waking me up. For enduring a life married to a writer, it isn't always easy. Thanks for being my best friend, an incredible father, and one surprisingly awesome plot-hole demolisher. I shudder to think where some of my characters would've ended up without you. My dreams wouldn't be possible without your support and willingness to supply me with coffee and double-cheeseburgers.

Thanks must be given to my amazing family. To Dad, for the years of encouragement. For always reading multiple versions of my stories, even the really awful ones, and telling me they were awesome. For the endless emails where I needed a pep-talk, and for the unflinching faith that I'd have my name on a book someday. Without your support, this book wouldn't be where it is now.

To Mom, for constantly telling me I could be anything I wanted when I grew up. I think I've figured it out now. And to my sister, for being a writer first and making my five-year-old self think it was the coolest thing ever! Naturally I would want to be like you.

I also need to give a HUGE thank you to these amazing

ladies:

To Rebecca, the Golden Goddess, you make me want to be a better writer, better mom, and better person all around. You are my hero and there is no amount of words for how much I adore you. Thanks for the countless advice, guidance, and willingness to talk about proper names for naughty parts.

To Mindy, for your sharp eye, your amazing encouragement, and awesome friendship. For reading it twice (including the time your iPad froze on the naughtiest scene in the book and had to be repaired with it staring the poor tech-kid in the face) And for making my lines stronger. You are simply the best.

To Sam, the one who catches all the things :) You are a rock star and I'm really sorry I made you cry on the subway. Hugs and all the chocolate to you!

To Kimberly Lovell-Chase, Prerna Pickett, and Aimee L. Salter, you ladies rock and continuously make my work stronger. I'm beyond lucky to have such a talented band of critique partners like you!

To Esther, the Hot-Mama I can't live without. You're my constant cheerleader and my soul-sister. Thanks for always being there, despite how many miles we live apart. Without our hour-long conversations, I'd lose my sanity. And speaking of losing, the boys are *still* behind in our never-ending Cranium tournament :)

I have to thank Cora Carmack, for not only reading the book, but blurbing it too, as well as offering me so much guidance in the profession of our dreams. And for finding me first. You're the absolute best.

To Kimberly Derting, thank you for providing an endless supply of inspiration and advice. It means the world to me. And for the cupcake.

To Jamie Bodnar Drowley, thank you for choosing my book when I thought all was lost.

Thanks must also go to my awesome PR Team over at Sassy, Savvy, & Fabulous. Linda you are my Obi-Wan and Yoda rolled into one!

A giant thank you to my editor, Karen Grove, without your sharp eye and amazing vision this would not be in the shape it's in. You are a delight to work with!

To Regina Wamba and Yuli Xenexai over at Mae I Design, thank you to the moon and back for giving me a cover intense enough to carry my storm chasers. You're beyond talented and there aren't enough ways to thank you for how stunning it is! And to the models, Ripp and Mackenzy, for making the characters I love real.

Thank you to Nichole and Christine at Perfectly Publishable for sharpening the inside of the book and making it sparkle! You are all so seriously talented!

And once again I'd like to thank you, the reader. Don't ever underestimate the power you have to bring life to the stories you love.

ABOUT THE AUTHOR

MOLLY LEE IS an author, editor, and mentor best known from *Pitch Wars,* a program that connects promising writers to established authors in the community. She writes NA contemporary and YA urban fantasy with strong heroines who are unafraid to challenge their male counterparts, yet still vulnerable enough to have love sneak up on them. Throw in high-octane action or any kind of supernatural element and she'll be hooked. A military spouse with two children and one stubborn English bulldog, Molly enjoys watching storms from the back porch of her Midwest home and digging for treasures at local antique shops.

Printed in Great Britain
by Amazon